"I saw a UFO

"What?" Pamela['s ...] ... became shaky.

"I was on a routine flight over the Eastern Washington desert," her friend continued, "when I saw this...this glowing silver capsule. Before I could report it to my commander, my instruments failed. I had to eject."

The familiar words sent a chill down Pamela's spine. Her father had spoken those exact same words before he vanished.... "And then what?" she prompted.

"And then this...thing landed near where I bailed out. And when I looked up, I saw a huge spider crawling out toward me...."

ABOUT THE AUTHOR

Vickie York has served as a commissioned officer in both the U.S. Army and U.S. Air Force. After an assignment to the Defense Language Institute, Vickie served as an intelligence officer for the rest of her military career. She was awarded a Bronze Star for service during the Vietnam conflict. Beginning with *The Pestilence Plot*, a 1982 hardcover, her novels have been based on her military experience. Vickie has traveled extensively and now makes her home in Tacoma, Washington, where she was born. She enjoys riding ferries on Puget Sound with special friends, singing in the church choir and taking long walks with her German shepherd.

Books by Vickie York

Don't miss any of our special offers. Write to us at the following address for information on our newest releases.

Harlequin Reader Service
U.S.: 3010 Walden Ave., P.O. Box 1325, Buffalo, NY 14269
Canadian: P.O. Box 609, Fort Erie, Ont. L2A 5X3

Moon
Watch
Vickie York

Harlequin Books

TORONTO • NEW YORK • LONDON
AMSTERDAM • PARIS • SYDNEY • HAMBURG
STOCKHOLM • ATHENS • TOKYO • MILAN
MADRID • WARSAW • BUDAPEST • AUCKLAND

FOR RUTH AND NICK

With thanks to my longtime Air Force friends
for their on-site Russian research

ISBN 0-373-22279-3

MOON WATCH

Copyright © 1994 by Betty Ann Patterson

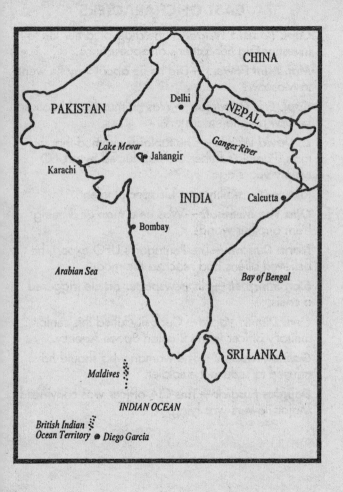

CAST OF CHARACTERS

Capt. Pamela Wright—She'd devoted her life to investigating her father's disappearance.

Maj. Matt Powers—Did he lie about why he went to Moscow?

Capt. Eric Goodman—Was he murdered because he saw an alien monster?

Lt. David Wright—The tabloids claimed that this man, Pamela's father, was abducted by a UFO twenty years ago.

Riker—Invisibility was his special talent.

Otto Von Meinhoff—Was he a man or a being from another world?

Norm Duncan—The Pentagon's UFO expert, he believed aliens had reached the moon.

Stan Sharplett—His newspaper article triggered a crisis.

Gen. Dimitri Vactin—Curiosity killed this senior military officer in the Russian Space Agency.

Galina Nazarov—The woman who should have refused to seduce the soldier.

Douglas Fosdick—This CIA officer was convinced Major Powers was lying.

Prologue

Tacoma, Washington

His head whirled. His damp palms clutched his Jaguar's steering wheel with the desperate intensity of a drowning man. Maybe his squadron commander was right. Maybe he did need to talk to a shrink. He sure as hell needed to talk to *somebody*.

For an instant, the terrifying images in Eric Goodman's head were replaced by the serene face of the only woman he considered a friend. Her oval face, with its frame of wavy golden hair, blanked out the monstrous spider he thought he'd seen. Hadn't she once told him that her father, also an air force pilot, had sighted a UFO before he disappeared twenty years ago? If anyone would understand his confusion, it was Capt. Pamela Wright.

Suddenly, Eric felt the urgent need to talk to her. Where was the nearest pay phone? Half-sick, he pulled into a deserted parking lot ringed by a theater and several small businesses.

Ahead, framed in the car's lights, were two pay phones mounted on the etched brick wall outside the theater lobby. He knew her number by heart and gave it to the operator, using his credit card. As the phone rang, he took a quick glance around, but saw nothing unusual in the early morning darkness.

"Hello?" Her melodic voice held a hint of annoyance. Eric didn't blame her. If anyone dialed *his* number at this hour, it better be a life-or-death matter.

"It's Eric, Pam."

There was a moment's hesitation. "You're not sick? Or hurt? Or in jail?"

"No, but I may be sick in the head." He tried to put a jocular note in his voice. "That's what my commander thinks."

He heard her sigh. "Don't tell me you've gotten another poor woman pregnant?"

"No. This is about a UFO I thought I saw last night."

She gasped. "Tell me about it." Her usually calm voice sounded shaky.

"I was on a routine flight over the Eastern Washington desert when I saw this...this glowing silver capsule. Before I could report it, my instruments failed, and I had to eject." He paused, wondering how she'd react to his fantastic story. "This saucerlike *thing* landed near where I bailed out. When I looked up, I saw a huge spider crawling out toward me."

"A spider?"

She didn't believe him. Not even after what had happened to her father. He'd been a fool to think she would. "Forget I called," he mumbled.

"Don't hang up, Eric," she cried. "Tell me about it."

He shuddered, picturing the towering monster. "The beast was ten to fifteen feet tall." He let his terror seep into his words. His skin crawled as he remembered the creature's long thin legs, its bulging brown belly and its blinking red eyes.

"What was it?"

"I don't know. It sure didn't look like anything I've ever seen on this planet." He took a slow breath. "You don't think I imagined the whole thing?"

He heard her hesitation. "Did you see anything else?"

He concentrated. The roaring in his head nauseated him, blanking out everything but her voice.

"If the spider came out of a capsule, a door must've opened," she prompted. "Could you see inside?"

"No, it was too dark." Then he recalled the flashing lights. "Yes. Wait. There *was* something inside."

"What, Eric? Tell me what you saw." Even with a thread of excitement in her voice, she sounded so steady and dependable that he almost sobbed.

"Flashing lights," he said. Just remembering made him break out in a sweat. "Flashing lights on a display board."

"Like an airplane's instrument panel?" she suggested.

"Sort of." He thought a moment. "Except that this panel took up most of the wall space I could see inside the saucer. And the lights had an interesting shape."

"What do you mean?" She spoke with an intensity that surprised him.

"Well, the flashing lights formed an outline around a shape something like an isosceles triangle."

He heard her expel her breath. "What did the Pentagon say?"

"I haven't reported it yet." He pressed a shaky hand against his throbbing head.

"Why not?"

"Because I'm not sure I saw the damned thing, Pam. When I landed, my helmet got knocked off and I hit my head. After I was picked up, they took me right to the hospital."

"Are you calling me from the hospital?" A new note of urgency filled her voice.

"No. I walked out before they could throw me in the booby hatch."

He heard her quick intake of breath. "You've got to go back to the hospital right away, Eric. And you've got to promise me you'll report what you saw first thing tomorrow morning."

"My C.O. thinks we should wait a few days." He forced himself to laugh. "When he heard my story, he advised me to see a shrink. Just between us, Pam, I think he knows something about the UFO he's not telling. Do you suppose I saw some kind of military experiment the Pentagon's conducting? I ejected over the nuclear reservation at Hanford."

"Is your commander the only one you talked to about the UFO?"

"Yes." He cleared his throat. "I must have blacked out. When I came to, the thing was gone, and I was in the chopper."

There was a moment of shocked silence. "Then it might still be out there." Pam sounded desperate. "If you won't report what you saw, I will."

Eric was already regretting his impulsive call. "All right," he agreed reluctantly.

Before returning to his car, he relieved himself in the shadows by the side of the building. As he headed toward his Jaguar, a vehicle turned into the lot and drove toward him. He stiffened, his senses instantly alert. The vehicle stopped between him and his car. Its two front doors opened.

Eric didn't wait to see who got out. Adrenaline spurted through his veins, shoving his legs into warp speed. Heart pounding, he ran toward the four-lane street on the shopping center's far side.

He heard the sound of running feet behind him. Then he was tackled and thrown to the ground. Somebody grabbed his arms. He tried to jerk away, but found himself held in a viselike grip. A rope tightened on his throat.

Air force captain Eric Goodman never got a good look at the men who killed him.

Lake Mewar, Jahangir, India

OTTO RECEIVED the telephone call in his secret laboratory carved out of stone beneath his island palace.

"Eric Goodman is dead." The voice on the phone belonged to Riker, a trusted operative.

"When?"

"Less than an hour ago. When the body is found, the police will believe Goodman was the victim of thugs who stole his car."

Since his unfortunate childhood, Otto had thought of himself as *the hairless bastard* because he had no body hair—not so much as an eyelash. Now, staring at his white, fleshy arm, he gripped the receiver more tightly. "Why did it take so long? You received the order hours ago."

"The pilot injured his head when he bailed out, and was taken to the hospital from the rescue helicopter. When we looked for him there, he'd wandered away without being released. He did not leave his car until late in the night to relieve himself. We had to be very cautious following him. The police patrol that area regularly, even late at night."

"But what did he tell his rescuers about the accident? Your source in the squadron must have told you. Did the pilot see anything *unusual* after he ejected from his plane?"

"Unusual? In what way?"

"There is no need for you to know."

Otto had trained Riker well. The assassin knew better than to pursue the matter. "Perhaps the pilot saw nothing unusual. Our source says he spoke to no one but his commander. The commander filed only the typical accident reports."

"We must assume the worst," Otto declared. "That the pilot saw something not meant for his eyes and told others about it."

"I will watch and ask questions," Riker said.

After Otto hung up, he could not concentrate on his work. What had the pilot seen? Had he been eliminated before he could put two and two together and sound an alarm? How unfortunate that a stupid navigational error had caused so much trouble.

Plodding ponderously to another microscope, Otto ordered himself to be patient. If the pilot had told anyone about the monster spider, that person would surface sooner or later. When he did, he would be eliminated.

Chapter One

Out of the drizzly gray dawn, the runner loped toward Pamela with the fluid grace of a young lion. Though he was still far off, she easily recognized him from his long stride and rhythmic body motion. He was Maj. Matthew Powers, commanding officer of Eric Goodman's fighter-interceptor squadron. Powers covered miles in minutes. He'd be here in no time.

Ignoring her nervousness, Pamela pushed her bike around a curve in the road where he couldn't see her. After observing him for the past two days, she'd found the perfect place to intercept him.

The road twisted here, so she'd be out of his sight long enough to arrange a convenient accident. She hoped nobody would come along and rescue her before Powers did. So far, no one else was headed toward her from either direction.

Pamela ripped a hole in the left leg of her tights, from the calf to the ankle. She rubbed grease from the bike's chain on her legs, and a fistful of mud on her brand-new white-and-green jacket. Then she sprawled on the road, the front wheel of her bike across her legs, waiting for him to find her.

With each passing moment, the bike on top of Pamela's legs felt heavier, the rocks beneath her thigh sharper. *Last chance to chicken out,* she warned herself, knowing Powers would be here any second. But she didn't move to get up.

It had rained off and on most of the three days since she'd arrived in Tacoma from San Antonio. This morning an early spring drizzle saturated everything. The wetness had already dampened her hair, removing whatever body it possessed. When she brushed a limp strand off her face, a fat drop of water rolled down her cheek. She'd be a bedraggled mess by the time Powers got here.

Why had he advised Eric not to report the unidentified flying object he thought he'd seen? Pamela wondered for the umpteenth time. Perhaps Eric was right and Powers was involved in the accident—or at least knew what was behind it. She'd have to be careful what she said. He mustn't guess what she was up to. If he were in any way responsible for what had happened, she'd be sure he paid. She owed that much to Eric's memory.

Pamela sensed his presence before she actually saw him. In the gray dawn silence, she heard the soggy pad, pad, pad of running feet on the wet blacktop, the deep breathing of a body working hard, and she knew he'd rounded the bend in the road. Lying with her cheek in the dirt, she couldn't turn her head easily. She twisted on her hip under the bicycle, pushing it away, hoping she looked as though she'd just fallen.

"Here, let me help," a deep male voice said.

Slowly, Pamela turned toward him. From the ground, she peered a long way up, taking in his running shoes, his bare muscular legs, his bright yellow-and-purple running shorts and tank top and, finally, his face.

He leaned closer and extended his hand.

"Thanks." She let him pull her up.

He's a lot better looking than his picture, she thought. An advantage of working at the Air Force Military Personnel Center was that she could get a peek at the routine information in almost anybody's file, which included an eight-by-ten official photo.

But the stern picture in Matthew Powers's file was black and white and unsmiling. In the flesh, he was much more attractive. As she focused on his face, her gaze roamed from his worried hazel eyes, to his patrician nose, to his full lower lip. The barely noticeable cleft in his chin gave him something of a devil-may-care appearance that was offset by his take-charge attitude.

"Are you okay?" His smooth baritone voice was full of concern.

Tentatively, she put her weight on her right foot and winced. She shifted off it, as if in pain. "Darn! I must have sprained something when I fell." She glanced sideways at him. Was her act convincing?

He knelt beside her. She felt his fingers gently kneading the flesh around her right ankle. He had beautiful hands, she noted, with long slim fingers and well-shaped nails.

"No swelling yet." Loosening her shoelace, he pressed a point on her arch. "Does that hurt?"

Pamela had never had a sprained ankle, so she had no idea what should hurt. She grimaced. "A little. If you could help me to my room in the visiting officers' quarters, I'll soak my foot for a while. I'm sure it'll be okay."

"Fine." He didn't sound upset that she'd interfered with his daily run. "Can you walk? If not, you can wait here while I get my car."

"With a little help, I'm sure I can walk." The last thing she wanted was to be left sitting by the side of the road alone at 0630 on a drizzly Thursday morning.

"Then I'll wheel your bike, and you can grab on to my arm." He smiled down at her. "I'm Maj. Matt Powers, by the way."

"Capt. Pamela Wright, Major Powers." Pamela took his arm with both hands. It was surprisingly muscular for a man with such slender hands.

"I'm Matt," he said.

"Pam," she returned, smiling. Congratulating herself, she hobbled along beside him. Phase one of her plan had

gone without a hitch. Now it was time for phase two, her
carefully worked-out plot to meet and talk freely with all
personnel in the major's squadron.

MATT FELT HER BESIDE HIM, hanging heavily onto his arm,
letting him support her when she shifted her weight to her
right leg. He wasn't positive, but would have bet a month's
pay she was faking. He'd seen enough sprained ankles to
suspect she didn't have one. The way she was lying when he
found her, with her right foot neatly placed under her left
leg, did not suggest a crippling fall. Just the opposite. She
looked as though she'd lain down very carefully in the
muddy road and pulled her bike over on top of herself.

Apparently, she'd wanted to intercept him. But why? No
woman who looked like this one—with the cool blond
beauty of a Swedish actress—had to feign a crippling accident to meet a man. Not that Matt hadn't had similar experiences. He was well aware that women found him
attractive, both physically and because he was an air force
pilot with an exciting job and a good future.

But this woman said *she* was a captain in the air force. If
she wanted to meet him, all she had to do was walk up to
him in the O'Club bar and say, "Hi." No, she had some
other motive for this little game she was playing.

He'd seen her out here riding her bike the past couple of
mornings. Had she been watching him? If so, she wanted
their meeting to look accidental. That must be why she
hadn't approached him in the O'Club. What was she up to?

Now that he'd gotten a good look at her face, Matt had
the nagging feeling that he'd seen her somewhere during the
past few months. But where? He felt a sudden warmth flow
through him as her slender form leaned against his side. No.
He wouldn't have forgotten this woman.

"You here TDY?" he asked, keeping his voice bland. She
must be at McChord on TDY—temporary duty—or she
wouldn't be staying in the visiting officers' quarters.

She smiled up at him. "No, I'm here on a thirty-day leave. I drove in from Randolph Air Force Base in Texas last Monday."

In spite of himself, Matt couldn't hide his amused surprise. "March isn't the best time of year to come to Western Washington."

"I'm finding that out." She sighed ruefully. "It's rained ever since I got here on Monday."

"Do you have friends or family in the area?"

She shook her head. "Not a soul. But I always wanted to see what Seattle was like. Things slackened up at the office, and I had a chance to take some leave. So I grabbed it and came on out."

"All by yourself?"

"I enjoy driving around the country alone." She sounded defensive.

He smothered a grin. She would never have devoted thirty precious leave days to come here, in March, all alone, simply to "see Seattle." Until he found out what she was up to, and what connection it had to him, he'd play along with her.

"Come back between June and September," he advised. "The rain stops then."

"I'm already wishing I'd waited till summer." She paused, and Matt detected a subtle shift in her weight on his arm. She was now favoring her left leg instead of her right. Suddenly, as though she'd recognized her mistake, her weight shifted back.

"So what do you do here at McChord, Matt?" Her question sounded like idle chitchat. He was sure it wasn't. Anyone who went to this kind of trouble to meet him knew exactly who he was and what he did.

"I'm commander of the F-16 fighter-interceptor squadron."

"A command position! Wonderful!" Her hazel eyes studied him expectantly.

Matt sensed she wanted him to ask about her job. "And what's your specialty, Pam?"

"Personnel. I'm stationed at the Air Force Military Personnel Center at Randolph." There was satisfaction in her voice. Obviously, their conversation was moving along the way she wanted it to.

The drizzle had changed to a steady rain, soaking them to the bone. Now that he'd slowed to a walk, Matt began to feel the chill. He stepped up his pace. In spite of her limp, Pam had no difficulty keeping up.

He waited patiently for her to get to the point. Maybe then he'd be able to figure out what she wanted and why it was so important to her.

"My office recommended the subject for the next commander's call lecture," she said conversationally. "It's about the changes in the former Soviet Union."

The commander's call, a monthly briefing for all military personnel, was usually voluntary. But this month's lecture had been made mandatory because of the serious nature of the subject.

He smiled to encourage her. Of all the matters he thought she might bring up to get to her point, a commander's call about the former Communist superpower was at the bottom of the list.

"Actually, I was the one who recommended that particular program to the air staff." There was a touch of pride in her tone. He knew how she felt. It wasn't every day an air force captain recommended a lecture topic to be discussed servicewide.

He eyed her thoughtfully. "You must be a Soviet specialist. Did you go through the Defense Language Institute?"

"No, I learned the language in college." She paused. "But you're right. I *am* a Soviet specialist. I was a political-science major with emphasis on the Soviet Union and its satellites."

"With an education like that, I'm surprised the air force didn't draft you into intelligence." He made the comment in an offhanded way to disguise his curiosity. "How'd you wind up in personnel?"

"Because personnel's the career field I wanted." Her reply was so quick that she sounded defensive. "I didn't tell the air force anything about speaking Russian, because I didn't want to be an intelligence officer."

Could she be here on some kind of assignment connected to intelligence? Was that why she was so quick to deny a role in intelligence?

Matt helped her around a puddle in the road. Her limp, which had almost disappeared, returned in full force.

He stiffened as an unsettling thought struck him. If she'd lied about her accident, everything else she'd told him was probably a lie, too—including her story about being a personnel officer on thirty days' leave to "see Seattle."

But if she was assigned to intelligence, why was she interested in his squadron? Mentally Matt reviewed his unit's operations for the past few months. He recalled nothing out of the ordinary except—Matt felt his gut tighten—except the mysterious circumstances surrounding Eric Goodman's F-16 accident. First, his jet had malfunctioned and crashed. Then, after he'd bailed out, he'd thought he'd seen a UFO and a monstrous spider. Less than twenty-four hours later, he'd been murdered—for his car, according to local police.

Matt had included information about Eric's UFO sighting in his report to the Pentagon. A special investigator, Norman Duncan, had spent several days in Eastern Washington checking out the UFO aspects of the report.

Matt took a deep breath. After he'd made the report to the Pentagon, he'd been ordered not to repeat the story or even tell anyone he'd reported it officially. So he knew how sensitive the information was.

Could Pam Wright be working undercover, sent by Norm Duncan, the investigator Matt had talked to? He'd heard of a secret room in the bowels of the Pentagon basement where military experts followed up on the work of the various public and private agencies that investigated UFO sightings. Could she be part of that operation?

Persistent rumors throughout the military during the past few years told of an alien presence on the moon. Allegedly, the watchers in the Pentagon basement monitored the aliens' progress and tried to establish contact. Maybe Pam Wright had come to search for a connection between the crash of Goodman's F-16, his UFO sighting and his murder—three incidents that were now being investigated by three separate government entities.

But why was she operating under cover? It didn't make sense.

"Who usually gives your commander's calls?" she asked, interrupting his thoughts.

So she was back on track again.

"My intelligence officer, who also doubles as my public affairs officer," he replied.

When she peered up at him, fat drops of water trickled down her cheeks. Even soaking wet, she was a good-looking woman. Matt caught a glimpse of her ripped tights clinging to her like a second skin, her muscles moving rhythmically as she walked. He let his eyes linger for a long moment. When he raised them, he saw she was watching him, her cheeks flushed.

He grinned at her. "Since you've got special Russian training, maybe you'd like to give this month's presentation." He made the suggestion to tease her, sure she'd turn him down. Nobody he knew would waste valuable leave time preparing a stodgy lecture for a bunch of airmen. He was definitely surprised when she slowly nodded her head.

"For the right incentive, I might be persuaded," she said, her cheeks still flushed.

"And what's the right incentive?" Unbidden, his mind jumped to a sudden vision of her with her shoulders bare, her blond hair fanned out on his pillow. He forced himself back to reality.

"Oh, maybe dinner together at the O'Club some night while I'm here." A note of shyness had crept into her voice. Matt wondered if she was acting.

"Dinner can be arranged, if you'll help us out with the commander's call. My public-affairs officer will be eternally grateful."

"Well, I suppose I could help out if you really need me." She gave him a satisfied smile. "Doing the lecture for your people will give me something to keep busy with while I'm here."

That's when Matt knew what she'd wanted all along: to present the next commander's call talk to his squadron. The knowledge didn't relieve his mind in the slightest.

What was *really* behind her offer?

As PAMELA GRIPPED Matt's muscular bare arm in the soaking rain, she found herself extremely conscious of his virile appeal. She was looking forward to their dinner date with uncalled-for enthusiasm. Over the meal, she'd get Matt to tell her about Eric's accident.

Eric. The memory of the dead pilot's boyish face shamed her. She wasn't here to enjoy herself. Admittedly, spending time with a man as attractive as Matt Powers wasn't the shabbiest duty in the world. But she must not let anything interfere with her investigation—especially not an adolescent physical attraction to the only other person who had heard Eric's UFO story.

The notion that Matt might somehow be involved in whatever had happened to Eric seemed almost laughable. But, then again, glancing at his face, she wasn't so sure. He was examining her with narrowed eyes, his brow furrowed and his mouth set in a straight, hard line.

Was he sorry he'd asked her to give the presentation to his squadron? Maybe he'd guessed she had an ulterior motive. After all, it wasn't every day that someone with exactly the right qualifications appeared out of the blue and volunteered to give a prescribed lecture.

"I'll get right to work on the talk," Pamela said quickly, so he wouldn't have a chance to back out. "Maybe I can come over to the squadron later this morning after I've soaked my foot and changed into my uniform." Tightening her grip on his arm, she kept her gaze on his face, radiating enthusiasm.

His eyes narrowed even more. "Do you really think soaking your foot for a few minutes will cure a sprained ankle?"

She forced herself to smile confidently. "Maybe not cure it, but I should be able to get around if I'm careful."

"Did you bring this bike with you?" Matt glanced down at the handlebars he was holding on to.

Leery of revealing too much, Pamela hesitated. She didn't even have a bicycle in Texas and didn't want him to guess she'd gotten this one for the sole purpose of following him.

"No. I bought it when I got here last Monday," she explained lamely. "I wanted to keep up with my exercise program while I was here."

"Have you tried running? You don't have to lug a heavy piece of equipment around."

She sighed—convincingly, she hoped. "I thought biking would be fun for a change. I run all the time at home—" another lie "—but not nearly as fast as you."

Pamela could have bitten her tongue as soon as she said the words. She'd as good as admitted she'd been watching him. Lying and being sneaky were a lot harder than she'd thought.

But if Matt Powers noticed, he gave no sign.

Lake Mewar, Jahangir, India

OTTO LOVED THE LAKE. From the center of the island, he could barely make out the opposite shore in any direction. In the serene stillness, he could hear the tiny waves licking the rocks, could smell the scent of jasmine and frangipani in the warm air. In many ways the lake was like a protective womb, cushioning his massive body from the hordes outside. In a country teeming with people, it amused him to live in a spacious stone palace, alone except for his women and his large professional and household staffs.

Now, searching the horizon from his bougainvillea-layered terrace, he spotted a boat headed toward the island. *Riker.* His serene mood vanished. Riker was bringing new information about the Goodman accident. Otto had asked him to deliver this report personally so he could study the assassin's face and sense his reactions in a way not possible over the telephone. This matter threatened to destroy everything Otto had worked for. He needed Riker's cold assurance that potential problems would be handled with the assassin's usual efficiency.

Ponderously, Otto rose and went to his tomblike library. Bad news wasn't meant to be heard in bright sunlight on a terrace shaded by vividly colored blossoms. Though it was gloomy inside, he didn't remove his dark glasses. They made him feel more normal, almost as though his eyebrows weren't missing. By the time Riker arrived, Otto's sensitive eyes had adjusted to the darkness.

He motioned for his operative to sit on the sofa next to him. As always, Riker stared straight at his dark glasses, deliberately avoiding any glances at his hairless head and arms. Otto wondered if Riker considered his hairless albino body, his massive shape and his pink eyes deformities. He thought of himself as deformed, had since he was a boy. *The hairless bastard.* Well, he'd show them all. One day he'd be remembered as the greatest genius of all time.

He didn't smile. "Tell me, Riker—what new information do you bring?"

"The pilot, Eric Goodman?" Riker paused.

"Yes, of course." Otto gestured impatiently. "Go on."

"He made a phone call just before he was eliminated." Riker's voice, like his appearance, was completely neutral. He disappeared in a crowd like a sardine in a barrel with a thousand other sardines.

"Why has it taken six weeks to discover this phone call?"

"The police kept it secret to protect the woman he contacted. They found the pilot's fingerprints on a pay phone and traced the call to her."

"So. A woman." Otto clenched his fists. "What did he tell her?"

"Nothing *unusual,* according to my police source. They interviewed her in Texas, where she's stationed, the week after the accident."

Otto studied his operative's chiseled features. Riker had more to tell. "Go on." He didn't hide his impatience.

"The woman's an air force captain named Pamela Wright."

Otto stiffened. *Wright* was a name he recognized.

Riker went on speaking. "Last Monday, Captain Wright arrived at McChord Air Force Base in Tacoma, Washington. The first thing she did was drive to the shopping center where the pilot died."

What unfortunate news. "She must have gone to Tacoma for some reason connected with Goodman's death."

"That's what I think," Riker agreed.

"But if the pilot told her nothing unusual, the woman is no threat."

"Perhaps she didn't tell the police everything she knows." As always, Riker focused on the worst possible scenario, one of his many useful traits.

"Watch her," Otto ordered. "Notify me at once if you discover she knows anything *unusual* about Goodman's accident."

Riker threw him a half salute. "Trust me, *Mein Herr,* if she is hiding something, I will find out."

Chapter Two

When a uniformed Pamela limped into the orderly room at
Matt's squadron, his first sergeant eyed her suspiciously.

"I'll need to see your ID card, Captain," he said after
she'd introduced herself. Since she wore captain's bars on
her shoulders and had told him who she was, it seemed like
a waste of time. But she handed the card over without protest.

Standing behind his desk, the noncom checked her ID
information carefully before he gave it back to her.
"Thanks, ma'am." A tall spindly man with black hair,
glasses and a mustache, he looked like his face would crack
if he smiled.

"Do you check every visiting officer's ID card?" Pamela asked.

He gave her a suspicious look. "Only when the major tells
me to."

Obviously this Mickey Mouse routine was Matt's idea.
Pamela glanced toward his open door. So he had some
questions about her, did he? Not half as many as she had
about him.

A few moments later, the sergeant ushered her inside
Matt's roomy office and closed the door.

"If you didn't believe I was who I said I was," she began, taking the offensive, "why didn't you ask me for the

name of my commanding officer at the Military Personnel Center? I've got the telephone number right—''

Before she could rattle it off, Matt repeated the number in his well-modulated baritone voice. "I've already talked to your commander. He confirmed that somebody with your name works at MPC. Of course, we didn't know you were that person until we checked your ID."

He gestured toward a chair beside his desk. "Sit down."

For half a second, she was too astonished to move. Then, gathering her composure around her like a coat of armor, she did as he asked.

Matt resettled himself behind his desk. "Please don't be offended by our security measures."

She studied his face. His firm mouth and somber expression seemed sincere. "I've visited a number of combat squadrons," she declared. "This is the first time I've been asked for ID."

"The other visits were probably in the line of duty," he pointed out, the epitome of cool logic. "You were preceded by official orders, and someone escorted you to the squadron. If you'd arrived here under those conditions, we wouldn't have checked, either."

Pamela met his gaze directly. His hazel eyes didn't waver. He's right, she decided, after a moment's thought. But she didn't intend to apologize for her questions. After all, she was doing him a favor by presenting the lecture.

"Anytime you don't like the way we do business around here, you can always walk away with no hard feelings." He gave her a narrowed, glinting glance. "After all, you *are* on leave. You're under no obligation to give this presentation."

She got the distinct impression he'd be relieved if she left. "I never renege on my commitments," she stated firmly, determined not to muff this chance to meet and talk to the people who worked with Eric Goodman. She smiled sweetly at Matt. "Now that you're satisfied who I am, maybe we can get to work."

Matt examined the cool woman opposite him, his congenial expression concealing his uneasy thoughts. Since her ID checked out, she probably wasn't an intelligence agent sent by the Pentagon to keep an eye on him.

Then just why *was* she here? She'd staged an accident to meet him, sweet-talked him into letting her give a presentation to his squadron—something she, obviously, wanted to do—and now she had the audacity to sit there, a regal lift to her lovely chin, acting as if she were doing him a favor just by being here.

To compound the problem, there was that annoying feeling he'd seen her somewhere before. Now that she was in uniform, the feeling was even stronger.

Somehow, in the short time since he'd deposited her at the door to her quarters, she'd managed to dry her blond hair. It waved bewitchingly over her left temple and below her ears. Just looking at it made him want to reach out and feel its silkiness beneath his fingers. He cleared his throat, unnerved by his unexpected desire.

She was staring at him, a curious expression in her hazel eyes. They were the same color as his, he noted. Right now, they held a bright sheen of purpose.

So, she wanted to get to work, did she? He stood. "My intelligence officer's been handling the lectures. I'll take you down to see him, and he can get you started."

"Fine." She followed him through the orderly room.

He could hear her limping along beside him, taking two strides for every one of his, her heels clicking on the tile floor leading to the small intelligence/public-affairs office. She was still limping, keeping up the pretense of the injured foot, though she was wearing low-heeled pumps.

The door to the intelligence office was open. The two men inside jumped to their feet as soon as Matt and Pam entered. One was the squadron intelligence/public-affairs officer, Capt. Tom Bolton, the other was Sgt. Calvin Stennis, who ran the office and did most of the legwork.

"As you were," Matt ordered, heading toward Bolton's desk. After a quick "Good morning, sir," the sergeant returned to his chair. Bolton remained standing, a broad grin on his face.

"Good to see you, sir." But Bolton wasn't looking at Matt, he was eyeing Pam. One look at her, and he was practically drooling. Matt reconsidered his decision to let Pam work with Bolton in the intelligence office. She might be more comfortable using the spare desk in the orderly room.

"Don't tell me my replacement has reported in already." Bolton had a smooth tenor voice that matched his handsome face.

"No such luck, Tom." Matt didn't return the other man's smile. "This is Capt. Pam Wright. She's going to give the commander's call next week."

"How very nice of you," Bolton said to Pam. "We have an extra desk—" he nodded toward an empty desk in the corner opposite his "—and I will devote myself wholeheartedly to ensuring the success of your endeavor." He glanced from Pam to Matt. "What stroke of good fortune brought Captain Wright to the 316th, sir?"

Matt shrugged. "Captain Wright brought herself here. For reasons known only to her, she volunteered to give the lecture."

Bolton's face lit up even brighter. "Ah, a mystery. She's keeping something secret. We intelligence types love mysteries."

Matt glanced at Pam, expecting a heated denial. She'd given him several reasons for her good deed, but he knew they weren't the real ones. Did she honestly think he'd believed her?

Instead of the blustering denial he expected, she looked him calmly in the eye, not giving an inch—she was as composed as she'd been in his office. Then she focused on Bolton. "There's nothing mysterious about why I volunteered.

I'm an expert on this subject and enjoy telling people about it."

Her words had the sound of a rehearsed speech. Matt suspected she'd put some thought into her reasons while she was changing into her uniform.

She smiled at Bolton. "Of course, when your C.O. found out I specialized in Russian studies, he *did* promise to take me to dinner tonight if I'd do this little chore for him." Deliberately, making sure Bolton saw, she grinned mischievously at Matt.

Staring back at her, Matt realized she'd just turned the tables on him. Her presentation now sounded like his idea. She might not be a very good actress, but she was certainly quick on her feet.

"I didn't realize we'd agreed on tonight," he said, matching her cool tone. "But if that's your preference, tonight it is. I'll pick you up at six-thirty."

"Six-thirty, then." She started toward the room's unoccupied desk.

"Make sure she gets anything she needs," Matt told Bolton.

"Yes, sir." The intelligence officer looked like a fox who had just spotted a plump jackrabbit. Matt had often wondered if Bolton was as much of a lech as he pretended. For the space of a heartbeat he again considered letting Pam use a desk in the orderly room.

Not a good idea, he told himself as he started back toward his own office. *She'd be too distracting for the men.* Not for a moment would he admit that the man who'd be most distracted was *him*.

PAMELA FELT TOM BOLTON'S eyes following her as she sat down behind the desk in the corner of his office. Was he going to be a problem? Not if she could help it. With a little work, maybe she could turn him into a buddy like Eric had been.

Eric. His memory haunted her. Maybe Bolton could tell her something about the accident. She flashed him a smile.

He needed no further invitation. In an instant he was perched on the side of her desk. She resisted the urge to push her chair away from him.

At the front desk near the door, the sergeant stood up and took some papers to the filing cabinet. He didn't look toward Bolton and Pamela in the back of the room.

Bolton glanced briefly in his direction, then turned to Pamela. "Since you're tied up with the boss tonight, how about some company tomorrow night? I give the best back rubs in the air force."

Pamela favored him with her sweetest smile. "Why don't you go give *yourself* a good rub, Bolton. Sounds like you need it."

He stared at her for an instant, as though unsure of her meaning. Then he chuckled. "Are you as tough as you sound?" But, jocular tone notwithstanding, he got up from her desk and went to his own.

"Judge for yourself," she returned, forcing herself not to speak abruptly. "Now, if you don't mind, I'd like to get to work on my presentation. You should have received some material from Air Force a week or so ago."

Bolton turned toward his sergeant's back. "Sergeant Stennis? Did we get that package Captain Wright's talking about?"

The sergeant rummaged around in his desk until he came up with a manila envelope. He swung his chair around. "We got this information last week, ma'am." Rising, he brought it to her.

Pamela stood up, leaning across the desk to shake his hand. "I'm Captain Wright, Sergeant."

"Cal Stennis, Captain. If you need anything else, let me know." He wore frameless glasses and had the well-rounded appearance of a man who enjoyed his wife's cooking. As he turned away, Pamela caught a glint of amusement in his dark brown eyes. He'd obviously enjoyed the exchange between her and Bolton.

"Thanks, Sergeant Stennis." Pamela sank slowly to her seat.

She spent the rest of the morning working on her lecture. Tom Bolton, properly chastised by her earlier comment, made no more suggestive comments. Sergeant Stennis went out of his way to help her. By midafternoon she'd established a friendly camaraderie with the two men and felt the time was right to broach the subject of Eric's accident.

Going to Sergeant Stennis's desk, she handed him an outline to type. "Maybe you can answer a question everybody at the personnel center's been asking."

The sergeant turned to face her. Out of the corner of her eye, she could see that Bolton's attention was focused on her, too.

"We heard about your squadron's aircraft accident last month. According to the initial report, the pilot said his flight-control system failed."

She paused, hoping Stennis would volunteer some information or that she'd catch a significant glance between Bolton and his sergeant. When there was no obvious communication, she went on.

"A few days later, we heard the preliminary investigation blamed the accident on pilot error." She paused again, but could detect no reaction other than interest. "That finding aroused everybody's curiosity at MPC. It didn't seem logical to us that pilot error could be responsible for a total system failure. What's the talk around the squadron? Do the noncoms agree with the preliminary report?"

Stennis nodded. "The government could find no evidence of any malfunction."

Pamela stared at the sergeant in disbelief. Eric had told her his instruments had quit for no apparent reason. He must have told Matt Powers the same thing on the helicopter after he was picked up. Powers had been aboard, Pamela remembered from her talk with Eric. That's how the information about the system failure appeared in the report Powers submitted.

"What did the pilot tell everybody else at the squadron?"

"Captain Goodman didn't talk about the accident to anybody but the major," Stennis said.

"Not anyone?" Pamela didn't believe it. According to Eric, only the major knew about the UFO. But surely he'd told others about the jet's malfunction. "How about the people who picked Captain Goodman up, before he talked to the major?" Intent on his answer, she leaned halfway across the desk. "Surely he told them something about the accident."

Bolton's tenor voice intruded. "Why so interested? You're not on some kind of undercover inspection trip, are you?"

She forced herself to sink back into her chair. "The air force would have to be pretty hard up to assign a personnel officer to investigate an aircraft accident."

Bolton didn't seem convinced. "No personnel officer I know has a background in Russian, Pam. Besides," he observed sagely, a new note of respect in his voice, "the best undercover agents are the ones who look innocent."

"First you say I'm tough and now, innocent," Pamela returned, keeping her voice light. "Make up your mind, Bolton."

Not until late afternoon did she get answers to her questions about Eric's F-16 accident. Bolton had left the office. Sergeant Stennis swung his chair around, facing Pamela's desk.

"Those questions you asked, ma'am—"

"What questions?" As though she'd been thinking of anything else during the past few hours.

"The ones about the major being the only one Captain Goodman talked to after he bailed out."

"Oh, yes," she said, keeping her voice bland.

"The major was aboard the rescue chopper that picked up Captain Goodman. When he was brought aboard, he was unconscious. He came to for a little while, but the major was the only one he talked to. He passed out again before he got to the hospital." Sergeant Stennis studied her speculatively. "I hope that answers your questions."

Pamela sighed. She'd known all along that nobody but Matt had heard Eric's story about the UFO, but she'd hoped he'd talked to squadron personnel about the jet's crash. Still, the squadron had been involved in the official investigation into the accident. Its personnel must have opinions about Eric's murder. Perhaps she could find somebody able to supply the kernel of information she needed to tie the two together.

"THE WOMAN'S BEEN SENT here by the Pentagon to spy on us, Major." Tom Bolton leaned across Matt's desk, his tenor voice taut with warning.

Matt eyed his agitated intelligence officer. He'd already heard Bolton's interpretation of Pam's questions about Eric Goodman's accident. Did her interest result from normal curiosity, or was she a special military investigator, as Bolton suspected?

"We examined Captain Wright's ID," Matt said. "There's no doubt she's who she says." When Bolton opened his mouth to protest, Matt held up a hand to forestall him. "We also called the Military Personnel Center at Randolph Air Force Base where she works. Her commander vouched for her."

A look of tolerant denial crossed Bolton's face. "Of course somebody at Randolph vouched for her, Major. That's part of her cover story. It was all arranged by the Pentagon. Her ID card is probably fake, too."

Matt shifted uneasily on his executive chair. Maybe Bolton was right. Hadn't similar suspicions crossed his own mind?

Concealing his doubts, Matt waved toward the chair Bolton had just vacated. "Sit back down, Tom, and let's talk about this logically." Without waiting for Bolton to settle himself, he went on. "Why would the Pentagon use cloak-and-dagger tactics in a routine accident investigation?"

"There could be a very good reason." Bolton dragged his chair close to Matt's. "I think the accident is being investigated by people assigned to a special Pentagon project with the classified code name *Moon Watch*." He lowered his voice to a whisper as he spoke.

"Moon Watch?" Though Matt had never heard the words, he guessed what Bolton was referring to—the Pentagon's UFO sighting center. He feigned total ignorance. "I've never heard the term."

Bolton smiled in the self-satisfied way of one privy to special information. "Not many people have. The only reason I've heard of it is because I dated a woman who worked in the Moon Watch operation when I was assigned to the Pentagon Intelligence Agency." He raised an eyebrow. "Of course, she didn't tell me anything about what she did, but I got the idea it was connected to UFOs."

Bolton probably knew more about the operation than he was telling, but Matt didn't press him to disclose classified information. Just by repeating the code word, he was probably revealing more than he should.

"Maybe I should have told you this sooner, sir," Bolton went on, "but I guessed there might be a UFO connection last month when I saw Norm Duncan on the desert, nosing around Eric's downed aircraft."

A warning alarm sounded in Matt's head. Duncan was the special military investigator who'd arrived in Tacoma two days after Matt had reported Eric Goodman's incredible UFO story to the Pentagon. Duncan had insisted on interviewing Matt in an obscure restaurant off base. Now he knew why. Apparently, Duncan wanted to avoid people like Tom Bolton, who knew he was connected to Moon Watch and might guess, just from seeing him, that the downed pilot had encountered a UFO.

Bolton was examining Matt's face with the intense interest of a man about to learn a juicy bit of privileged information. "What puzzles me is why the Pentagon thinks a UFO was involved in the accident."

Matt couldn't reveal the truth about Eric's sighting. Duncan had made that painfully clear. His order to keep quiet had been followed by a written communication from the air force chief of staff confirming what Duncan said.

"Now that Captain Goodman's dead, we may never know the whole truth," Matt declared noncommittally. "But I don't think we should speculate on something that's none of our business."

"How about Captain Wright? What should we do about her?" Bolton clearly thought she posed a threat to the squadron.

Matt shrugged. "I don't see that we can do much of anything about her, especially if you're right and she's here on Pentagon authority. Just watch what you say around her, so she'll take home a good impression of the squadron. After she gives her presentation, we'll be done with her. If she really is investigating some aspect of the accident, she'll make sure any clandestine snooping she wants to do is finished by then."

"But her lecture's not scheduled until the end of next week." Bolton's voice rose in an audible protest. "Do you think it's wise to have her around the squadron that long? She might report us for some fool thing like sexual harassment."

"I think the squadron can put up with Captain Wright for the next eight days," Matt said. "Once she gives her lecture, she'll have no excuse to hang around our area. Even if she doesn't leave Tacoma right away, she shouldn't bother us."

But he couldn't ignore the oddly unsettling possibility that, since he was the only person who talked to Eric about the UFO, she might be here to spy on *him*. So she might be *bothering* him for a lot longer than eight days.

He leaned back in his chair. On second thought, if that were the case, he certainly knew how to handle *her*.

Chapter Three

Matt held the door of the visiting officers' quarters open for
Pam. He watched her pull the hood of her raincoat over her
shining blond hair as she stepped into chill drizzle outside.
Though she was of above average height, her coat—belted
at the waist—emphasized her slimness, making her seem
fragile and, somehow, vulnerable. Her slight limp added to
the impression.

Don't be fooled, he warned himself. *She's only playing a
part.* He couldn't let himself be taken in, not if he expected
to spring tonight's trap on her successfully.

"Let's go into town for dinner," he suggested, taking her
arm to guide her toward the parking lot. The questioning
glance she threw him made him wonder if she suspected he
had a reason for this change of plans.

"I thought we agreed on the Officers' Club." Her voice
held a hint of suspicion.

"I figured you'd be tired of the place," he said. "I know
I definitely am. So I made reservations at a place a friend
recommended in town."

Shrugging, Pam smiled up at him. "Well, if you don't
mind the drive—"

He shook his head. "It's only about ten miles."

Glancing down at her, he saw no reaction. When would
she realize where he was taking her? Matt was pretty good
at sensing other people's feelings. Any unusual reaction

from her, and he'd know Bolton was right: she was an undercover investigator from the Pentagon.

Opening the car door, he helped her inside. She fumbled with her seat belt.

"Let me help you with that." At her nod, he reached across to fasten it for her. Inadvertently his arm touched her breast. Even through her raincoat, there was no mistaking the softness.

His physical reaction was immediate—and totally unexpected. Matt had brushed against other women without a jolt of awareness like this. He caught himself wondering how Pam would look in a filmy negligee, her breasts peeking saucily through the transparent material.

Quickly he blotted out the image. *I've been working too hard,* he told himself, hastily locking her belt in place.

Since Matt had been transferred to McChord six months ago, he'd been too busy to do any serious dating. Until this moment, he hadn't realized how much he missed having a special woman in his life. Too bad Pam Wright wouldn't be staying. And even if she were, she wasn't his type. He liked women who talked and laughed a lot to complement his conservative nature.

He dismissed his chaotic thoughts. *She's nothing but trouble,* he warned himself. Besides, no matter what game she was playing, she'd be out of his life in a few days. When they got to town, he'd have a better idea what she was up to.

Matt slammed her door and went around to the driver's side of his seven-year-old Chevrolet station wagon. The dependable old Chevy was a comfort he couldn't bring himself to give up. The car was another reflection of his conservative nature, he thought wryly. For years he'd tried to be more outgoing but had finally given up.

"So tell me about yourself, Pam," he said, after he'd started the car and turned toward the base's main gate. "How did you end up in the air force?"

It was a trite question, one Pamela had been expecting. She didn't have to think twice about her answer.

"I haven't had the most interesting life in the world." She was determined to volunteer as little personal information as possible. The less he knew about her, the less likely he'd be to associate her with her father, Air Force Lt. David Wright, who had disappeared after reporting a UFO twenty years ago.

Eventually, Pamela learned her father had been returning from a top-secret, high-altitude reconnaissance mission over the USSR when he disappeared. The tabloids blamed his disappearance on aliens. Hogwash. Somehow the Soviets had sabotaged his plane. She'd spent the years since then determined to learn everything she could about the country that had taken her father from her. Someday, she was sure, that knowledge would help her find out the truth about his disappearance.

"I joined the air force shortly after I graduated from the University of California at San Diego," she said. "Before that, typical college experiences. After, typical air force training and life."

Hoping that would satisfy his questions, she stole a look at Matt's profile. With his trench-coat collar turned up at the neck, he looked mysterious, fully capable of hiding Eric's monstrous secret—or even of being involved with whoever or whatever was behind his accident. But she couldn't reconcile her suspicions with the air of honest dependability Matt projected.

"Is that where you grew up?" he persisted. "San Diego?" The drizzling rain on the windshield cast weird shadows on his face when an oncoming car passed.

She nodded, a sudden chill racing across her shoulders. "Yes." Why had he insisted on eating in town when the O'Club was so convenient? She sensed a purposefulness about him, as if he were a lion waiting to pounce on an unwary gazelle.

"Your parents still there?" His voice was low, composed.

Pamela warned herself to be careful. "My mother is." She didn't want to talk about her family and thought about changing the subject, but decided not to. That might make him suspicious.

"How about your dad? Is he in San Diego, too?"

Pamela hesitated, tempted to lie and say yes. She decided not to, sensing the man beside her would know. "My dad died when I was eight."

"That must have been hard on you and your mother." There was a note of genuine sympathy in his voice.

Hearing it, Pamela almost let her guard down. *It was the hardest thing that's ever happened to me. It turned my whole life upside down.* She shrugged offhandedly to conceal her troubled thoughts. "We had Dad's insurance. And Mom was into real estate. She ended up making a small fortune."

An overpass crossed the interstate. On the other side stood Lakewood, a suburban community renowned in the area for its elegant lakeside homes. No elegance was evident, however, along the road leading from the base. Gas stations and flat-roofed, one-story businesses, all brightly lit in the drizzling rain, lined the four-lane highway.

Traffic lights appeared with annoying frequency. At the first one, Pamela felt Matt's gaze on her face and turned to meet his hazel eyes.

"How did your father die?" he asked.

Pamela's stomach clenched. This was the question she'd been hoping he wouldn't ask. She looked down at her hands clasped tightly in her lap. "In an automobile accident," she lied.

Though he seemed to buy the story, Pamela didn't let herself relax. From the corner of her eye she caught him stealing glances at her. Was he weighing her reactions to his questions? How easy this evening would be if they were two people who'd just met and simply wanted to get better acquainted. She concentrated on her breathing so she wouldn't seem tense.

The car's delayed-action wipers whoosh-whooshed, straining to clear the light drizzle from the windshield. They'd left Lakewood and entered a dark stretch of highway bordered by towering firs. Why was this drive taking so long?

"How far is it to town?" she asked.

He gave her a sideways glance. "Didn't you drive into Tacoma when you got here Monday?"

She tensed, wondering what to say. The first thing she'd done Monday was investigate the shopping-center parking lot in Tacoma where Eric had been killed.

"Yes," she admitted slowly. "That's when I bought my bike. But I took the interstate, so this road's not familiar." She sensed that he wasn't satisfied with her answer.

"We've only a few more miles to go." He glanced at her again.

"I've told you all about me," she said, feeling the time was right to finally change the subject. "Now how about you? Are your parents still living?"

He nodded. "They retired to Florida from Chicago."

Pamela knew most of the basic facts about him from her peek at his file, but kept up her questioning so he wouldn't guess she'd checked up on him. "What route did you take to get to the air force from Chicago?"

"Air Academy." His reply was terse. Pamela noticed that his breathing had sharpened, like he was expecting something to happen. Was her lion about to pounce?

"Know where you are yet?" he asked unexpectedly.

Startled, she glanced out her side window. Judging by the inexpensive residential housing along the road, they'd obviously reached the city. "No. Should I?" Her early chill returned.

He shrugged, but his tense posture was anything but relaxed. "I thought you might have gotten over into this neighborhood when you came to town last Monday."

She gave a feeble laugh. "Is the Tacoma Mall around here somewhere? That's where I bought my bike." She knew it

wasn't. The Tacoma Mall was visible from the interstate.
They weren't anywhere near there. From the direction
they'd come, she guessed they were somewhere near the
Narrows Bridge.

The Narrows Bridge. Eric had been killed in the Narrows
Plaza Shopping Center parking lot, only a mile or so from
the bridge.

An instant later Matt turned into the same parking lot
she'd visited last Monday—the place where Eric had died.
Tensing, Pamela felt the blood drain from her face.
Through the drizzling rain she saw the theater with the two
pay telephones mounted on the wall outside the lobby. Eric
had called her from one of them.

She swallowed hard. For one horrible moment, she
thought she was going to be sick. Why had Matt Powers
brought her here?

As soon as the theater came into view, Matt knew he'd
guessed right. From Pam's shocked reaction, he was pretty
sure she recognized it.

So Bolton was right. She *was* here in connection with
what had happened to Eric Goodman. Why else would she
have come to this out-of-the-way shopping center during her
first hours in Tacoma?

He parked in a space near the one Goodman must have
used the night he'd been murdered. The sidewalk in front of
the theater was brightly lit, a beacon in the drizzly semidarkness.

"Why are we stopping here?" Pam's voice sounded
faintly accusing, as though she suspected him of some sin-
ister ulterior motive.

He had an ulterior motive, all right. He wanted to find
out what the heck she was up to.

He got out of the car and glanced around, pretending to
look for the restaurant. "It's over there," he said, nodding
toward the place, "on the other side of the parking lot. I
knew it was around here somewhere."

He backed slowly out of the parking space and threaded his way through the incoming movie traffic to the nearest lane across the big lot. The restaurant's entrance faced the street on the side opposite the theater. He drove around the building and parked in front.

After helping Pam out of the car, he guided her toward the wooden steps leading up to the Western-style covered porch. Two men sat on rocking chairs near the dimly lit entrance. On this drizzly, cold March night, they seemed out of place. Matt eyed them warily.

Too late, he saw the camera on one man's lap and recognized his companion. A moment later, the brilliant glare of an exploding flashbulb shattered the darkness.

"Evening, Major," one of the men said. He had a gravelly voice, like a two-bit gangster in a B movie. "In case you don't remember me, I'm Stan Sharplett." He stuck out his hand. Matt ignored it.

Smiling, Sharplett thrust his hand in his raincoat pocket. "Your duty NCO told me we might run into you here tonight. That's a great system you military types have—always letting somebody know where you are." His smile broadened. "So we took a chance and came on over. If we could have a few minutes of your time, the *Morning News Herald* would be eternally grateful."

Pamela's eyes had snapped shut a millisecond after the flashbulb went off. But she couldn't erase the image of the dazzling light, burned black against her retina. Instinctively, she edged closer to Matt. Whatever these newspaper people wanted, their business was with him, not her.

"I'm sorry, Sharplett," Matt said. "I can't talk now. Our reservations are for seven. Call me at the base tomorrow."

The reporter moved to block the entrance. "Calling you doesn't work, Major." Sharplett's voice turned whiny. "Your sergeant says you're not available and refers me to your public information officer, Captain Bolton, who doesn't know zilch."

Pamela felt Matt tense at being intercepted by Sharplett, as though an electric shock had jolted through him.

"He knows as much as I do." Pamela heard the anger in Matt's voice. "And if you think you're going to bully me into an interview using tactics like this, think again." He stepped toward the door. "Move aside, Sharplett."

Matt was six inches taller than the other man and at least forty pounds heavier. For an intense moment, Pamela thought he was going to pick the reporter up bodily and heave him off the porch. But nothing happened.

"Look here, Powers." Sharplett's voice lost its wheedling tone. "Your picture's going to be in the *Herald* whether you talk to me or not. You can tell how important we think this story is by the fact that a photographer's along. Wouldn't you rather have me write something accurate instead of a bunch of speculations about these *interesting* rumors we've been hearing? You can bet I'll include my ideas as to why you won't talk to me about the aircraft accident."

The aircraft accident? In spite of herself, Pamela felt her body go rigid. She edged farther behind Matt. So that's what the reporter wanted. Matt's story about Eric Goodman's F-16 malfunction and crash. But what were these rumors Sharplett mentioned? Could the press somehow have gotten wind of Eric's UFO sighting?

"I gave you a statement six weeks ago," Matt growled. "My conclusions haven't changed. As for these *rumors* of yours, I don't know what the hell you're talking about. If you've got any kind of in with the police, you probably know more about what happened than I do." He took a purposeful stride toward Sharplett.

This time the reporter stepped aside. "Who's your friend, Powers?" He nodded his head toward Pamela.

Ignoring Sharplett, Matt swung the restaurant door open.

"Is there some reason you don't want her name in the paper with yours?" The question was soft, almost a whisper.

Turning, Pamela looked straight into the reporter's eyes. They were black and beady, a ferret's eyes.

"Of course not," she said, guessing that Sharplett could easily find out her name with a call to the same duty NCO who had told the reporter how to reach Matt. "I'm Air Force Capt. Pamela Wright."

Sharplett threw her a sloppy half salute. "Thanks, Captain. You've saved me some time checking you out."

"Glad to cooperate." Pamela gave him what she hoped was a pleasant smile. But deep down the thoughts of this ferretlike man checking her out sent anxious tremors racing through her.

THE RESTAURANT HAD pegged wooden floors, fires blazing in several fireplaces and photographs of World War I era Puget Sound scenes on the walls. It smelled of mesquite smoke and garlic.

Maybe the reporter had done her a favor after all, Pamela thought. She wanted Matt to tell her what he knew about Eric's accident. What better excuse to talk about it?

"What was that all about?" Pamela asked Matt, after they'd been shown to their table.

Matt studied her through narrowed eyes. "Why ask? I'm sure you guessed." He sounded accusing, almost as though he suspected her of collusion with the reporter. But that was ridiculous.

She shrugged off her guilty feelings. "I suppose I did have a pretty good idea. But why should that reporter be after you six weeks later? Like he said, the paper wouldn't send a photographer unless they considered this an important story."

Matt scowled. "The final report on the cause of the accident came out yesterday."

Pamela tried not to appear too eager. "Did it agree with the preliminary report? That the accident was due to pilot error?" That much information was in every newspaper that carried a story about Eric's accident.

Matt nodded. "The local paper got hold of the final re-port. They want me to comment on it." He paused, and Pamela got the feeling he was wondering how much to tell her. "I've got no idea what these rumors are he's talking about."

She studied him thoughtfully. "Since the plane crashed on the Hanford Nuclear reservation in Eastern Washington, there can't have been any close-up observers."

He leaned toward her. For a breathless moment, she thought he might confide in her. Instead, his expression turned suspicious. "You seem awfully well-informed about the accident."

Disagreeing would be pointless. "I found it interesting that your pilot crashed in a restricted area." She studied his face. He was examining her with his stalking-lion look. "I can see why you didn't want to talk to that reporter," she said, to throw him off balance.

"You can?" His eyebrows lifted in surprise.

The waiter brought coffee for both of them and took their orders.

"Sure," she said, when the waiter had left. "You're in the wrong, no matter what you say. If you agree with the inves-tigators that the accident was pilot error, you're throwing blame on one of your people—who now happens to be dead. If you disagree, you jeopardize the whole system—and make them wonder if you know something they don't."

She gave him a critical look. "Just between you and me—two air force officers—what do you really think hap-pened?"

He didn't hesitate. "It had to be pilot error. The govern-ment searched the wreckage and found no evidence of mal-function."

"But what did the pilot tell you?" Pamela knew the question might give her away, but she had to ask. "The pa-pers in San Antonio said he talked to his commander aboard the helicopter right after he was rescued. He must have told you what happened." The newspaper stories she'd read had said no such thing. She'd gotten that information from Eric himself.

Matt's mouth twisted cynically. "What the pilot said is in my official accident report, so I suppose there's no reason not to tell you." He took a long swallow of coffee.

Pamela waited, almost holding her breath. This was one of the things she'd come so far to hear.

"The pilot claimed something made his flight-control system go hard over." Matt paused. "Do you know what that means?"

"I've no idea." She leaned across the small table toward him, intent on what he was saying.

"It means the pilot no longer had control of his aircraft." His voice was soft, but alarming. "That's why he bailed out."

She sucked in her breath, remembering Eric's fantastic tale about a monstrous spider. Had the spider been an alien creature that had somehow interfered with the jet's sophisticated instruments? To conceal her shock, she asked the first question that popped into her head. "How could the flight-control system get fouled up like that?"

He shrugged. "Over U.S. territory, with no hostile aircraft around, it couldn't. That's another reason the cause of the accident had to be pilot error."

"But why would the pilot tell you a thing like that if it weren't true?"

Matt shrugged again. "To protect his own tail. Or maybe he misread the instruments. Or maybe something did go wrong with the flight-control system that cleared itself up later, after he'd bailed out."

Pamela frowned in disbelief. "Do things like that happen to jet airplanes?"

"Not to any I've ever flown." He gazed at her with a bland half smile. "But, then, you and I both know anything's possible."

Matt's cryptic remark was the closest he'd come to admitting that something unusual had happened on the Eastern Washington desert the night of Eric's accident. But why had he included her in his assumption? There was no way he could guess that she, like Matt himself, had heard the unbelievable details of Eric's fantastic tale. *He mustn't find out,* she warned herself. *Not as long as there's a chance he might be involved.*

MATT ATTACKED HIS STEAK, determined not to give Pam any more information about Eric Goodman's accident. Right after he'd talked to Goodman, he'd decided to keep the downed pilot's story as quiet as possible in order to protect Goodman's career and reputation. The Pentagon's military UFO investigator, Norman Duncan, had given him another good reason for his vow of silence.

"Don't say anything to anyone about the possible UFO sighting," the dumpy little man had ordered. "We don't want to scare the public to death, now do we?" The next day, Matt had received a top-secret TWX from the air force chief of staff repeating Duncan's order.

Bolton's news that Duncan was connected with Moon Watch only strengthened Matt's resolve to keep a tight lid on the UFO aspects of Eric Goodman's strange story. Whoever Pam Wright was—and whatever she was up to—she wasn't going to find out anything about UFOs from Matt.

Sitting across the table from her, watching her blond hair reflect the light as she bent over her plate, he had to keep reminding himself that this woman was trouble. She was here to spy, probably on him. And every other word she said was a lie.

Still, he couldn't keep himself from wondering, as he was doing this instant, if her cool outer reserve hid a blazing furnace within. Would she give herself to a man with the disciplined passion of a Victorian princess? Or with the unbridled ardor of a mysterious Mata Hari?

"Do you have some dark, secret reason for helping out the 316th with our commander's call?" he asked. "Or are you always this cooperative when you're on leave?'' He kept his tone light, with just a touch of insinuation.

She gave him a questioning look. ''Of course I have a reason, Matt. You don't think I'd give up all this leave time without one.''

As their eyes met, his senses quickened. Surely she wasn't going to tell him what she was up to—just like that. ''Well, what is it?''

Her expression remote, she glanced down at her half-empty plate. ''I probably shouldn't admit this, but...''

He waited impatiently.

She cleared her throat and straightened her shoulders. ''What would you say if I told you I'm helping Stan Sharplett get your statement about the result of the accident investigation?'' She shot a sideways glance toward Matt. ''He thought I might have better luck than he's had, so he got me phony ID and uniforms.''

For half a second Matt believed her. Then she lifted her head. Amusement flickered in the eyes that met his.

''You're not serious,'' he said, knowing he'd been had.

''Of course I'm not serious.'' Her amusement swiftly died, and her expression turned accusing. ''I can't imagine why you thought I was.''

Matt was caught off guard by the sincerity in her voice. *Don't be fooled,* he warned himself again. *She lied to you before and she will again.*

''Just tell me one thing,'' she went on. ''Be honest with me, and I'll be honest with you. Why are you so sure my motives aren't exactly what I said?''

So she wanted the truth, did she? ''Because you lied to me this morning.'' Matt growled out the words, tired of keeping his suspicions hidden. ''You staged that accident on purpose. There was nothing wrong with your foot.'' He pierced her with his most penetrating stare.

He heard her quick intake of breath. Stains of scarlet appeared on her cheeks—stains so bright, they rivaled the pink in her turtleneck sweater. There was no way she could be faking her embarrassment unless she was a master of the trade.

"You've caught me trying to put one over on you, Matt." She gave a nervous little laugh. A tremor touched her lips. "My fall this morning was nothing but an act."

UNABLE TO MEET Matt's demanding gaze, Pamela looked down at her plate. How could she get him to believe her? As long as he thought she was a liar, he'd tell her nothing.

Besides, she didn't want him to think she was a liar. She wanted him to respect her for what she was: an honorable fellow officer.

So why was she going to tell him the biggest lie of all? The blood began to pound in her temples. Her cheeks burned as a humiliating, deflated feeling swept over her. Matt would think less of her after he heard her explanation.

That can't be helped, she told herself fiercely. It was the only logical reason for her faked accident—other than the real one, of course.

Across from her, Matt was studying her with an expectant expression, his forearms resting on the table's edge.

She cleared her throat. "This is sort of hard for me to admit, Matt."

His eyes narrowed.

Pamela cleared her throat again. "When I was out riding my bike last Tuesday morning, I spotted you and decided you were somebody I'd like to know better." She paused, watching him closely. With his brows drawn together over his narrowed eyes, he looked about as sympathetic as a police officer arresting a multiple offender.

She tried to smile, but her face felt frozen. "Back at the quarters after my ride, I asked a few questions—found out who you were and that you're single." To her dismay, her voice quavered. Her gaze returned to the half-eaten fish on her plate. "I'm not too clever at contrived introductions. The only way I could think to meet you was that clumsy accident."

Without lifting her head, she stole a glance at him from under her lashes.

His eyes studied her with a curious intensity. This time she didn't look down.

"You went to a lot of trouble for nothing," he said. Pamela could hear the skepticism in his voice. "If you wanted to meet me, why not just walk up and say hello in the O'Club?"

"That's probably what I should have done," she admitted, playing her part. "But I'm not used to picking men up in bars—not even in the Officers' Club."

She paused, then forced herself to shrug offhandedly. "I figured you'd probably guess what I was up to."

If he didn't believe her story, so what? She already had access to his squadron. Still, she couldn't believe how pleased she was when the lines between his brows vanished.

He leaned toward her with a slow smile. His hazel eyes sparkled with warmth.

"You wouldn't have had to pick me up in the bar," he said, his voice a raspy purr. "One look at you, and I'd have been at your table introducing myself five minutes after you sat down." He lifted an eyebrow and grinned, rather wickedly, Pamela thought.

She shifted uneasily on the padded bench seat. "Just because I went out of my way to meet you, don't get any ideas." She kept her voice light, but with enough authority to let him know she meant what she said.

Unexpectedly, he reached across the table and took her hand. "I promise you'll love every idea I come up with." Before she could jerk her hand away, he brushed her palm with his lips.

When Pamela felt his breath, warmly moist on her sensitive hand, something electric trembled deep inside her. Even after he released her, she could feel the soft pressure of his lips. Her blood surged to the place he'd kissed. It tingled warmly, almost as though he'd left a tangible mark on her palm.

Chapter Four

Much as Matt wanted to accept Pam's explanation, he couldn't. In the car after they left the restaurant, he warned himself not to believe her. If just the faked accident was involved, he probably would have. He would even have accepted as coincidental her offer, complete with credentials, to give his commander's call lecture.

The one thing he couldn't accept was her startled reaction to seeing the place where Eric Goodman had died. So, her appearance at McChord had nothing to do with an attraction for Matt Powers—and everything to do with Eric Goodman's aircraft accident and death.

Why couldn't she just be honest with him? Perhaps if he confronted her with his suspicions...? But he'd have to play his cards carefully. Turning onto the street from the restaurant's parking lot, Matt headed in the direction opposite the base.

"Where are we going?" Pam asked, a thread of tension in her voice.

He glanced down at his watch, deliberately casual. "It's still early. Now that we know your foot's okay, how about walking off our dinners along the waterfront?"

"My foot might be okay," she said, "but my shoes aren't right for the beach."

Matt grinned to himself. She hadn't said no. Was it possible she'd come here to investigate Goodman's F-16 crash and subsequent death, as Matt's intelligence officer claimed, but was still telling the truth about why she faked her accident? Maybe she'd done it because she admired him, just as she said. The thought sent a shaft of excitement racing through him.

"A sidewalk parallels the beach, so the shoes you've got on are fine," he said.

Staring at her profile in the lights from the oncoming traffic, Matt wanted very much to believe she was as attracted to him as he was to her. With her face turned straight ahead, he could see the aristocratic line of her nose, the regal tilt of her head. She looked every inch an air force officer. That should have turned him off, but somehow it made her more desirable. But when she shifted toward him and smiled, she reminded him more of a high school homecoming queen than a military officer. Maybe it was her pink turtleneck sweater showing through her raincoat's open collar. Strangely, he liked that look, too.

The nearer they got to the beach, the more he dreaded their coming confrontation.

SITTING BESIDE MATT in the darkened car, Pamela forced herself to look straight ahead into the oncoming headlights—anywhere but at Matt Powers. Strapped in next to him, with his lean, muscular body tantalizingly close to hers, she couldn't help wishing that what she'd told him tonight in the restaurant was the honest truth. Then she could stop fighting the attraction drawing her to him.

Though Matt wasn't the type of man she usually dated, something about him fascinated her. If she didn't resist, she could find herself falling for him. But she mustn't do that. Not until she uncovered the truth about Eric's aircraft accident and what part, if any, Matt played in it.

He parked across the road from the beach. Getting out of the car, Pamela drew her raincoat tightly around her. In the drizzly darkness, the place felt spooky, like a cemetery in a strange city.

Above, on a steep hill, rows of wooden dwellings towered, their lighted windows peering toward the water like
giant eyes. Off in the distance, she heard the lonesome
whine of a train whistle and the click, click, click of big
wheels on steel rails. The sound grew louder. Looking
around, she discovered tracks running along the bottom of
the hill, not twenty feet from where she stood. A moment
later a train thundered past, shaking the ground beneath her.

What had possessed her to agree to a walk in a strange
area with a man she hardly knew? She turned toward the
car. "This place doesn't look safe to me, Matt. Let's go back
to the base."

He took her arm. "The sidewalk's well lit, and police cars
drive along here all the time." He paused. "But if you're
afraid, of course we'll go back."

Pamela didn't miss the challenge in his voice. She took
another look down the road. Several restaurants on pilings
jutted out over the water. Now that the train was past, she
heard rhythmic drumbeats coming from one of them. On
the sidewalk next to the beach, a man ran with his dog.
What appeared to be a small park was directly opposite the
car.

"No, I'll take your word for it that it's safe." She started
across the asphalt road with him beside her.

"I'm glad we're taking this walk," he said when they'd
reached the sidewalk on the far side. "There's something I
want to ask you."

She glanced up at him, half-afraid of what was coming.

He gripped her arm more tightly. "I noticed you reacted
when we drove up to the theater in the Narrows Plaza. Is
there something you're not telling me?" There was almost
a look of pleading on his face.

For a heart-stopping moment, Pamela could hardly take
a breath. She had to force herself to keep walking. Could
she afford to deny, once again, that she'd been there before?

No, she decided. She'd have to come up with something better than a denial.

"I…uh… This is going to sound pretty gruesome, Matt," she began, stalling to organize her racing thoughts.

"Let me be the judge." He sounded more sympathetic than he had all night. Their shadows lengthened as they moved farther away from the streetlight.

She took a deep breath. "You've got to understand that your Captain Goodman's murder—so soon after he bailed out of his fighter—aroused a lot of curiosity at the personnel center."

"So?" In the muted light, Pamela saw his narrowed eyes, the frown lines between his brows.

"So, I wanted to see where it happened." She breathed deeply, letting the fresh salty air strengthen her resolve.

"When I checked in at the visiting officers' quarters, I asked a few questions about the accident. Since I didn't have anything better to do Monday afternoon, I went to see the place the pilot was killed after I bought my bike at the mall."

Pamela felt like a ghoul, confessing to such morbid curiosity. But Matt didn't seem to think it odd. In the glow from another street light, she could see relief wash over his rugged face, smoothing his skin.

"And that's the only reason you went to the Narrows Plaza?" he said. "Curiosity?" There was a new lightness to his step.

"Yes." She gave a nervous little laugh. An elderly couple, huddled together, passed them going the opposite direction. Pamela waited until they were out of earshot before continuing. "I seem to be confessing to all sorts of embarrassing secrets tonight. You can see why I was reluctant to admit I'd been there."

He smiled and inclined his head. Tiny beads of water trickled down his temples off his straight brown hair.

"You've been honest with me, and I want to be honest with you," he said, his mouth curved in a half smile. "Your story isn't half as bad as the one Tom Bolton's peddling about why you're here."

A stab of apprehension made Pamela stiffen. "That sounds ominous. What's he saying?"

Matt squeezed her arm. "He thinks you're a secret agent sent by the Pentagon to investigate Captain Goodman's aircraft accident and death."

Pamela forced herself to grin. "That's the stupidest thing I ever heard."

"That's what I thought." He stopped walking. His gaze traveled over her face and searched her eyes. "Sometimes I wonder how intelligence officers come up with the off-the-wall stuff like this."

"Good imaginations, I guess." Inside, Pamela was limp with relief that Matt believed her instead of Bolton. Suddenly, she didn't want the night to end. She took Matt's arm.

"It's not even ten yet," she said, scarcely believing what she was saying. "Let's go somewhere for dessert."

His eyes widened with surprised delight. "We could probably get a cup of coffee or a brandy at that place." He nodded toward a modernistic structure leaning out over the bay on stilts. Raucous snatches of hard-rock music echoed across the water from the place. "There's a discotheque on the second floor, but a nice restaurant downstairs," he explained.

She nodded, pleased for this chance to know him better. "You can have the brandy. I'll take dessert."

Her arm in his, they headed toward the restaurant. In the misty drizzle, the streetlights were ringed with hazy halos. Off in the distance, Pamela heard the dull bleat of a ferry horn. The night, which seemed so threatening only minutes before, had become strangely peaceful now that he believed her.

Neither of them spoke, appreciating the comfortable silence between them. Matt was the most down-to-earth man she'd met in a long time, Pam thought. She leaned closer to him, enjoying the solid feel of him beside her.

He put his free hand on her arm. "Even though we've only known each other a few hours, I suspect we're a lot alike, Pam." His words were as soft as a caress.

In spite of herself, Pamela felt her heart give a little lurch. "In what way?"

He didn't answer right away. When he did, his voice echoed her own longings. "I'll bet you've always wanted to be the life of the party—you know, the kind of person everybody clusters around."

"You, too?" she asked slowly.

He nodded. "But when I play that part, I'm simply not—"

"Not yourself," she finished for him. "I feel that way, too."

He squeezed her arm in silent empathy, as they entered the restaurant. Decorated in a nautical motif, the place featured lots of thick rope, shiny brass and a huge laminated fish on the wall over the entrance.

Seated at a window table, Pamela could see the lights on the far shore through the misty drizzle. While she nibbled on her wickedly rich pecan pie and Matt sipped his brandy, they found other things in common.

Like violent movies with daredevil heroes. "Maybe we're making up for the lack of excitement in our own lives," she suggested.

And big family gatherings on holidays. "Better than a cocktail party anytime," Matt commented.

Also, animals and the environment. "We've got to save the rain forests or the human race will cease to exist," she insisted solemnly, with no objection from him.

And, finally, golf, which they both played as often as they could.

Pamela didn't notice how late it had gotten until everyone else had gone and the staff began setting tables for tomorrow. The disco upstairs wasn't closed, though.

Drumbeats swirled around them, as they passed through the lobby on their way out. She glanced at Matt and saw her own distaste reflected on his face.

"Let's try out the disco," she said, teasing him.

His mouth spread into a thin-lipped smile. "Sure, if that's what—" His forced smile changed to a grin. "You're kidding."

"Of course," she said. "By now you ought to know that if you don't like the music, neither will I."

After they'd walked back to the car, Pamela still didn't feel tired. Being with Matt quickened her senses, and she didn't want to let him go. Not yet. Not until she'd really gotten to know him.

So instead of going directly back to the base, Matt took her around Browns Point, which was across Commencement Bay from Tacoma. On a promontory above the city, they looked down at the gleaming lights on the industrial Tideflats. From their lofty perch, the Tideflats seemed like a giant glowing stage with downtown Tacoma as a sparkling curtain rising on the hill beyond.

When Matt took her hand, Pamela didn't object. She knew he'd never take advantage of her in this out-of-the-way place. They were alike, she and Matt. She knew how he felt because she felt that way, too. They sat there for nearly half an hour, hand in hand, enjoying the music on the radio and the wonderful closeness that comes when two people instinctively understand each other. Finally, it was time to go.

Not until they reached McChord's main gate did Pamela realize that she'd done what she'd set out to do tonight, which was to earn Matt Powers's trust—in spite of all her lies. That thought brought her back to reality. How would she feel if he'd lied to her the way she had to him? Like she'd been betrayed. And that's how he was going to feel when he found out. Twice she found herself on the verge of blurting out the truth. But each time she heard Eric's voice accusing Matt of involvement.

Matt pulled the station wagon into a vacant spot near the visiting officers' quarters, but made no move to get out. Pamela unfastened her seat belt and reached for the door handle. Before she could twist it, she felt his hand on her shoulder. Something warm and deep responded to the feel of his hand sliding down her arm and drawing her closer. After the wonderful evening they'd shared, an undeniable magnetism was building between them. How like him to wait until they were safely on the base before showing his desire. She tried to hide her own feelings, but couldn't.

He leaned toward her, his mouth curved with tenderness.

You can't let him kiss you, she told herself, trying to throttle the dizzying current racing through her. *Not after all the lies you've told him.* But she didn't move away when he slid nearer.

"Don't," she whispered weakly, putting her hands on his shoulders in a halfhearted attempt to push him away.

He paused, his mouth inches from hers. "Are you sure, Pam?"

She could smell the sweet hotness of his breath, could feel the smoothness of his fingers caressing her neck.

No, she mouthed silently. *Dear God, no. I'm not sure.*

As though he could read her thoughts, his mouth descended on hers, taking her lips with an aching tenderness. Hesitantly at first, then more forcefully, he pulled her against him.

Pamela wanted to resist, but she couldn't. Her body seemed made of molten metal, eager to fuse with his. Her hands found their way around his neck, holding him ever more tightly. She thrilled to the feel of her body against his—her sensitive breasts against the hardness of his chest, her fingers on the muscular tendons behind his neck.

Matt moaned with pleasure as her resistance crumbled. He turned her in his arms so she was molded more firmly to the contours of his body. For a long moment, nothing mattered except his kisses and the erotic sensations shooting through her.

Suddenly, the door to the visiting officers' quarters slammed. The sound brought back her reason. How could she let this happen with a man she'd deliberately lied to? A man who might be involved in Eric's aircraft accident? She pushed herself away, his chest hard under her fingers.

Breathing heavily, Matt gave her a surprised look. "What's wrong? You want this as much as I do, Pam. I know you do. If you didn't, you wouldn't have stayed out until 3:00 a.m. with me, and you certainly wouldn't have faked your accident this morning."

Pamela felt like crying. "I should never have told you," she blurted out.

Without waiting for him to come around and open her door, she scrambled out and fled up the sidewalk.

Matt didn't chase after her, but sat watching until she was safely through the door. What a fascinating woman she was—cool as ice outside, but, if she was as much like him as she seemed, hot as an erupting volcano when she was with the right person. Not for a second did he doubt he was the right man—or that Pam had been telling the truth when she said she'd faked her biking accident this morning because she was attracted to him.

CAPT. TOM BOLTON, the squadron intelligence officer, was waiting in the orderly room when Matt arrived at work the next morning. Under his arm, he was holding a copy of the morning newspaper.

"We've got to talk, Major." He waved the paper in the air. "There's an article in this morning's *Herald* you'll be interested in."

Matt grimaced and nodded to Bolton. "Come on into my office, Tom."

Once inside, Bolton laid the newspaper on Matt's desk. "You made the front page, sir."

Seated behind his desk, Matt took a good look at the photo Bolton was pointing to. Spread across four columns was a big picture of him and Pam. He cursed Sharplett under his breath. Then he noticed the half-inch-high headline over the picture: UFO Coverup?

Matt froze in shock. Had the reporter managed to ferret out Eric Goodman's strange tale?

Matt stared at his intelligence officer, who was studying him with unabashed curiosity. "What's going on, Bolton?"

"You tell me, sir." Bolton sat down in the chair next to Matt's desk. Leaning back, he crossed an ankle over the opposite knee and folded his hands in his lap. "According to the article, you and Captain Wright are suspected of covering up a UFO sighting Captain Goodman made in Eastern Washington the night his F-16 crashed."

"Captain Wright?" Matt reminded himself to keep his voice down. "What in the world does she have to do with this?"

"That reporter dug up some very interesting information about her."

Bolton looked so smug, Matt knew the article's "interesting information" confirmed the intelligence officer's theory that Pam was here to investigate Goodman's accident and death.

Matt's gut hardened into a lump of concrete. Last night he'd been so sure she was attracted to him, he'd ended up believing everything she said. Could his intuition have been that far off? Deliberately, he leaned back in his chair and folded his arms behind his head so Bolton wouldn't know how disturbed he was.

"What kind of 'interesting information'?" Matt knew he could find out from the newspaper article, but he wanted to hear Bolton's interpretation before he read Sharplett's story.

Bolton straightened. "For one thing, sir, Goodman called Captain Wright just before he was killed. The police found his prints on one of those pay phones outside the theater and traced the call through his credit card."

Matt got up and went to the window, afraid his troubled thoughts would show. In the distance, he caught a glimpse of Mount Rainier, its cap enshrouded in clouds.

So, Pam was a friend of Eric Goodman's. Suddenly, it hit Matt where he'd seen her before—in a photograph at Goodman's apartment, in her uniform, with Eric. What was her relation to the downed pilot? Had they been lovers? Probably, Matt thought with a twinge of jealousy. Goodman's reputation as a ladies' man was legendary. Why else would she come all the way to Tacoma from San Antonio to find out more about his accident and murder?

"What's her UFO connection?" Matt asked tersely.

Bolton got up and came toward him, obviously eager to answer. "You remember that story about an air force pilot named Lt. David Wright? Disappeared—along with his bird—over the Indian Ocean about twenty years ago. One of my instructors at the intelligence school spent half an hour talking about him."

Matt searched his memory, but no light clicked on. "Was he a relative of Pam's...er...Captain Wright's?"

"You've got it, sir. He was her father."

Her father! Hadn't she told him her father had been killed in an automobile accident? What a fool he'd been to believe anything she said.

"So what does Captain Wright's father have to do with UFOs?" Matt went back to his desk and sat down. "Don't tell me he reported one before he bought the farm."

"Not only that," Bolton returned, following Matt from the window, "but neither he nor the plane were ever found. He ditched in the ocean, of course. But even in deep water, there's usually some wreckage. Our investigators searched for weeks but found nothing." Bolton shrugged. "There are those who believe both he and his Blackbird were transported aboard a UFO and taken somewhere away from the planet."

A cold chill tightened Matt's back. Though recently retired from service, the SR-71 Blackbird was still the world's most advanced reconnaissance aircraft. Twenty years ago the plane was so secret that a special code word protected its photography. Could aliens have stolen it, along with its pilot? And where would they have taken it? To the moon, maybe?

Rubbish. But was that notion any more unrealistic than Eric Goodman's space spider?

"Just because her father reported a UFO, and now Captain Wright shows up here after talking on the phone to Captain Goodman—that's no reason to connect Goodman's accident with a UFO." Maybe Sharplett had screwed up.

Bolton shook his head. "There's more, sir. Some people saw the UFO just before Goodman's plane crashed. They claim to have seen it land near where his parachute came down. They say the saucer took off half an hour or so later."

Matt felt like he was seeing a movie in slow motion for the second time. First Goodman's version and now this article's. Still, his mind refused to accept either story.

"That reporter's sources must be crazy," he said doggedly. "Why wait nearly two months to report what they saw? And why tell Stan Sharplett?"

"You knew the plane crashed on the nuclear reservation over at Hanford?" Bolton's confident smile showed even white teeth against his olive skin.

Matt nodded impatiently. "Of course."

"Apparently some antinuclear people were over there snooping around an off-limits area. They were afraid they'd get arrested if word got out. Sharplett's keeping their names secret." Bolton shrugged. "I imagine they told him, instead of somebody else, because they knew he'd give their cause some publicity."

"Is that all they saw? Some sort of saucer from a distance?"

"Isn't that enough, sir?" For the first time that morning, Bolton looked bewildered.

Matt nodded, careful to keep his thoughts hidden. The Pentagon had told him to keep quiet about Eric's monster. He intended to tell no one about it. Apparently, the observers hadn't seen it, or Sharplett would have mentioned it.

"Send Captain Wright in here as soon as she comes in," Matt said. "And don't say anything to her about this article. I'd like to see how she takes the news."

As Bolton rose to go, a smile lit his face. "Yes, sir."

Matt picked up the newspaper and began to read.

OTTO WOULD BE FURIOUS.

Postponing the inevitable telephone call, Riker lingered in the restaurant's high-backed booth and read the article for the third time. So, the woman's father had disappeared twenty years ago after reporting an unidentified flying object. Riker's police source—contacted first thing this morning—said he never knew that. The information was closely guarded—limited to the Tacoma police officers involved in the investigation of Goodman's death.

Regardless, Otto was sure to blame him for the oversight. Setting his coffee cup down on the restaurant's Formica tabletop, Riker balled his hand into a fist. Maybe he needed to put more pressure on his source. Better yet, maybe it was time to recruit a new police contact.

Riker concentrated on the facts in the story and what he'd learned from his employer. Goodman, the downed pilot, must have seen a UFO. That must have been what Otto had been trying to find out. Riker remembered his exact words. Had the downed pilot seen "anything unusual" after he ejected from his plane?

Riker pictured Otto's massive body, devoid of hair or color. Sometimes he reminded Riker of a grubbing white worm, probing joylessly in the dank depths of his stone mansion.

Otto was a genius, of course. In the shadowy circles where Riker traveled, he'd heard that Otto Von Meinhoff was the richest human being on earth—able to buy almost anybody or anything he wanted. Even kings and presidents. What had he done to earn his fortune? No one could say. But there was one thing nobody doubted: Otto's enemies disappeared without a trace.

Something inside Riker shuddered. Was Otto really a man? Or did that ungainly form contain a being more—or less—than human? Was that why he was involved in this strange business with a UFO?

The waitress appeared at his table. "More coffee, sir?"

Riker nodded. He'd have one more cup before facing Otto's wrath.

Half an hour later he made the call from a pay telephone on Sixth Avenue. His employer answered in the oddly high-pitched voice Riker knew so well.

"The local paper claims the woman and Goodman's commander are covering up a UFO connection," Riker said.

Otto let out his breath in a huge sigh. "How much else do they know?"

Riker's spirits rose at his employer's mild tone. "I'll read you the article." Riker repeated the story over the long-distance phone line, stopping only once to turn to an inside page.

When he was finished, he heard only silence. Instead of the fury he'd expected, he sensed a cool judgment being rendered, a sentence passed.

"Find out how much Powers and Wright know about the unidentified flying object and whom they've told. Then, eliminate them." Otto gave the order without a pause.

"Yes, *Mein Herr*," Riker said, smiling to himself as the line went dead.

WHEN TOM BOLTON WALKED into the intelligence office on Friday morning, Pamela resisted the temptation to ignore him. After all, this *was* his office.

"Good morning," she said, intending to glance up at him briefly and then return to the work on her desk. But something in his expression held her gaze. He seemed to bulge with important information that he was, obviously, dying to reveal. Leaning back, Pamela waited for him to tell her whatever it was.

When he approached her desk, he came toward her like a cat stalking an unwary mouse. "The old man wants to see you."

In the military service, *the old man* was a term of respect for a unit commander. But something about the knowing way Bolton said the words made Pamela wary.

"Major Powers wants to see me?" she asked, her heart in her throat.

Grinning, Bolton nodded. "There's no other 'old man' around this squadron."

A stab of anxiety pierced her insides. "What does he want to see me about?"

Bolton's smug smile was distinctly unpleasant. "I can't say."

But he obviously knew. That certainty made Pamela more anxious than ever.

Chapter Five

The door to Matt's office was open. Ignoring the first sergeant's cold stare, Pamela marched toward it.

"Come in and sit down," Matt called, standing behind his desk.

After one look at his frowning face, she struggled to ignore the fluttery feeling in her stomach. If this was how spies felt—constantly afraid they'd been found out—she felt sorry for them. The notion that her flutters might be a reaction to Matt himself seemed too ridiculous to contemplate. Smoothing her blue uniform skirt, she entered the office.

There was a newspaper in front of him. She'd barely lowered herself to the chair beside his desk, when he shoved it toward her.

"We made the front page," he said, his voice accusing. "Read the article." His hazel eyes shot daggers at her.

Pamela picked up the paper, glanced at the first word in the headline, and immediately felt sick to her stomach. She had to force herself to take a long, slow breath.

UFO! the headline screamed. How had the reporter found out? Eric said nobody knew about the UFO but her and Matt.

Pamela glanced at the picture, and her stomach clenched tight with apprehension. Had Eric talked to someone after he called her? Or had he indicated somehow that Pamela and Matt were the only ones who knew his secret?

Impossible. So how had the reporter connected them both to Eric's UFO?

With trembling hands, she held up the paper. When she finished reading, she felt her cheeks burning with shame. Most of her lies were exposed. What must Matt think of her? At that moment Pamela felt like something slimy, hunting for a rock to hide under.

Straightening her shoulders, she cast her guilt aside. If anyone was guilty here, it was Matt Powers. He was the one Eric had blamed for his accident. Like the reporter's sudden appearance last night, this article could be a blessing. It would force Matt, finally, to admit Eric had told him about the UFO. Maybe, after that barrier had been removed, she'd know whether she could trust him.

TO CONCEAL HIS ANGER, Matt picked up a pencil and began tapping the eraser on his desk. How dare she sit there, a regal tilt to her blond head, staring at him as though he was the one responsible for this damnable article? After their closeness last night, didn't she feel at all ashamed that she'd told him nothing but lies from the minute they'd met?

Not Pam, he thought bitterly. *She'll probably lie again and claim the article is wrong.* God, if only it *was* wrong. But Matt knew Sharplett's stories rarely contained mistakes. The reporter had probably been on the phone most of the night checking and rechecking his information.

Pam was studying him like a lab technician examining a specimen under a microscope. His attempt to shame her seemed to be having the opposite effect. He dropped the pencil and folded his arms.

"I think you owe me an explanation, Pam," he began. To his surprise, he found himself hoping she had one—something he could believe for a change. "From the time we met," he went on, "most of what you've said's been a lie.

How about leveling with me? What are you *really* doing here?"

She met his accusing eyes without flinching. "I'm here for the reasons stated in this article. What it says about me is correct—the phone call from Eric, my father's UFO sighting before he disappeared. It's all true."

He stared at her in disbelief. "Then you admit everything you've told me is a lie."

She shook her head. "Not everything. My name is Pamela Wright. I'm an air force officer and I work at the personnel center at Randolph Air Force Base. Like I said, I'm on a thirty-day leave."

He took a deep breath. "But you didn't come to see Seattle."

"No," she admitted. "Sharplett guessed right. I came to investigate Eric—Captain Goodman's—accident and death."

"Why, Pam? What was Eric Goodman to you?" Matt leaned across his desk toward her, wondering if he truly wanted to hear her answer.

Boldly her hazel eyes met his. "He was a friend." Her voice faded, losing its confident tone.

"Only a friend?" Matt didn't believe her. They had to have been lovers. "You're going to an awful lot of trouble for someone who was only a friend."

Her eyes glistened, but she didn't look away. Instantly, Matt felt like a brute for asking. No matter how many lies she'd told, it was obvious she'd lost someone dear to her. His accusations were bringing back her grief.

He felt his anger ebbing but resisted the urge to reach out and touch her. "Don't you think I have a right to know?"

She swallowed hard, obviously controlling herself with an effort. "Yes. After all the lies, you've got that right." She cleared her throat. "Eric and I were more than good friends."

Matt saw the sadness in her face. His compassion overrode the twinge of jealousy.

After a moment's pause, she went on. "Eric was like the brother I always wanted but never had. When he was murdered—"

Her voice choked. Matt felt like even more of a brute but wasn't able to release his anger. She had gotten to him. At the core of his indignation was an unexpected hurt. He glanced away until she'd regained her composure.

"I knew I'd never rest easy until I found out what or who was behind his death," she said. "That's why I'm here. That's why I volunteered to give your lecture. So I could mix around in your squadron—talk to your people, ask a few questions—without arousing suspicion."

She paused. Waiting.

Now that she'd made her confession, Matt sensed she expected him to do likewise. He remembered what Sharplett said in his article—that Goodman called her before he was murdered. The pilot, undoubtedly, told her about the giant spider. But had he also told her that Matt was the only other person who knew about the creature? Studying her pale intense face, he knew the answer was yes.

Tensing, he glanced through the open door to the orderly room. No one could hear what they were saying, but with the door open, someone might come in. He quickly closed it and returned to his desk. Pam sat forward and watched him intently.

"On the phone, Goodman told you what he saw, didn't he?" Matt asked. "After he ejected from his fighter?"

If she acted dumb, Matt intended to say no more about the pilot's strange sighting. He was on orders from the Pentagon to keep quiet about the alleged monster. Maybe Goodman hadn't said anything about it to her, after all.

But she nodded, fear glittering in her hazel eyes. "From the way Eric described it, he must have seen an alien creature." Shuddering, she drew her chair closer to his desk.

Matt felt an odd, prickly sensation on the back of his neck. *Don't be a jerk,* he told himself. *There are no such things as UFOs and alien monsters.* But the prickly feeling didn't go away.

"He was probably hallucinating," Matt said. "His eyes were playing tricks on him because of his rough landing."

She shook her head, a frown darkening her features. "Then why was he murdered, if not to shut him up about what he saw?"

"Maybe the police are on track. Maybe it *was* a simple case of car theft. He drove a fancy sports car, you know." Matt leaned back in his chair. "But assuming you're right, don't you think radar would have picked up a UFO entering our airspace?"

She drew her chair closer, her jaw tightening. "Even if radar saw it, do you think the information would be released?" she countered. "That's why the government classifies information about UFOs. To keep the public from finding out about them."

Remembering the Pentagon's warning to keep quiet, Matt felt the skin on the back of his neck prickle again. She had to be wrong. Norm Duncan—the Pentagon investigator— was simply trying to stop an outlandish rumor before it had a chance to take off.

"I checked," he said quietly. "Nothing came to earth from outer space that night."

Her eyes widened. He could tell she hadn't expected this. "What do you mean, you *checked*?"

"I've got a friend at the Goddard Space Center." Once again he resisted the urge to reach out and touch her, to assure her everything was okay. "Nothing entered or left earth's atmosphere during the time frame we're discussing."

She didn't look convinced. "Don't tell me the space center tracks every little plane that flies anywhere on earth."

"Of course not," he returned quickly. "But they *do* track everything in outer space—from the smallest piece of space trash to the multi-ton satellites orbiting the earth. If anything had entered earth's atmosphere, the people at Goddard would have seen it."

"Maybe your friend's covering up," she persisted doggedly. Her brittle smile betrayed her frustration.

"Anything's possible," he agreed. "But I really don't think so." Again he remembered the order to tell no one what Eric Goodman had seen. Had his friend at Goddard received similar instructions about an unknown UFO?

PAMELA STARED AT MATT'S rugged face. Was he telling the truth about checking with someone he knew at the space center? She sensed he wasn't—at least, not the whole truth. Either that, or he was keeping something secret.

"Then you think Eric imagined the whole thing?" she began cautiously. "And he was murdered so someone could steal the car?" She watched his face carefully.

"You've got to admit it's—"

A quiet knock on his door interrupted Matt's answer. He crossed the room, his lip twisting with exasperation.

His first sergeant stood outside. "Something's come up you should know about, sir," he said. Then he lowered his voice so Pamela couldn't hear the rest of his message.

"Thanks, Sergeant Newton," Matt said. "You should have buzzed me on the squawk box." He shut the door and returned to his chair. "It's a phone call," he said, picking up the receiver. "Should only take a minute."

Pamela made no move to leave. Apparently, the sergeant thought this telephone call was one Matt would prefer she not know about, so he hadn't announced it over the intercom. That gave her a very good reason to be interested.

"Yes, sir," Matt said, without any of the usual pleasantries. When he'd repeated the same "yes, sir" a few more times, she let herself relax. The call must be from a senior officer with a lot of dull instructions. As Matt listened, he kept scribbling notes on his desk pad.

Then he glanced at her. "She's right here in the office with me."

Pamela stiffened. Nobody knew she was in Tacoma except her office at Randolph and her mother. *And everybody who'd read that stupid article.*

"She's here on leave, sir." Pause. "Said she came to see Seattle."

So Matt wasn't betraying her confidence. Score one point for him.

"Ten-hundred hours tomorrow morning? We'll be there, sir." Matt hung up the receiver with a grim look on his rugged features. "As you probably guessed, that was the Pentagon. Some bird colonel named Reed from the Pentagon Intelligence Agency wants to see us tomorrow morning at ten o'clock. He'll send a car to meet us at whichever airport we choose."

This was happening too fast for Pamela, who never took spur-of-the-moment trips. "There's no way we can get there that soon."

Matt grinned bitterly. "Tell that to the Pentagon."

"We don't have orders," she protested. "Besides, I'm still on leave."

"Your leave's cancelled. The orders are probably coming in on the fax machine right now."

Pamela was too surprised to do more than stare at Matt. The military she knew didn't move this fast. Through her astonishment she forced out one word. "Why?"

"That blasted article, of course." His brow furrowed. "The brass have already heard about it and want to question us."

Pamela felt the blood rush from her face. The Pentagon could make or break an officer's career. How could she tell the Pentagon that she suspected Matt of involvement in Eric Goodman's accident?

RIKER CALLED HIS HOTEL from a pay telephone outside the main gate at McChord Air Force Base. Well aware that his ability to blend in did not extend to a military facility, he'd made no attempt to get on the base. Instead, he waited for the Wright woman and the squadron commander outside the main gate. Sooner or later, they would come. When they did, he would be ready for them.

Every couple of hours he checked in with the hotel operator. This time his call bore fruit. His informant at the F-16 squadron on the base had left a message. Though the words were cryptic, Riker knew exactly what they meant. Pamela Wright and Matthew Powers were leaving from McChord that afternoon for Washington, D.C., on an air force jet. They'd arrive at Andrews Air Force Base outside Washington about midnight and were scheduled to meet with Pentagon intelligence officials the next morning.

Riker sneered, as he balled his hand into a fist and pounded the phone. They had to be eliminated before they talked to intelligence professionals. Too bad they'd managed to find space on a military flight. He'd have had no trouble finishing them off if they were booked aboard a commercial plane. Going to the airport, they'd have been easy targets.

So what? he told himself. According to his informant, their plane made a couple of stops en route. By chartering a jet, he'd have no trouble getting to Washington ahead of them. But timing was critical. For his plan to work, he'd need a car with an experienced driver as soon as he touched down at Washington National. Fishing more coins out of his pocket, he dialed the unlisted number of his D.C. operative.

PAMELA STRAPPED HERSELF in the webbed canvas seat of the KC-135, her stomach churning. Try as she would, she couldn't put down the feeling that disaster loomed just over the horizon.

To make things worse, her new slacks, purchased two hours ago at the base's uniform store, were so big she'd been afraid they were going to fall off as she boarded the plane. The store had been out of slacks in her size, so, treacherous though they were, she had to wear these. She couldn't sit in a low-slung seat for nine hours in her stylishly short uniform skirt.

Every pull-down seat along the sides of the KC-135—a military tanker version of the B707 airliner—was filled. Some of the passengers were military women, of course, either active duty or retirees. But the majority of the plane's fifty-plus passengers were male.

Next to her, Matt adjusted his seat belt. In his baggy flight suit, he looked as much at ease in the plane's cavernous interior as a polar bear on an ice floe. She admired the adventurous picture he cut with his flight cap perched jauntily on his head, his major's oak leaf pinned precisely on the right side. Matt Powers might be as conservative as she—at least, that's the impression she had of him—but right now he projected an exciting image of the dashing fighter pilot.

Pamela could just imagine the image *she* projected. Droopy slacks. Wrinkled raincoat. Limp blond hair. All she needed was to get sick on the flight. She looked around but couldn't spot one of the familiar airsickness sacks. Since the seatbacks were against the inner sides of the tanker, there were no pockets in front of each seat where such items were usually kept. Instead, passengers stared into the cargo bay, which was filled with an assortment of wooden crates. Her one suitcase—she'd left the rest of her things in her car—was tied down near the plane's tail section with the other passengers' luggage.

Also at the rear was a curtained-off latrine area. In her eight years in the air force, Pamela had never been aboard a cargo plane, but she imagined the toilets were like the portable chemical ones on recreational vehicles. Lord! She hoped she didn't have to use one.

Matt grinned at her. "Need some help with that seat belt?"

Pamela's cheeks grew hot at the memory of his arm brushing her breast when he'd helped her in his car last night. She knew she was blushing and hated herself for it. "Thanks. I've got it fastened."

A uniformed male sergeant walked down the aisle between the cargo and the passengers, checking seat belts. A
moment later the jet's four turbofan engines roared, and the
KC-135 hurtled down the long runway, ten minutes ahead of
schedule. When it reached cruising altitude, the deafening
roar subsided.

"I'm not sure taking this tanker was such a good idea,"
she began, once Matt could hear her over the engine noise.
"United's red-eye flight would have gotten us in at six
o'clock tomorrow morning."

He unfastened his seat belt and turned toward her.
"That's six hours later than this one, Pam, and we need the
down time. We're lucky this baby came along when she did.
We'll be rested when we match wits with the intelligence
people. They'll be looking out for any discrepancies in our
stories." He gave her a warning nod.

Suddenly Pamela's neck burned with humiliation. "I
hope you don't think I'm going to lie to the Pentagon." Did
he really think she'd be that foolish?

"Quite honestly, I don't have a clue about what you'll tell
them," he said, watching her intently. "All I've got to go by
is what you told me. You've got to admit, you weren't exactly truthful."

"I was trying to protect Eric's reputation." She tried not
to sound defensive. Why did it seem so important to convince him she had good reasons for her lies? "Telling people Eric thought he saw a monster makes him sound like he
was crazy."

She paused, wondering if this was the right time for a
confrontation. *Yes,* she told herself quickly. *The sooner I
find out where Matt's coming from, the better.*

"By the way, what excuse do you have for not reporting
what Eric saw?" she asked. "He made his official statement to you. Shouldn't you have reported it to the proper
authorities?"

He seemed strangely upset by her questions, but didn't hesitate. "The same reason you had. Like you, I thought I'd do some checking on my own before I said anything."

Pamela was certain he was holding something back. But before she could ask any more questions, he looked past her to the young enlisted man at her side. She'd been so anxious that she'd forgotten they might be overheard. Turning, she glanced at the airman. He was sound asleep, his mouth half-open, his booted legs sprawled in front of him. She swung around, again facing Matt. The seat next to him was empty, its occupant wandering around the windowless cargo bay.

"So what did you find out?" she asked Matt. At his questioning glance, she added, "When you investigated what Eric saw?"

"Not much," he admitted somewhat sheepishly. "Until I read that fool article, I didn't realize anyone else spotted the UFO."

"You really didn't check on anything, did you?" Her accusing voice stabbed the air.

She'd caught him and he knew it. He'd answered her questions impulsively to avoid telling her he *had* reported Eric Goodman's sighting to the Pentagon. He shook his head. "I thought Goodman was seeing things, so my investigation stopped almost before it started."

"Whenever I think of Eric I think of my dad." Rancor sharpened her voice. "Everybody thought *he* was seeing things, too, until they realized both he and his plane had disappeared without a trace."

Matt hesitated, measuring her reaction. "Sharplett's article said your father was returning from a reconnaissance mission over the USSR, when he broke radio silence to report a UFO."

"That's right." Her brow furrowed.

Matt nodded to encourage her. Thank God her anger at him was fading.

"Sharplett certainly hit that nail on the head," she said.

Suddenly alert, Matt studied her face. "Hit *what* nail on the head?" he asked.

"Remember, I told you everything Sharplett said about me in his article was true?"

Matt leaned closer. "Of course." She'd lowered her voice, and he could barely hear her over the deafening throb of the jet's engines.

"The article claimed my father's UFO sighting was one of the reasons I came to Tacoma." She shrugged. "Well, Sharplett was right."

Matt expelled his breath in a disbelieving snort. "The article hinted at some kind of connection between Goodman's UFO and what happened to your father. So they both saw UFOs. So what?"

The sergeant acting as steward picked that moment to deliver their sack lunches. Matt put his under his seat. He'd eat later, after he'd heard her out. He was grateful when she did the same.

"There's more of a connection than that," she said, her voice louder now.

Again, Matt glanced around them to assure himself they weren't being overheard. The seat next to him was still empty. The airman beside Pam had roused and was opening his foil-wrapped sandwich. Matt doubted the enlisted man could hear Pam and him over the roar of the engines, but moved his head closer to hers, anyway. She was so near, he could feel her warm breath in his ear when she spoke. Responding physically, he forced himself to concentrate on what she was saying.

"That night on the phone, Eric told me about something he saw inside the capsule," she said.

Adrenaline shot through Matt's veins. "Goodman said nothing to me about getting a look inside."

"I know. He told me he'd forgotten about it." She hesitated, as though wondering whether or not to go on.

"Something he saw inside the capsule reminded you of what happened to your father?" Matt prodded patiently.

"In a way," she said. "Eric saw what seemed to be a huge instrument panel. Part of the display was lit up with flashing lights in the general shape of an isosceles triangle."

Matt could barely control his excitement. "Were the lights an outline around the triangle?" Apparently, Goodman had seen something not meant for human eyes. Was that why he'd been killed?

She shrugged. "He wasn't clear about it. The whole thing sounded pretty farfetched, until I remembered some sketches my dad had framed in his den. One was in the general shape of an isosceles triangle."

"Could be a coincidence," Matt said. But the prickly feeling on the back of his neck told him that this was no coincidence. She was right. There was a connection between Eric Goodman's accident and what happened to her father.

"Did your father tell you what the sketches were of?" he asked.

"No. I tried to pin him down, but he just laughed and said they were his little secret, and that in twenty years he'd tell me all about them." She stopped speaking, and the animation left her face.

Twenty years. That would have been right about now, Matt thought.

"Is there a chance your mother might still have them?" he asked.

She shook her head. "Mom remembers them vaguely but said she got rid of them ages ago. A year or so after Dad disappeared, she disposed of all his things. Said she couldn't bear to have them around."

Matt nodded sympathetically. "I wonder if she ever asked him what the sketches were of."

"She said he told her the same thing he told me."

"They were something he wanted kept secret," Matt said.

"So it would seem."

Over the roar of the jet's engines, he could hear the weariness in her voice. She was tired and hungry, and it was time to drop this subject.

He sensed that she hadn't yet told him everything, but there'd be time later. With two stops en route, this was going to be a long flight.

PAMELA WOKE UP with a crick in her neck, her head resting against Matt's firm shoulder. His flight suit, oddly smooth under her cheek, smelled of the outdoors—like windblown laundry dried on an outside line. All around her, the jet noise throbbed and vibrated, turning the darkened cargo bay into a pulsating cradle.

She straightened, twisting her head back and forth until the tightness was gone. She wished the way she felt about *him* would go away this easily. "How long did I sleep?"

He glanced at his watch. "A little over an hour."

She stifled a yawn. "I can't imagine why I'm sleepy. It's only seven o'clock Pacific time."

"The engine noise does it." He patted his shoulder, an invitation for her to use it as a pillow again. "Go back to sleep. You'll feel better tomorrow with some shut-eye now."

Resolutely, Pamela shook her head. Before she dozed off again, she needed to get something squared away.

"Matt . . ." she began cautiously.

He leaned closer with alert interest. "I'm listening."

"Before we get there, I think we ought to share everything we know. We might not have a chance once we land at Andrews."

"I agree," he said heartily. "Is there something you haven't told me, Pam?"

Of course there was. She'd never told him Eric thought he was involved with whoever or whatever was behind his accident. But she couldn't say that.

"Not me, Matt." She didn't flinch as she told the lie. "I've told you everything Eric said." Eric had to be wrong. She couldn't be falling for a man involved in her best friend's aircraft accident—an accident that probably led to his murder.

Resolutely, she went on. "But I have the feeling you're holding back something I ought to know."

He didn't flinch, either. "Eric told you more than he told me, Pam. You know everything I do."

It sounded like a lie, even to him. But he couldn't violate his orders.

Tomorrow, at the Pentagon, he'd be able to tell her the whole truth.

Tomorrow ...

Chapter Six

Andrews Air Force Base, Maryland

A few minutes before midnight, Pamela and Matt emerged from the KC-135's cargo door near the front of the aircraft.

After more than nine hours on the plane, Pamela's body throbbed from the jet's incessant vibration. She found herself clutching Matt's arm, glad he was beside her. Despite her suspicions, she knew that whatever disasters lay ahead she wouldn't have to face them alone. A very female response, she thought wryly. But that's how he made her feel—feminine and worth protecting.

A bus took the passengers from the aircraft to the terminal area, where the bags were unloaded.

Matt pointed to an unmarked black sedan parked outside the building. "That must be our car." He picked up their bags and headed toward it. As they approached, a tall, gaunt man in civilian clothes got out.

"Major Powers and Captain Wright?" the man asked tersely.

"That's right," Matt returned. He leaned forward, sizing the man up. Then he smiled and nodded.

The driver held the sedan's back door open. "Get in, please. I'll take care of your bags."

Out of the corner of her eye, Pamela caught a movement. A captain and a lieutenant walked up to Matt and saluted. "We're going into D.C., sir. Could we hitch a ride with you?"

The driver came around the car. "Sorry. I can't take anyone else." His tone was courteous but uncompromising.

"Sharing rides is part of the air force tradition," Matt said with open disapproval.

The driver stiffened. "I have my orders, Major. If you want to complain to my superiors, use the car radio."

"That won't be necessary," Matt grumbled as he helped Pamela get in.

Observing the brief exchange between Matt and the driver, a warning alarm sounded in Pamela's head. On her many official trips, she'd often used motor pool vehicles but had never run into a driver who refused to take other passengers. In the air force, everybody went out of their way to share transportation.

Once inside the vehicle, she could see it was more luxurious than it had appeared. The plush velveteen seats had drink holders in the armrests, and a small television monitor was mounted behind the center of the front seat.

She leaned forward. "Does the Pentagon give this kind of treatment to every officer who comes in from the field?" she asked the driver.

He turned his head so she could hear his answer. "You and the major got lucky, ma'am. This is a VIP car. All the other vehicles were out." He backed away from the terminal building and started down a road that, presumably, led to the main gate.

Pamela lowered her voice to a whisper. "Something's not right about this setup, Matt."

His body stiffened. "Why?"

"The government doesn't use its VIP cars for low-ranking officers like us." She hesitated. "And why didn't the driver let us take anybody else along? Didn't that seem odd to you?" She crossed her arms over her chest, her eyes holding his.

He nodded, a watchful frown on his face. "In all the years I've been flying, the number of people we could take was only limited by the size of the car."

The lights at the main gate loomed ahead. Matt tapped the driver on the shoulder. "Go to the checkpoint."

Slowly the car circled to a one-story, flat-roofed building on the extreme side of the entry-exit road.

"Now, let's all get out and go inside." Matt's voice was calm but full of authority.

"Whatever you say, Major Powers." The driver preceded them into the small building.

Though it was after midnight, an air policeman was on duty inside the building. Expectantly, he leaned across the counter. Since Matt was the senior officer, the AP directed his question to him. "What can I do for you, Major?"

Matt inclined his head toward the driver. "Call the Pentagon Motor Pool and ask if this man works there."

"Can I see some ID, please?" the AP said to the driver.

The driver flashed a card. "Fred Altman. Tell the dispatcher I'm with the CT Unit."

"The CT Unit?" There was a new note of respect in the AP's voice. "Yes, sir." A moment later, after a quick phone call, he glanced at Matt. "The dispatcher says Mr. Altman was scheduled by Col. Ted Reed of the Pentagon Intelligence Agency."

"Thanks," Matt said. Outside the building, he turned to the driver. "Sorry to be so suspicious, Altman, but I'm a cautious man."

The driver smiled, his skeletal face softening for the first time that night. "I wish there were more like you, Major."

"What's a CT Unit?" Pamela asked when they were back in the car, headed down a tree-lined road.

"Counterterrorist," Altman said.

A flicker of apprehension coursed through Pamela.

Beside her, Matthew tensed. "Why did Colonel Reed send someone from the Counterterrorist Unit after us?" he asked.

Altman shrugged. "I already told you, sir. I was the only driver available. It *is* Friday, you know."

Pamela didn't believe him. Tomorrow, when she and Matt talked to Colonel Reed, she'd find out why he was lying.

IN THE BACK SEAT of the sedan, Matt took a quick look at Pam. She was nervous, her face tight with tension. He slid his arms around her shoulders. For a moment she stiffened, eyes startled. Then, like a rag doll, she relaxed with a faint sigh. Feeling protective, he drew her close to his side. His blood surged at her nearness.

"I'm sorry I got you involved in that scene with Altman," she whispered, her breath hot against his ear.

"There's nothing to be sorry about," he whispered back, hugging her shoulder. She fit against him like one spoon against another. "I should have checked his ID before we got in the car. You were right to be suspicious." Through his flight suit he could feel her softness.

"I'm glad we're together in this, Matt."

The touch of her body against his sent a warming jolt through him. God help him, he was aroused again. In the back of a government sedan where he could do nothing about it. By a woman he'd known only two days—a woman who'd told him nothing but lies until she was forced to admit the truth. The worst part of it was that he was enjoying every minute with her.

"I'm glad, too," he said, unable to resist stroking her hair, so silky beneath his fingers. For a moment she stilled, pulling away slightly before relaxing back against his body.

"Do you think they'll talk to us together?" she asked. "Tomorrow at the Pentagon, I mean." Her voice wavered. Was it because of his touch or was she still nervous?

Matt continued stroking her hair to soothe her. Its liveliness shot sparks through his hand. He had to steady his voice to answer her question. "Probably not. But we've got nothing to hide. We can't go wrong as long as we tell the truth."

Her breathing quickened. Was she feeling what he was? He turned so he could see her face. In the dim light from the passing traffic, a shadow of uneasiness crossed her features. She pulled away. He felt bereft, but forced himself to ask, "You've told me everything Goodman said, haven't you, Pam?"

When she hesitated, a wave of disappointment splashed over him. So, she was still keeping secrets from him—and wondering if she should hide them from the Pentagon, as well.

She turned her head so he could see nothing but her profile. "You know everything I do." But her voice trembled. He was certain she was lying again.

Why couldn't she trust him? Matt wanted to shake her and hug her at the same time. Didn't she know he was on her side? Eric Goodman was one of his people. Matt wanted to find out what had happened out there on the desert as much as she did. Frustrated, he turned away, giving his aroused body a chance to cool down.

Flashing colored lights behind the car interrupted his thoughts. Matt twisted around so he could peer out the back window.

"What is it?" she asked.

"A police vehicle, I think. He wants us to pull over."

"Whatever for?" Her voice rose indignantly. "We're not speeding."

Matt shrugged. "I expect we're about to find out." This wasn't their problem. He wasn't going to worry about it.

But their car didn't slow down and pull over the way he expected. The flashing lights of the police car drew up close behind, then swung into the lane next to them.

Sensing trouble, Matt started to ask their driver why they weren't stopping. Before he could speak, Altman began talking into the car's radio.

"Operator seven-seven requests check on police tail."

Matthew felt himself go rigid. Was their driver's request standard operating procedure for the CT Unit?

"Roger seven-seven," came the answer. "What is your location?"

"Two miles west of Andrews Air Force Base on the Suitland Parkway." Altman paused. "Make it quick, Control. This guy means business."

The radio went silent. The police car pulled alongside, dangerously close to their left front fender. Matt tried to get a look inside, but it was too dark. He clenched his fist, feeling suddenly helpless. Something was terribly wrong, and there wasn't a thing he could do about it.

Suddenly the police car struck their left front fender and there was a screeching, metal-on-metal sound.

The government vehicle jerked sharply to the right, but Altman managed to keep it on the pavement.

A moment later, the police car rammed their vehicle again. This time, the government car swerved off the road, onto the grass beyond the narrow roadside strip of dirt. In half a second, they were back on the road, heading west again at the same speed.

Matt felt Pam clutch his arm. She stared into his eyes.

I'm scared, Matt. Her fear was so tangible, he almost thought he could hear her. A second later, she spoke.

"What's going on?" The intensity of her voice confirmed what he'd already guessed—she was terrified.

His own stomach was doing push-ups, but he managed to squeeze her hand reassuringly. "I'm sure as hell going to find out."

"Seven-seven, this is Control." The radio was back on line.

"Go ahead," Altman said.

Matt glanced out the window. The patrol car, moving abreast again, was going to ram them a third time.

"No official police vehicles are in your area," reported the radio voice. "Two are en route to assist you. This bugger's caused trouble before, and they'd really like to catch him." The neutral male voice brightened. "Take evasive action."

Altman didn't bother replying.

One minute, they were moving along at fifty miles an hour. The next, their speed increased to something over one hundred. From the way Matt's seat belt pressured his gut, he figured they must be going at least that fast.

A mile or so away, two police cars hurtled toward them in the opposite lane, lights flashing and sirens screaming. Matt peered out the back window. There was no sign of their attacker. He'd apparently turned tail when Altman stepped on the gas.

Their car slowed.

Matt took a deep breath to steady his voice. "What was that all about, Altman?"

"The carjackers in the D.C. area are getting more and more creative, Major." The driver's voice was as calm as a TV news anchor's.

"Then you think that's what this guy was up to? Carjacking?" Matt didn't believe it.

"No doubt about it," Altman replied. "He's been giving the locals a hard time for a couple of weeks now. Folks think it's a police car and pull over right away when they see the flashing lights." He hesitated.

"But?" Matt supplied.

"He usually doesn't operate this close to town," Altman said thoughtfully. "And he usually doesn't pick parkways. They've got so few access roads, it's hard to get on and off."

Beside Matt, Pam shifted on the seat. He sensed her near panic.

"Could they have been after us?" she asked.

Altman didn't reply for a long moment. "Anything's possible," he said finally.

Washington, D.C.

COLONEL REED HAD MADE reservations for them at the old Hotel Washington, a historic landmark within walking distance of the White House and the Washington Monument. Like the hotel itself, the lobby's furnishings were old but well cared for.

At the registration desk, Pamela stared into the apologetic eyes of the young desk clerk.

"We weren't able to get you adjoining rooms on such short notice," he said. "But you're on the same floor."

"That'll be fine," she said, realizing that Colonel Reed must have requested adjoining rooms for them. She hadn't even considered the possibility, but a deliciously warm feeling flowed through her at the thought of Matt in the next room, his bed only inches from hers.

What would it be like to feel his hands caressing not only her hair, but her entire body, as well? His hands, his warmth, his flesh against her own had felt so good last night when he'd kissed her. She shrugged the feeling aside. It wasn't to be, and maybe it was just as well. With a desolate sigh, she signed her name on the guest register and handed the pen to Matt.

A bellboy, his black hair flecked with gray, loaded their bags on a luggage cart and led them to the polished brass elevator. The beautifully maintained old car ascended slowly to the fourth floor.

Matt followed Pamela into her room when the bellboy took her bags inside. "We need a few minutes to talk before tomorrow morning. I'll stow my gear and be right back."

"Good." After her nap on the plane, she wasn't tired. At least, that's what she told herself. But something deep inside her thrilled at the prospect of the two of them together, late at night, in her hotel room.

She'd barely opened her suitcase and started hanging a neatly folded shirt inside the closet, when there was a light knock on the door.

She peered through the peephole. Matt stood outside, still dressed in his flight suit. Quickly, she threw the night latch and let him in.

After Pamela sat down on the bed, he pulled the room's one chair close to her and dropped into it. An uncomfortable ripple of awareness coursed through her. She forced herself to ignore it. This was neither the time nor the place to succumb to an adolescent attraction that was certain to cause problems she didn't want to deal with right now.

His face was grim. "After what happened tonight, I've come to some pretty frightening conclusions." His voice held a rasp of excitement.

A shiver of anticipation mingled with her heightened awareness of him physically. "This is about the carjacking?" She forced her face into a cool mask.

He nodded. "I think our driver was wrong about that. They were after us, Pam. Did you see the way they seemed to be waiting for us? The question is why."

She drew a long breath. "I hope you're not right. But if you are, there's no mystery as to why they were after us—for the same reason Eric was killed. *They,* whoever they are, know we're the only ones he talked to. They don't want us to tell anybody what he saw."

"After six weeks?" Matt's voice rose with disbelief. "By now we could have told the whole world what Eric Goodman saw."

"But we didn't, did we, Matt?" She studied his face for some sign of guilt, because he hadn't reported Eric's story to the Pentagon first thing—the way he should have. As Eric's commander, it was his responsibility. But instead of displaying guilt, Matt met her gaze directly, with an air of competent efficiency that fascinated her.

"No, we didn't tell anyone, and we both know why." A puzzled frown crossed his face. "Do you really think he was killed to keep him quiet?"

Matt pulled his chair closer to the bed—so close that Pamela could smell the toothpaste he must have used as soon as he got to his room. She inched away from him on the mattress, keeping a safe distance between them. But she was unable to ignore the vibrant chord he struck within her.

"That's what I've thought all along." She paused, forcing her mind back where it belonged. How could he sit there, so close their knees were almost touching, and not feel disturbed—the way she did?

"But nobody suspected he'd told us about the UFO," she went on. "Until that dratted article came out, that is."

Pamela saw a hesitation in Matt's sober eyes. A muscle quivered in his jaw. For a long moment, he was silent. Finally, he spoke. "I'm going against orders to tell you this, but somebody else *did* know, Pam." He spoke so softly, she wasn't sure she'd heard him right.

"What are you saying?" She forced out the words, every part of her being intent on his answer.

"I reported what Goodman told me to the Pentagon—a man named Norm Duncan. Afterward, I was ordered to tell no one. That's why I kept it from you." He slumped in his chair, as though he'd been punctured with a giant pin.

She stared at him wordlessly, her heart pounding. So this was what he'd been hiding. No wonder he'd been torn—not wanting to lie to her, but unable to go against his orders. Impulsively, she leaned toward him and took his hands. "I understand," she said, inexplicably happy that he had a valid reason for withholding information from her.

"I wasn't going to tell you," he said. "I was going to let the Pentagon do the honors, but the more I thought about what happened tonight—"

Pamela tightened her grip on his hands, uncomfortably aware of the warmth and security his nearness gave her. "Could we have been set up, somehow? Would someone in the Pentagon want to get rid of us? Or scare us half to death, so we wouldn't talk to any more newspaper reporters?"

He straightened. "The only thing I know is that we've got to be very careful till we find out what the score is. If the Pentagon didn't suspect something was going to happen tonight, why send a trained, counterterrorist driver? And why did Altman say he hadn't been specifically picked to meet us, when it's obvious to us that he had been? If Colonel Reed thought we were in danger, why not tell us the truth?''

Pamela couldn't stop the trembling that shook her body. "If... if Altman hadn't been driving our car, we'd probably be dead right now.'' She stared in horror at Matt.

He quickly moved to the bed and put his arm around her. "We might have been dead even with Altman driving. That other car almost knocked us off the road.''

She couldn't seem to stop shaking. "We've got to stay together, Matt.'' Suddenly, any doubts she may have had vanished. Pamela knew what, subconsciously, she had known all along—no matter how hard she'd fought against it, she and this wonderful man were meant to be together.

She saw the heartrending tenderness of his gaze and knew he'd be there for her whenever she needed him. Right then, she knew she could never tell the Pentagon anything that might hurt him. The realization sent a shudder of warm relief pulsing through her.

Instinctively, she moved closer to him. Putting both arms around her, he turned her toward him.

"Pam?"

Her heart lurched when he whispered her name. She forgot she'd known him only two days. She forgot Eric had implied he was involved in the F-16's crash. She remembered only what her heart had just told her. The smouldering desire she saw in his eyes blazed inside her, as well.

She turned her face up. "Yes, Matt."

His mouth covered hers hungrily. Pamela's surface calm evaporated, and she leaned into him, reveling in the feel of his lips against hers. Shocked at her own eager response, she wanted to back away, but found she couldn't. She felt molded to him, like hot, burning metal.

All at once, she smelled the sweetly intoxicating musk of his body and wanted to drown herself in it.

Matt sensed her readiness. The desire that never burned too far under his conservative exterior burst forth.

"My sweet Pamela," he murmured. His fingers fumbled with the buttons on her uniform shirt.

The garment opened. She felt his hands and mouth on her breast, but was powerless to resist. She wanted him too much.

Her baggy pants had already slipped halfway to the floor. He pulled them the rest of the way. Pamela was barely conscious of what was happening to her clothing. All she could think of was his burning, hungry mouth and the erotic sensations coursing through her. She lay back on the bed.

He leaned over her. "You're so warm, so ready. Just the way I knew you'd be." His voice was thick with passion.

Pamela smelled the sweetness of his breath on her face. She drew his face closer, tracing his fiery lips with her own.

With new urgency, he started to unzip his flight suit. In his haste, the zipper caught. Quickly he got up from the bed. With both hands, he yanked at the heavy twill fabric until it parted, ruining the zipper. In a moment, his clothes had joined hers in a pile on the floor.

The bedside lamp softened his craggy features as he lowered himself to her. He was such a striking man. *But a stranger,* she warned herself. Or was he? He must trust her, or he'd never have confided in her tonight. And she trusted him, too—more than she'd ever trusted anyone. In some mystical way, the strange secret they shared removed the barriers between them.

For an instant, he hovered over her, his lean frame a tangible shield between her and tomorrow's looming uncertainties. Then their bodies touched, and all concept of tomorrow left her. There was only this moment, and the incredible feeling of his hard body on top of hers.

"I've dreamed of you like this from the first minute I laid eyes on you," he breathed, taking her face in his hands. "Having you, touching you—it's more wonderful than I ever imagined."

"Hold me tightly, Matt," she whispered. *I've let no one hold me like this for such a long time.*

He stared deeply into her eyes, seeming to understand that her need went beyond desire. Then he wrapped his arms around her, holding her against his warm, pulsing body.

When they kissed, their passion was too great for tenderness. He took her mouth roughly, almost violently, and she gloried in his hunger.

She arched her hips to meet him, needing to feel him inside her. For an instant, he hesitated. She moved again, inviting him in.

Unable to control himself any longer, Matt shed all restraint. He slid inside her, fevered by her eagerness and the passion she aroused. Under her spell he felt wild, untamed and high-flying—the way he felt when he was flying, alone, in the stratosphere. Yet even as he brought them both to a shuddering climax, he felt the strong urge to shelter her from harm. It was a feeling he'd rarely experienced.

Later, he tried to put his thoughts into words. "I want you to know that if you're ever hurt or need help, I'm here for you," he said, his voice hoarse.

Her hair looked like lustrous glass in the pale light. His hand moved to trail through the silky strands. Seeing her lips swollen from his kisses made him want to kiss her again.

"I know," she said. "I'd never let anything hurt you, either, Matt."

"Of course you wouldn't," he replied. But a nagging red light flashed on in his brain at her words. *I'd never let anything hurt you,* she'd said. Why had she put it that way? He'd sensed all along that she was still hiding something. After all the lies she'd told, why should he believe her now?

Irritated with himself, he cast the thought aside. After what had just happened between them, how could he doubt her?

"I feel a special kind of rapport with you," he said thoughtfully. "It's never happened with anybody else."

"I know." Her eyes were so wide with wonder that he wanted to drown in them.

He leaned toward her and kissed her gently, almost reverently. She came to him this time with a tender passion, a moon's reflection in a still stream compared to her first response. But when the end finally came, it was deeper and more satisfying than before.

Exhausted, he turned off the bedside light and fell asleep with her in his arms.

WHEN PAMELA AWOKE the next morning, Matt was gone. Vaguely, she remembered him whispering that he'd be back soon, after he'd unpacked and put on his uniform. Or had she dreamed it?

Her lips hurt, her chin burned from his emerging beard, and she ached all over. But she also felt incredibly happy. She hugged Matt's pillow, smelling his musky scent on it, and wished he were still here.

Any minute now he'd be calling or knocking on her door. The thought brought her fully awake. She needed to shower before he got here. She sat upright in the bed. What time was it, anyway? She glanced at her watch on the nightstand. *Nearly eight-thirty*. A staff car was picking them up at nine-thirty in front of the hotel, and she still wasn't unpacked. Why hadn't Matt called?

Hastily she arose, yanked a robe out of her suitcase, and put it on. Then she dialed Matt's room. There was no answer. He'd probably gone out for some breakfast. She wished he'd woken her so they could have gone together, but he'd obviously decided to let her sleep.

She called room service and ordered breakfast. By the time it arrived, she'd unpacked, showered and dressed in a clean service uniform.

She rang Matt's room again. There was still no answer. Maybe he was waiting for her downstairs in the lobby. A flash of irritation tugged at her. After last night, he should have come by her room to pick her up. Was something wrong between them that she didn't suspect?

You haven't known this man very long, she reminded herself grimly, as she ate her eggs. *Maybe he's the silent type who gets upset and won't tell you why.*

Before she headed down to the lobby, she dialed his room again. Nothing. Where was he? She had to find him. Maybe he was waiting for her downstairs.

The well-polished old elevator seemed to take an eternity getting down to the lobby from the fourth floor. When it finally arrived, Pamela stepped off and glanced around her. Several men in business suits eyed her from the sofas in the lobby, but there was no sign of Matt's familiar lean frame. An odd mixture of apprehension and anger knotted inside her.

She glanced at her watch. It was almost nine-thirty. The Pentagon staff car would be here any minute.

She rang Matt's room from a house phone near the elevators. No answer. Where could he be? Frantically, her mind searched for an answer. Could he have gone on to the Pentagon? Perhaps he'd left a message for her at the desk so he wouldn't waken her.

"Are there any messages for Captain Wright?" she asked one of the clerks. Nervously she bit her lip as she waited for an answer.

The clerk checked Pamela's box and shook her head.

"Would you mind ringing Maj. Matthew Powers's room for me?" Pamela repeated Matt's room number. "I've been calling all morning, but there's been no answer. I'm afraid something's happened to him." She took a deep breath and tried to relax, but her heart wouldn't stop pounding.

The clerk, a young black woman, punched a couple of numbers on her computer. Then she looked up and smiled. "Here's your problem, Captain Wright. Major Powers checked out at six thirty-five this morning."

Chapter Seven

"There must be a mistake!" In confused exasperation, Pamela glared at the young woman behind the hotel's registration desk. "Major Powers was planning to be here until tomorrow."

The woman eyed her coolly. "Maybe he moved to another hotel."

"He wouldn't do that. Not without telling me." Pamela struggled to keep her voice even. "You must have made a mistake."

A middle-aged man appeared. He smiled at Pamela in the patronizing way of a manager used to dealing with difficult guests. "Is there a problem?" he asked the clerk.

"Captain Wright thinks our recorded checkout time for Maj. Matthew Powers is incorrect," the clerk replied.

"I don't think he's left the hotel," Pamela said, lifting her chin. "You must have gotten him mixed up with someone else."

The manager's thin eyebrows drew together. "It's always possible we've made a mistake, Captain. Would you like to inspect the room he checked out of?" His words were as unctuous as a used-car salesman's.

"Yes." Pamela's breath burned in her throat. This couldn't be happening. Matt wouldn't simply disappear like this. Not after last night.

Silently she accompanied the manager to the elevator.

RIKER STUDIED THE WRIGHT woman from behind his
Washington Post as she hurried through the lobby. She ap-
peared agitated. Apparently, she hadn't known Major
Powers intended to leave the hotel early this morning.

How odd. Riker shifted uneasily on the hotel sofa, already dreading his next conversation with Otto. During his
surveillance outside the hotel early this morning, he'd seen
Powers leave with two men in dark suits. He didn't recognize either of them, but he did recognize the diplomatic
plates on the car that picked them up.

Russians. What was Powers doing with Russian diplomats? The two had shielded Powers so well in his short walk
from the lobby to the car that Riker had been unable to get
a clean shot at him. So Powers had gotten away—for the
time being, at least. But Riker doubted he'd be keeping his
appointment with the Pentagon. And that seemed to be
what Otto feared most.

That left the woman. She wouldn't be keeping the Pentagon appointment, either. Smiling confidently, Riker fin-
gered the Magnum in his jacket pocket.

MATT'S BED HAD NOT been slept in. Silently, Pamela moved
through the room to the closet. There was no luggage inside—no sign of a flight suit with a broken zipper or any
other clothing. Her throat ached at the sight. How could he
have calmly taken his bags and left, without a word of
goodbye?

Trembling inside, she followed the manager to the bathroom. The towels had been used, and the shower curtain was
still damp. Pamela detected a lingering reminder of the
woodsy scent Matt used—like pine boughs at holiday time.
She swallowed hard, holding back her tears. They'd been so
close last night—with no secrets between them. And now he
pulled a stunt like this. Why had he done it without telling
her?

Maybe he was acting on Pentagon orders again. Some of
her hurt evaporated, leaving more questions. He'd con-

fided in her before against orders. Why not now? Could something terrible have happened, forcing him to leave?

A wave of helpless anguish swept over her. What if he were dead? Killed like Eric? Not possible, she told herself angrily. Hadn't he taken a shower before he left? Hadn't he walked calmly out of the hotel with no sign of coercion? No, the Pentagon had to be behind this.

The manager gave her an I-told-you-so smile. "Satisfied, Captain?"

Pamela masked her troubled thoughts with a deceptive calmness. "Yes. Thank you for your time." Stoically, she returned with him to the elevator.

When she reached the lobby, she glanced around, searching for a tall, lean major in a blue air force uniform. Matt wasn't there. With a sinking heart, she started for the street door. She could delay no longer. It was past ninethirty, and the Pentagon staff car would be waiting outside.

A familiar face approached—Fred Altman, the driver from the night before. He'd apparently been lounging near the door, his skeletal frame out of sight behind a potted palm.

He fell into step beside her. "Where's Major Powers? I was supposed to pick you both up."

A sudden chill enveloped her. If the Pentagon was behind Matt's disappearance, why didn't Altman know he wouldn't be here?

"I don't know," she said. "According to the desk, he checked out of the hotel at six-thirty this morning." She felt helpless, empty, afraid.

Altman gave her a questioning look. Did he think she was hiding something? "We'll have to go without him." He preceded her through the lobby door, holding it for her from outside.

On the sidewalk, a uniformed concierge commanded a small army of drivers and bellboys. Horns honked. People hurried in and out of cars standing three deep near the lobby door on the busy downtown street. Nervously, Pamela accompanied Altman across the sidewalk.

The staff car was illegally parked at the curb, a couple of car lengths from the entrance, with its engine running. Altman handed a bill to the concierge. "Thanks for the parking space."

But Pamela noticed Altman wasn't looking at the concierge when he spoke. He was surveying the people around them the way Secret Service people did on TV, their eyes constantly moving. Did Altman think she was in some sort of danger right now, on this bright summer morning in the nation's capital? A jolt of fear spurted through her as she started for the car.

A second later, Altman kicked her legs out from under her. She slammed to the concrete on her left side, hitting the pavement so hard the breath was knocked out of her.

Frantically, she fought the blackness. She couldn't breathe, couldn't see, couldn't think. There was only the sharp pain in her hip and the rough, hard concrete beneath her. Through the mist shrouding her mind, she heard screams and knew something dreadful had happened.

Altman, whose thin body seemed to have developed abnormal strength, jerked her up and yanked her to the car. "Get in!" His voice rang with urgent command.

Still gasping for breath, she let him shove her across the back seat. Her cheek rubbed across smooth upholstery, tinged with the faint scent of cigar smoke.

Altman slammed the door behind her and scooted across the front seat to the driver's side. Pamela was jerked backward as they took off, the wheels screaming against the pavement.

"Keep your head down," he yelled. "They might have a car waiting to chase us."

Pamela wanted to ask who Altman was talking about—and what had just happened—but she didn't. With her cheek pressed flat against the car's seat, she concentrated on keeping her head down. When the car's erratic movements evened out, she began breathing normally again. But she didn't lift her head.

"This is seven-seven, Control." It was Altman's neutral voice, speaking on the car radio. "Leaving the hotel, we were attacked by a lone gunman. We were not injured, but my passenger was shaken when I knocked her to the ground."

Pamela sank into the seat cushions. How could Altman be so cool? Had someone really fired a shot at them?

"A passerby may have been hurt," Altman went on.

"We'll check on that," the radio voice said. "Did you recognize the attacker?"

"Negative. He was very ordinary—white, male, five foot eight, medium build, mid-thirties. A face you see everywhere and never remember."

"We'll have some mug shots for you to look at." There was a pause. "Can your passenger walk?"

Altman glanced over his shoulder. "Are you all right, Captain?"

"I'm fine." Her voice sounded shakier than she'd have liked.

"She hit the deck pretty hard," Altman said into his radio. "Somebody should meet her."

"Roger, seven-seven." The radio went silent.

Several moments had passed before Pamela realized that Altman had said nothing about Matt's unexpected departure from the hotel. Why hadn't he reported it?

WHEN THE STAFF CAR drew up in front of the Pentagon's River Entrance, a stocky man in a green army colonel's uniform hurried down the steps toward them.

Altman came around the car to open Pamela's door. She climbed out, her bruised hip and leg protesting every move she made.

"Colonel Reed, this is Captain Wright," Altman said.

Pamela saluted. "Good morning, sir."

Colonel Reed returned her salute. He was wearing glasses with black frames that gave him a bookish look. "I hear you had some excitement on the way over here. Are you okay?"

"Yes, sir," she said, carefully controlling her voice. "I'm not sure exactly what happened."

"Frightening experience." Frowning, he bent and looked inside the car.

"Where's Major Powers?" he asked Altman. "You were supposed to pick him up with Captain Wright at the same hotel."

Pamela's nerves tensed. A wave of black despair swept over her. If Colonel Reed didn't know where Matt had gone, something dreadful must have happened to prevent him from keeping this appointment.

"According to Captain Wright, he checked out of the hotel early this morning," Altman returned. "I figured he was probably following your orders, sir. That's why I didn't mention it when I reported the attack on the car radio."

Colonel Reed turned to Pamela. "Did Powers say anything about leaving the hotel early?"

"Nothing, sir." Her voice didn't betray the sick, clenching pain in her stomach. What could have happened to him? "I expected to meet him in the lobby and didn't find out he'd left until I asked at the desk around oh-nine-twenty."

"Did the desk tell you if he was alone when he checked out?" Reed's sharp eyes bored into hers.

Pamela shook her head, starting to feel dizzy. "I didn't think to ask." Why was Colonel Reed throwing questions at her out here in the parking lot where the sun was so bright?

"That could be important." Colonel Reed nodded sagely. "We'll send somebody over to the hotel this afternoon to find out."

"I can ask the hotel people myself when I go back to my room tonight." Pamela made the suggestion wearily, hoping he wouldn't take her up on it.

"You won't be staying at the hotel tonight," Colonel Reed corrected abruptly. "The agency keeps an apartment in Alexandria for VIP guests. You'll be safer there."

Pamela's heart dropped. *If I'm not at the hotel, Matt won't be able to find me tonight.* An instant after the thought occurred to her, she kicked herself mentally for being illogical. Whatever was preventing him from keeping this appointment would also prevent him from returning to the hotel.

Colonel Reed caught Altman's eye. "I'll need you later this afternoon to take Captain Wright to her new quarters." He grasped the driver's hand and shook it vigorously. "Thanks for getting her here in one piece."

Pamela did her best to smile. "That goes for me, too." Suddenly, her service blues felt too warm, and her body ached in places she'd never even thought of. Her dizziness increased. Swaying, she raised her hand to shield her eyes from the sunlight.

Colonel Reed took her arm and turned her toward the row of massive mahogany doors that marked the River Entrance. "Let's get you inside, out of the sun."

Gratefully, Pamela let him help her up the stairs.

On the long trek across the huge building, she forced herself not to think of Matt. With these intelligence people watching her like hawks, she couldn't afford to feel sorry for herself because he was gone. Neither could she let herself be scared to death that something might have happened to him. Those emotions would have to come later, when she was alone.

As they walked, Colonel Reed explained that most Pentagon Intelligence Agency offices were located in the building's mezzanine basement, a windowless area guarded twenty-four hours a day. Since Pamela didn't have the required clearances, he said, she'd be interviewed near the PIA director's E-Ring office.

To Pamela's surprise, a number of uniformed officers— men and women—and one bearded man in civilian clothes waited for them in the bright, comfortable conference room, its windows overlooking the Potomac. After everyone was seated around an oak table, Colonel Reed introduced them.

Only one name was familiar—that of Norman Duncan, the civilian. Last night, Matt had told her he'd reported Eric's story to a man named Norm Duncan from the Pentagon. Pamela swallowed hard, remembering last night. *Sweet, passionate Matt.* Then, aggravated with herself, she thrust Matt's smiling image from her mind.

This meeting's important, she told herself, still not convinced the Pentagon wasn't somehow involved in his strange disappearance. *Something that happens here might help me figure out where he is.*

Unobtrusively, she stole a closer look at Norm Duncan. In his rumpled brown suit and garish yellow tie, the bearded civilian stood out among the uniformed colonels and lieutenant colonels like a middle-aged professor among youthful lab assistants. She pegged him as *the* expert on UFOs.

To start the session off, Colonel Reed—standing at the head of the table behind a briefing podium—held up a copy of the *Morning News Herald*.

"As you all know," he began, "this newspaper article is why we brought Major Powers and Captain Wright to Washington." After a brief announcement that Major Powers had been detained but would, hopefully, address them later, Reed passed out copies of Sharplett's article so everybody could read it.

Though she recalled many of the reporter's words, Pamela studied the article carefully. She didn't want to confuse anything it said with what Matt had told her or what she'd figured out for herself. She still wasn't sure what the Pentagon Intelligence Agency wanted from her. Until she knew, she intended to reveal nothing that might hurt Matt or her father or Eric.

When everyone had read the article, Colonel Reed smiled brightly at Pamela. "Now, Captain Wright, please tell us exactly what Eric Goodman said the night he called you and what happened afterward. Newspaper reporters aren't always as careful as they should be about the accuracy of their stories. We'd like to hear your version."

He gestured toward the podium. "Would you mind stepping in front so everyone can hear you?"

Her mind spinning, Pamela barely heard his question. Why had Colonel Reed implied the article was wrong? Matt had already confirmed Eric's UFO sighting in his report to Norm Duncan. And everything Sharplett said about her father was verified by Pentagon records.

"Captain Wright?" The colonel sounded concerned. "Are you okay?"

Pamela rose. "Yes, I'm fine." She went to the podium. "Which part of the article did you think might be inaccurate?" She stared pointedly at Colonel Reed, who was now sitting in the seat she'd left.

He hesitated a moment before answering. "The part about the UFO Captain Goodman saw. That had to be pure fabrication. God knows where the reporter dug up his witnesses, but those people must have been seeing things."

The colonel isn't going to acknowledge Matt's report. Pamela could see it in his manner, hear it in his hesitation. The realization stiffened her spine.

A spark of anger flared inside her. Why wasn't he leveling with her? She wanted to pin him down, make him admit he'd known about Eric's UFO weeks before he read Sharplett's article in the *Herald*.

But she couldn't. That would betray Matt's confidence. He'd been under orders not to tell anyone.

"Before I start, I've got one other question," she said, still eyeing Colonel Reed.

"Shoot." He wasn't smiling now.

"Why did our driver lie and say he wasn't specially chosen to pick us up?" She held Reed's eye, not letting him look away. "Since two attempts have been made on my life in the past twenty-four hours, it seems obvious somebody's out to get me and that your trained CT driver was used purposely.''

The colonel cleared his throat. For an instant, Pamela thought he was going to repeat the same lie Altman had told. Then he nodded. "We didn't want to alarm you unnecessarily. Your driver was instructed to tell you what he did.''

Pamela took a long breath. These intelligence people were experts at prevarication by omission. The fact that they were lying to protect classified information didn't make the lies more palatable. She'd have to question everything they told her.

"One more thing, Colonel," she said. "Why did you think we were in danger?''

Reed looked her straight in the eye. "Until the incident on the parkway last night, we really didn't think so. But since the newspaper article implied the pilot's murder was connected to a UFO sighting only hours before he was killed, we didn't want to take any chances." He paused. "It was possible someone might try to silence you the way they did him.''

Pamela kept her face composed as the colonel dug himself in deeper by claiming the article was his first indication of the UFO sighting.

During the next few minutes she summarized Eric's conversation with her, including his description of the monster spider, her interview with the police officers, who questioned her after they found Eric's prints on the phone and traced the call to her through his credit card, and her conviction that her father had been shot down by the Soviets, not abducted by the mysterious UFO he'd reported.

But she did not mention Eric's insinuation that Matt knew more about the accident than he was telling. Or Eric's description of the triangular-shaped lighted display panel. Eric's description was too close to the sketch her father had made. What if her father had been involved in something illegal—or *immoral*—and the sketches were some sort of clue that could betray him? *And destroy my mother.* Pamela pictured her mother's serene face and shuddered inwardly. She couldn't afford to take the risk.

BACK IN HIS MEZZANINE basement office, Norm Duncan answered the phone.

"Major Powers left the hotel with two men," the lieutenant reported. "A clerk was outside having a smoke and saw the car that picked them up. It had Russian diplomatic plates."

Duncan jerked forward, hardly believing his ears. What a bombshell! When he'd sent the lieutenant to the Hotel Washington to follow up on Major Powers's early checkout, he'd never expected news like this. If Powers had walked out of the hotel with Russian diplomats, he had *espionage* written all over him.

Duncan put his hand over the receiver and turned to his boss, Colonel Reed, who was eating a sack lunch at a nearby desk.

"The lieutenant says Powers left the hotel this morning in a Russian staff car," Duncan said. "Looks like he had information to sell and knew the Russians would pay plenty to hear it."

"What the hell!" Colonel Reed put down his sandwich and grabbed his extension. "What's up, Lieutenant?"

Duncan didn't hang up. As the colonel's deputy, he knew his boss wanted him to listen in. This was a UFO matter, and he was the agency expert. After thirty years in this business, he ought to be, he thought grimly. Soon he would have the answer to the strange sightings on the moon in recent years. The giant spider was the key.

While Duncan listened, the lieutenant gave a few more details about Powers's unexpected departure from the hotel.

He'd been wearing a dark, civilian suit when he checked out, not a uniform. He'd carried one bag and a briefcase. The two men with Powers were also dressed in dark suits.

"Check around to see if anybody else saw them," Colonel Reed ordered.

After he hung up, he swung his chair around toward Duncan. "Looks like Powers has sold out, Norm."

"When I talked to Powers in Tacoma, he didn't strike me as a man who'd sell out," Duncan said thoughtfully, knowing the crime was not lessened because the former Soviet Union was no longer an enemy. "But they say almost everybody has a price."

"What do you think we should do about this?"

Duncan considered the question. "If we charge the major with espionage, the pilot's UFO sighting—including the information about the giant spider—will get in all the papers."

"It's already in the papers."

Duncan nodded. "The UFO sighting *is* in one paper, Colonel. But, so far, there's nothing about the monster." He paused to let his words sink in. "According to Captain Wright, the reporter made a lot of shrewd guesses based on her arrival in Tacoma, her father's experience and the word of these so-called observers, who saw the UFO out in the desert. The reporter admits they were in the area illegally and are afraid to come forward. In effect, they're nobody." Duncan cleared his throat. "This thing'll die out in a few days, if we treat it like all the other sightings. The important thing is not to jeopardize the security of Moon Watch."

Colonel Reed got up and began pacing back and forth in their cubicle. It was set off from the rear of the branch's operating area by a couple of movable partitions. Outside the partition, the room was partly dark since it was Saturday, with only a few lights burning.

"We've got to get Powers back here, Norm. That pilot might have told him something he didn't report to you last February." Colonel Reed paused in front of Duncan's desk. "My God! With what he knows about the spider, he might hold the key to our operation. Maybe that's why the Russians want him."

"There's no way we can force him back without them guessing how important he is," Duncan said, with wry logic. "Even if we claim he's simply an officer who's deserted, the Russians'll suspect we want him in connection with the UFO sighting."

"But they won't know we think *this* sighting is connected to an alien presence on the moon." Colonel Reed resumed his pacing. Duncan nodded thoughtfully. "Maybe we can talk him into coming back on his own."

The colonel stopped in midpace. "How the hell can we do that?"

Duncan took a long swallow from the coffee cup on his desk. The stuff was cold, but there was no sense letting it to go waste. "Why don't we let Captain Wright talk him into coming home like a good little boy?"

The colonel shook his head in annoyance. "You mean send her to Russia? How would she ever find him?"

"We'll find him for her," Duncan said. "That's what we pay the CIA for."

"She'd never go." The colonel sounded incredulous, but he stopped pacing and went back to his desk. "And we can't force her to do something like that. She'd have to volunteer." He took a deep breath. "My God, Norm. In effect, we'd be asking her to bring home a turncoat."

Duncan nodded sagely. "She's perfect for the job. You heard her this morning when she was talking about her father. She's already been to Moscow twice, so she knows her way around. She speaks fluent Russian, and there's nothing illegal about what she'd be doing—simply visiting an American friend."

Unconvinced, the colonel shook his head. "Somebody's been gunning for her, Norm. What if they follow her to Moscow?"

Duncan waved off the objection. "How will they know where she's gone? She'll be safer there than she is here in Washington."

The colonel's resistance was crumbling. "She'll never do it," he repeated lamely.

"Sure she will," Duncan said softly. "We'll make her an offer she can't refuse."

THE CT DRIVER, Fred Altman, brought Pamela to the hotel to pick up her things, and then back across the Potomac to the town house in Alexandria. Her mind wandered as he showed her around the place.

How wonderful it would be to fix dinner with Matt in the well-stocked kitchen. Afterward, they could snuggle on the comfortable sofa in the living room in front of the big TV screen.

If only he's all right, she thought. *Please, God, let him be alive.* Then she swallowed her sentimental prayers. Of course he was all right. Otherwise, he could never have left the hotel under his own stream.

But Matt didn't want to snuggle with her in a town house in Alexandria or anywhere else. He was gone. Out of her life. She hated him for making her so happy one night and reducing her to ashes the morning after. Half angry, half scared for him, she forced herself to keep her troubled emotions in check awhile longer—at least until Altman left.

"Is there a subway station around here?" she asked him. "Since tomorrow's Sunday, I thought I'd look around the Smithsonian."

He narrowed his eyes. "You'd better check with Colonel Reed before you go out. People who use this house usually stay put."

"But nobody knows I'm here. Why can't I go out?" Pamela caught her breath. "It almost sounds like I'm a prisoner."

He shifted awkwardly. "Since you were shot at, the colonel's taking precautions. It's for your own safety. If someone weren't after you, you wouldn't be here."

So that's why the place was so well stocked—from the current issue of the *Washington Post,* to the cupboards full of dishes, to the refrigerator loaded with vegetables and dairy products. Nice as the town house was, her heart sank at the thought of being forced to stay here for God knew how long.

As soon as she was alone, Pamela dialed the number Colonel Reed had given her. "Yes, I thought I made that clear," he said. "You're under orders to stay inside until you hear otherwise. We'll call you when we need you."

So, in effect, she *was* a prisoner. Pamela managed to say, "Yes, sir," and hang up before she burst into tears.

Chapter Eight

Pamela spent the next three days watching TV and reading. Altman stopped by about noon each day to see if she wanted anything from the store. By the end of the third day, all she wanted was to get out of there.

The place had a screened porch in back, overlooking a tiny fenced yard. She sat on the porch for hours every afternoon, smelling the scent of lilacs in the air and wishing Matt were here to smell them with her.

Much as she tried not to think of him, she felt a sickening sense of loss. Half of her couldn't believe he'd walk out on her and was certain he was in deadly peril. The other half scoffed at her for being a gullible fool.

Never again would she let herself be smitten by a man she barely knew. She refused to admit what her secret self believed—that after a night with Matt Powers, she would never again be smitten by anybody.

Colonel Reed finally called at 0800 on Wednesday morning. He said Altman would pick her up at ten o'clock, and he gave her a room number to report to.

When Pamela got there, she found both the colonel and Norm Duncan waiting for her in a spacious briefing room outside the main entrance of the Pentagon Intelligence Agency. The two stood at the far end of the room, next to a polished wood briefing podium with the agency's logo emblazoned on it.

The expert, Pamela thought uneasily, eyeing Duncan. Did he and the colonel suspect she hadn't told them everything she knew? She renewed her vow not to reveal anything that would hurt Matt, her father or Eric.

Rich with scarlet draperies and carpeting, the room reminded Pamela of an elaborate theater. Unfortunately, in this theater she would be the star performer. Squaring her shoulders, she threaded her way through the neat rows of red leather chairs to the front of the room.

Colonel Reed nodded and smiled. But his eyes, narrow behind his black-framed glasses, did not reflect his congenial welcome.

"We've got some news I think you'll be interested in," he said with quiet emphasis. Pamela was sure she wouldn't like his news, whatever it was.

The colonel pulled a couple of chairs out of the first row and swung them around. Then he gestured for her to sit on another. From the way the chairs were positioned, she'd be facing the two men. She resisted her urge to shift nervously from one foot to another.

"Sit down, Captain Wright," he said. "We might as well be comfortable for our little chat."

Careful not to betray her anxiety, Pamela sat where he'd indicated. The colonel and Norm Duncan took the other two chairs. Apprehensively, she studied the men.

Colonel Reed's bland expression revealed nothing. But Duncan's eyebrows were raised, and his pudgy body was leaning toward her in obvious interest. His tie was crimson, almost the same color as the scarlet in the plush room. Pamela wasn't surprised when he, not the colonel, took the lead.

"We've found out what happened to Major Powers," he began, a serious expression on his buttery face.

Pamela stiffened with shock. Her usual cool demeanor failed her. "Is he okay?" She heard her heart pounding in her ears and took a deep breath to quiet it. "What— Where is he?"

"Moscow. He's gone over to the Russians." Duncan's mild voice pierced her senses like a steel-tipped arrow.

For an instant, she was struck speechless. Then her shock yielded to anger. "I don't believe it, Mr. Duncan." No matter that Matt hadn't shown up for his Pentagon appointment, he didn't deserve this. "How dare you say such a thing about a loyal air force officer?"

"Because it's true." Duncan's tone held a note of sympathy for her obvious agitation. "When Major Powers left the hotel Saturday morning, he was spotted getting into a car with Russian diplomatic plates."

Pamela thrust her chin out. "Then he was being kidnapped."

Duncan shook his head. "Both the desk clerk who checked him out and the one who saw him get in the car said there was no sign he was being forced."

"Were the two clerks the only witnesses?" She couldn't keep her voice from trembling. "They must have made a mistake. He wouldn't—"

Colonel Reed held up a hamlike hand to stop her. "There's no mistake, Captain Wright. We've checked this out thoroughly." His brows, which had been drawn together, relaxed. "Believe me, I appreciate your concern for a fellow officer, but there's no doubt about this—none at all." He nodded to Duncan. "Tell her the rest."

Duncan stared at her questioningly, his blue eyes bright in his puffy face.

"Yes, please go on," she said, taking a deep breath.

"A Russian general named Dimitri Vactin is the top military man in the country's space agency. Major Powers has been in touch with him."

Pamela's stomach clenched. "How did you find out?"

Colonel Reed leaned toward her, his mouth twisted in a confident smile. "Classified sources."

Classified sources. Pamela looked away from Reed so she wouldn't be tempted to make a sarcastic comment. Classified sources, indeed. It was the stock answer of intelligence people.

Still, Duncan's accusations made a dismaying kind of sense. If the capsule Eric saw had, indeed, come from outer space, Matt's information might be worth a substantial amount to General Vactin, the senior military officer in the Russian space program.

"Go on," she said, steadying her voice.

"We've also found out where Major Powers is staying in Moscow," Duncan said.

Pamela stared at him, unnerved by this unexpected revelation. "Why are you telling me this, Mr. Duncan?"

Colonel Reed leaned forward. Pamela took a quick glance at him. For an instant, his bookish face glowed with alert interest. But when he caught her watching him, his shuttered expression returned.

"We're letting you know everything we do," Reed said, "because we need you for a significant mission. It's the most important thing you'll ever be asked to do for your country."

Significant mission? Pamela shoved her chair backward, away from them. They couldn't be suggesting what she suspected. She'd never betray Matt, no matter what he'd done.

Norm Duncan's beard moved in what she interpreted as a smile. "We need Major Powers back here," he said softly. "We can't force him to come. You're the perfect one to talk him into returning of his own free will."

Shaking her head, Pamela pushed her chair back farther. "I'm sorry. I'm simply not qualified." Trembling, she got to her feet, her legs shaky under her. "Can I please be excused, Colonel Reed? I'd like to get back to my job in Texas." Thankfully, her voice sounded as cool as ever.

Colonel Reed rose from his chair. Norm Duncan got up ponderously from his.

Moving quickly, the colonel positioned his stocky body between her and the door. "Not so fast, Captain," he said.

"We can't let you leave until we're certain you're out of danger."

Pamela shot a defiant glare at Colonel Reed, feeling her face flush with anger. "What's going on here, Colonel? One day you lock me up in a safe house because someone's trying to kill me, the next you ask me to risk my life by going to Moscow. Doesn't that seem a little hypocritical, even for the Pentagon?"

Norm Duncan cleared his throat. "You'll be safer in Moscow than you are here, Captain Wright."

She stared at him in disbelief. "That doesn't make sense."

"It does if you remember that whoever's after you here will have no idea you've gone to Russia." Duncan moved a step closer. "Even if he finds out, he's not likely to follow you to Moscow. And once you're there, you won't be doing anything illegal. Just talking to a friend and encouraging him to come home with you." His eyes narrowed. "As a matter of fact, we don't want you to do anything illegal or dangerous. If you do, and you get into trouble with the Russian authorities, you're on your own."

"You'll be safer in Moscow than Washington," Colonel Reed affirmed, parrotlike. "If you don't go, you'll have to spend more time in Alexandria—until we find out who's behind Saturday's sniper attack."

"Does that mean I'm still a prisoner, Colonel?"

"You were never a prisoner, Captain Wright." But his lips were pressed together in a firm, hard line, belying his words.

Norm Duncan spoke again. "Hear me out, Captain. You'll like the rest of what I have to say."

"Not if it means you want me to lure Major Powers back here so you can court-martial him for espionage." They'd never force her to change her mind.

"He won't be court-martialed, I promise you." Colonel Reed sounded sincere, but Pamela didn't believe him.

"We need him for the same reason the Russians need him," Duncan said. "To find out everything we can about that UFO Captain Goodman saw. Major Powers is the only person who had a face-to-face meeting with the pilot. It's vital we talk to him.''

Why don't you go read the report he sent you? The retort was on the tip of her tongue, but she couldn't divulge Matt's confidence. Instead, she let Duncan lead her back to her chair. There was an earnest, down-to-earth quality about the pudgy little man that lowered her resistance.

When they were seated again, he leaned back and folded his arms. ''If you do this for us, we're prepared to do something for you in return.''

She eyed him suspiciously. His eyebrows were lifted in an expression of sympathetic helpfulness.

''What?'' she asked. Would they be so foolish as to offer her a bribe?

''Saturday morning when you briefed us, you said your father's disappearance had influenced the course of your life.''

Pamela felt herself go rigid. ''That's right.''

''If you'll do this for us, we're prepared to release to you all the classified information we have about your father's mission, his disappearance and the resulting search for him and his plane.''

For an instant, Pamela stared at him speechless. This was what she'd been trying to accomplish ever since she joined the air force. But she could never betray Matt.

As though reading her thoughts, Colonel Reed spoke up. ''I'll sign a notarized statement that Major Powers will not be court-martialed when he returns.''

''Will you also give me leave orders for him that I can take along?'' With the orders and notarized statement, Pamela figured Matt would be covered.

Colonel Reed hesitated. Pamela could almost see the wheels spinning in his brain.

Finally, he nodded and turned to Norm Duncan. ''Give her what she wants and get her over there ASAP.''

RIKER PUT OFF the phone call as long as he could. When four days had gone by with no sign of the Wright woman, he was forced to call Otto for help. He couldn't believe she'd escaped from him outside the hotel. It was all that blasted government driver's fault. What he didn't understand was how she could just disappear without a trace.

"So the woman isn't dead yet?" Otto's high-pitched, androgynous voice sounded vaguely accusing.

"No, *Mein Herr*. She's disappeared."

For a long moment, Otto didn't speak.

Riker rarely sweated. But now, in this steaming phone booth on Wisconsin Avenue, he was sweating. Profusely.

"So, that is why you did not call sooner," Otto said finally.

"Yes." Riker didn't like to admit he'd failed. He'd make sure the woman suffered for the humiliation she'd caused him.

There was an odd squeaking noise coming through the receiver. Riker stiffened. The sound meant Otto was laughing.

"The woman has not disappeared, my friend."

Disbelieving, Riker stared at the receiver in his hand. How could Otto know where she was? He had eyes everywhere, but that didn't mean he was omniscient.

Otto squeaked again. "The woman is in Moscow."

"How do you know that, *Mein Herr?*"

"Because that's where the major is." Otto's cackle vanished. "You should have no trouble finding her. She'll be registered with the Intourist Bureau. I have a contact there who will help you locate her."

Moscow

WILL HE BE THERE?

Pamela repeated the question over and over again in her mind as she rode the subway from her hotel to a station close to the address Norm Duncan had given her. What if Matt wasn't there? What if something awful had happened to him and she never saw him again?

"He'll be there," Colonel Reed had assured her in the Pentagon Intelligence Agency's scarlet briefing room. "If nobody answers the door, or if he's with someone, stay and visit for a while, then go back later. Keep trying until you talk to him alone."

Pamela had raised no more objections, keeping her darker doubts to herself. If Matt wasn't there, he might be dead. If he *was* there, he'd be a traitor. What if he slammed the door in her face and refused to talk to her? Did she simply walk away? Even worse, what if he were with a woman in the apartment? How would she handle *that?*

Her head aching with fatigue, Pamela struggled to answer the painful questions that had played havoc with her mind during the twelve-hour trip from Washington, D.C. Only two hours ago, she'd landed at Sheremetyevo Airport. The international terminal, layered with dirt and smelling faintly of marijuana smoke, was as grimy as she remembered from her last visit two years ago.

On the bus to the hotel, she'd stared tiredly through the smudged window at the rows on rows of monotonous high-rise apartment buildings. Would she find Matt in a building like one of these, with its concrete flaking, its iron balconies lopsided, and apparently too weak to stand on? Tired as she was, she couldn't rest until she'd sought him out. She had to know if he was okay.

Taking time only to shower and change out of her jeans into tailored black slacks and a pink shirt, she headed for the nearest *Mitro*. From her earlier visits, she knew the subway was the best way to get around Moscow. Safer than taxicabs for a woman alone, it provided comfort, speed and—above all—anonymity. As she rode, she planned for various contingencies. What would she do if Matt were with another man? A woman? What if someone else opened the door? Carefully, she mapped out strategies for every situation she could think of. Even with a transfer near Red Square, the ride, on a remarkably clean train, took less than forty-five minutes.

Pamela emerged from the elaborate Byelorusskaya Station to find herself on a street corner only blocks away from the address Duncan had given her. The unpainted, concrete, fifteen-story apartment building, when she reached it, looked like all the others in Moscow. The tiny patch of grass in front was muddy brown—the color of the city in April. The rest of the ground around the building was covered with gravel.

Inside, she found herself at the bottom of an unheated concrete stairwell that felt damp and cold. A clammy sense of foreboding settled over her. What secrets were hidden in the apartment on the sixth floor? Would she find Matt there, in this decaying old building? With all her heart she hoped so—even if it meant he was a traitor.

As she climbed, she smelled onions, and cabbage, and potatoes—cooking odors that made her stomach tighten with hunger. She'd had nothing to eat for hours. Relentlessly, she shoved the thought from her mind.

On the sixth floor, she found the apartment on the left side of the landing. Her heart thudding madly, she knocked on the door. There was no answer. She knocked again, more loudly. If Colonel Reed was right, Matt would open the door. What would he say? How would he look? Would he be glad to see her?

"Who is it?" The male voice spoke Russian. It wasn't Matt's. Would the man inside let her in if he knew she was an American?

Probably not. Implementing one of the strategies she'd worked out on the subway, Pamela said hello in Russian and gave a phony Russian name. The door opened. A young man in an army uniform grinned at her. He wore enlisted insignia.

"Yes?" he said in Russian, opening the door wider. He was a big, strapping kid with blue eyes and brown hair about the color of Matt's. From his welcoming smile and the head-to-toe examination he gave her, Pamela could tell he liked her looks.

"I'm from the population bureau," she said, forging ahead with her plan. "The bureau is doing a survey of residents in this building. We need to know their ages and occupations, and to interview them personally."

"Come in," he said, grinning at her.

Head high, she strode into the room. The soldier pushed the door until it closed behind her with an ominous click. But, she noticed gratefully, he didn't slide the two bolt locks into place. If she had to leave in a hurry, at least she wouldn't have to fight those.

The room smelled of sweat and cabbage. She gazed around. Heat radiated from an iron stove in one corner. A bucket heaped with coal stood nearby.

The tiny, sparsely furnished living area opened onto a crude kitchen. Soiled rag rugs covered the plywood floors, and there was a small TV set near the outside door. Several doors opened off a short hallway lighted by a bare bulb. One door stood ajar. Pamela heard vague rustling sounds coming from the room, as though someone were inside.

After the cold stairwell, the room was much too hot. Pamela started to perspire but didn't remove her lined raincoat—it provided protection from the soldier's interested gaze.

Standing in the center of the room, she drew a tablet and pencil from her black leather bag. She could hear the rustling sounds more clearly now. Was Matt back there, watching through the tiny crack in the door, not wanting to see or talk to her?

"Now, we'll start with you," she declared, in as officious a tone as she could manage. "Do you live here alone?"

"No," said the soldier, who seemed to buy her population bureau story. "I am staying with a friend."

"Then who *does* live here?"

A suspicious glint appeared in his eyes. "If you are from the government, you should know the name."

A shiver raced across Pamela's shoulders as she remembered Norm Duncan's warning. *Don't do anything illegal,* he'd said. *Just try to convince Powers to come home with you. If he turns you down or some problem develops, walk away.*

Yet here she was, in spite of his warning, doing something very illegal as soon as she got here. She was a U.S. Air Force officer on a tourist visa. If she were caught pretending to be a Russian government official, she could be imprisoned for espionage. Russia might be more democratic now that communism had fallen, but she doubted the country was any more tolerant of foreigners lying about their identities.

Hastily, she thumbed through her blank tablet, her mind racing. Colonel Reed said Matt was in touch with a Russian general named Dimitri Vactin. Maybe General Vactin arranged for this apartment.

She pretended to find the information she was looking for. "Yes, here it is," she said. "Of course we know the name. The apartment belongs to a family named Vactin."

The soldier relaxed against the sofa back. "Yes. He is a general, you know."

Pamela nodded. Relief surged through her. She'd guessed right about General Vactin leasing the apartment. Did that mean Matt was nearby?

From the hallway came a thumping noise. Was Matt back there? If so, he was being held prisoner and this soldier was his guard. She had to know for sure.

Pretending to be startled, she glanced behind her. Then she turned toward the soldier and lifted an inquiring eyebrow.

The soldier shrugged apologetically. "It is the cat. She jumps up and down off the furniture."

Pamela turned back toward the hallway. "Oh, I love cats," she gushed. "May I see her?" She moved forward.

Before she'd reached the door, the soldier grabbed her arm. "The cat doesn't like strangers."

"I'm sorry. I didn't mean to be nosy." Attempting to ease the sudden tension, she smiled at him. Her brief glance through the slit in the door revealed nothing but darkness. But she heard a disturbing grunting sound. Someone—or something—was inside that room.

The soldier thrust her away from the door. He pulled it closed before following her back down the hall.

Pamela tucked her tablet in her purse. "I'll come back when the family is here," she said. "When will they return?"

"General Vactin will be here tonight at six."

When Pamela headed out of the apartment, the young soldier went onto the landing with her. As she turned to go, he grabbed her arm, the way he had before. For one frightening moment, Pamela thought he was going to drag her back inside.

But he released her arm and flashed her a toothy grin. "Next time come and see *me,* not the general."

Next time I'll have a delightful surprise for you, my friend, Pamela thought, already planning to return with someone who could be counted on to keep the soldier occupied while she took a good look into the back bedroom.

WITH HER APPLE-RED cheeks, freckled round face and innocent blue eyes, the girl looked like a peasant fresh off a Ukrainian farm. *Which only proves that looks are deceiving,* Pamela thought, as she rode the *Mitro* back to Byelorusskaya Station, with the girl beside her.

This wholesome-looking young creature was a prostitute, highly recommended to her by a hotel bellboy at the Rossia, a huge downtown hotel on Red Square. Pamela wasn't staying at the Rossia. Her hotel was many miles from the immediate downtown area. By hiring a prostitute from a different hotel, where she wasn't registered, Pamela hoped to cover her tracks.

The prostitute's name was Galina, and Pamela had had to pay the bellboy a small fortune for her. The money came from the ten thousand dollars Colonel Reed had given Pamela to handle situations like this. "Emergency cash," he'd called it. At the time, she'd wondered if the money was a bribe. Now, she realized it was simply a necessary cost of doing business in the shadowy world where she found herself.

Would Galina help her find Matt? Maybe not. But at least the prostitute would give Pamela the time she needed to check out the apartment's back room. Until she knew for sure whether Matt was being held prisoner there, she didn't dare report what she suspected to the U.S. Embassy. One misstep, and she'd wind up in some Russian prison.

No. She had to do this alone and right away—before the young soldier told his boss about the blond woman from the government's "population bureau," who tried to get into the back bedroom. Once they figured out Pamela was a phony, they'd move Matt somewhere she'd never find him. And the Russian police would hunt her down for espionage. The thought sent anxious tremors racing down her spine.

On the remote chance she'd need it, Pamela had dropped a small pocket knife into her leather shoulder bag before she left her hotel. The knife was a gift from Norm Duncan. "It opens bottles, in addition to cutting things," he'd said when he handed it to her. Though only a few days had passed since then, it seemed like decades.

The strong fruity smell of Galina's cologne brought Pamela back to the swaying subway car.

"We are almost there," the prostitute announced in Russian. She had a high-pitched child's voice that went along with her girlish appearance. "This General Vactin must be a generous man to provide such a service as mine for his soldiers." Her giggle was totally unselfconscious.

Pamela nodded. "This soldier has been very faithful. You must tell him that to make him proud." She studied the woman's face. Tiny lines around her eyes and mouth had already begun to betray her youth and seeming innocence.

"Does the general want you to remove something from the apartment while I keep the soldier occupied?" Galina's eyes narrowed shrewdly. She'd probably guessed that General Vactin knew nothing about this afternoon's treat for his randy young enlisted man. "If you take something, I will be blamed."

Pamela hoped to remove something from the apartment, all right. If Matt was a prisoner in that back bedroom, she intended to bring him out with her—or die trying.

"To show you how much I appreciate your help, I'll give you more cash," Pamela offered, so the woman wouldn't back out.

"How much more cash?"

Pamela named a sum that made the prostitute smile and promised to give it to her when they reached the building.

The cash transfer was completed in the deserted stairwell. Then Galina went up the stairs alone. Pamela waited the ten minutes they'd agreed on, then climbed the six flights to the apartment. Pausing, she listened. The sound of voices filtered out through the closed door, battering her.

Pamela froze. Had Galina failed to lure the soldier into the bedroom? Worse, had she taken the cash and fled?

Listening more closely, Pamela heard women's voices and snatches of music. She expelled her breath in a huge sigh. The television set must be on. The realization did nothing to steady her erratic pulse.

Ever so gently she pushed on the door. As instructed, Galina hadn't closed it tightly, so the latch hadn't caught.

For a moment, Pamela stood motionless, hardly breathing. The lingering odor of sweat and of Galina's cloying cologne hung in the overheated air. Pamela put a tissue to her nose and held it there, forbidding herself to sneeze. She heard no sound but the chattering on the TV.

Half expecting the soldier to come charging across the room toward her, she tiptoed to the hallway. Both bedroom doors were tightly closed. Gingerly, she crept past the first door. The creak of bedsprings told her Galina was living up to her end of the bargain. Pamela quickened her pace.

When she reached the second bedroom door, she paused with her hand on the knob. Adrenaline kicked her heart into overdrive. What if someone else, not Matt, were inside, waiting to pounce on her as soon as she opened the door? What if the rustling sounds she'd heard were made by some kind of animal? Or the monstrous spiderlike creature Eric had seen?

Fighting these dark images, Pamela gripped the knob and slowly turned it. Cautiously, she pushed the door open far enough so she could peer inside.

The room was almost totally dark. Black material tacked across one window blocked the outside light. She opened the door wider to allow illumination from the hallway's bare bulb.

An appalling, stale, slept-in smell enveloped her. Something or someone alive was being kept in this room. She squinted to see in the almost total blackness.

The only furniture was a bed and a metal locker. Since the bed was behind the door, she had to step into the room to get a good look.

Someone lay on the bare mattress. Her breath caught in her throat. Could it be Matt?

Chapter Nine

A man dressed in boxer shorts and a T-shirt was tied, spread-eagled, to the bedposts. A rag covered the lower half of his face, but his hazel eyes were wide-open with surprise.

It was Matt. Pamela ran to him, her breath ragged. She was so relieved, she could hardly keep from sobbing.

"Oh, Matt," she whispered, running her hand over his head. "What have they done to you?"

Frantically, she grabbed Norm Duncan's knife from her bag and opened its longest blade. Sharp as a razor, it sliced cleanly through the heavy cotton rag stuffed in his mouth. When it fell away, he started to speak. She put her hand over his lips. A noticeable growth of whiskers brushed against her sensitive palm.

"Don't talk," she whispered, her mouth very close to his ear. "The soldier's in the next room." In an instant, she'd cut through the ropes tying his hands to the bed.

He took the knife from her and cut the leg bonds himself. Then he swung his legs over the side of the bed.

Her heart thumping madly, Pamela examined his lean body in the semidarkness. Though he'd been tied, she saw no rope burns or abrasions on his skin. For a man who'd been held prisoner for close to a week, he seemed in remarkably good shape. Obviously, they'd let him exercise. When he stood beside the bed and stretched, he looked as muscular and vital as ever.

Where were his clothes? Panicking, she cast her eyes around the room. They had to hurry. She focused on the wall locker opposite the bed. Could his captors have been so foolish as to leave what he'd been wearing inside? Trembling, she crossed the small room. The metal door opened with a raspy screech. She froze, holding her breath, listening.

When no shouts erupted, she peered into the locker. Dark pants, a white shirt and a suit coat hung inside—the clothes he'd been wearing when he checked out of the Hotel Washington. His wallet was in his pants pocket, his passport in his suit jacket.

How odd that they'd leave them there, she thought, vaguely disturbed at finding them. She removed the garments and brought them to where he stood reviving the circulation in his arms and legs. He slipped into his shirt and pants.

She gazed around, searching for his shoes. There was a chamber pot in one corner, the source of the bad odor. Kneeling, she looked under the bed and saw the shoes tumbled together near the headboard. She pulled them out, finding the socks stuffed inside. He sat down on the bed to put them on. When she tried to help, he waved her away.

Dressed, he followed her to the bedroom door. After a cautious look down the hallway, she led the way through the living room and then to the landing beyond. She eased the outside door closed. A tiny click told her the latch had caught.

They hurried down the stark concrete stairwell. When he started to say something, she put her finger to her lips. No one must hear them speaking English. Not until they were well away from this building.

Pamela should have been grateful that Matt had come out of this ordeal in such good shape. And she was. But a niggling doubt chewed at her elation as they ran down the stairs to the street.

If he was truly the prisoner of an important Russian general, why had he been so easy to find and rescue? And if he wasn't a prisoner, why was he tied to the bed?

"WHAT THE HELL ARE YOU doing here?" Matt exploded as soon as they were off the train and no one was within earshot. He couldn't believe she was really beside him.

"Save your strength," she urged, moving toward a long flight of crowded concrete stairs, which led out of the most ornate subway station he'd ever seen. "We'll talk later."

"I'm fine." Matt ignored the mass of people around him. "If you don't answer, I'm going to stop right here and kiss you the way I wanted to when I saw you in that bedroom. I thought I'd gone crazy when you waltzed in and started cutting my gag off." He stopped. "So what the hell *are* you doing here?"

She offered him a slow smile. "Rescuing you, of course."

"All by yourself?"

She mounted more stairs, and he followed. "No one's with me here, if that's what you mean."

They emerged at the top of the long stairwell. The overcast sky held a hint of drizzle. Ahead Matt could see what looked like an ancient church, with five domed spires.

"How did you find me?" He felt her tremble when he touched her arm. She held on to his hand, keeping him close.

"The Pentagon Intelligence Agency found you," she said. "They sent me to talk you into coming home so they can question you about Eric's accident."

Her words roused his apprehension. "If they found out where I was, they must realize I was forced to come."

She hesitated. He sucked in his breath. The air that had tasted so fresh and clean moments ago, now had a bitter quality. "They think I deserted, don't they?" His gut clenched as he spoke. "And that I'm selling information about the UFO?"

She nodded, her eyes full of sympathy. "When you tell them what really happened, they'll change their minds." There was a husky note to her voice.

They started across a wide street.

"Are we going to your hotel?" he asked.

"No. The U.S. Embassy is in the next block. We'll be safe there."

They reached the far side of the street. No one was near, but Matt sensed someone watching, someone they couldn't see. He jerked to a stop. "I'm not sure this is a good idea, Pam—"

The next instant, he heard the distinctive crack of a rifle firing.

PAMELA HEARD A SHARP noise, like a car backfiring. Then Matt grabbed her hand and took off back across the street, dragging her behind him.

A scream died in her throat, and she gasped for breath. What was happening? Why was Matt running? A yellow city bus swerved around them. Instead of blaring his horn, the driver shook his fist as he passed.

On the far side of the street, Matt still clutching her hand, they headed back in the direction they'd come. At the end of the block he slowed.

"Somebody took a shot at us," he said, panting.

Pamela gasped for air. "How do you know?" Though they'd slowed to a walk, her legs felt like lumps of wood.

"I've fired enough rifles to know what they sound like."

A frisson of fear slid down her spine. "Maybe they weren't aiming at us."

"Sure they were." His grim face chilled her. "General Vactin sent somebody to keep an eye on the embassy. He knew that's the first place I'd go."

"But we came straight here," she declared. "They wouldn't have time to get here before—" She pictured a diagram of the Moscow subway system. "No, that's wrong," she corrected herself. "The embassy isn't that far from where you were being held. It took us nearly an hour to get here because we had to go clear into center city to transfer."

"But someone in a car could've gotten here in minutes."

She stared at his tense face with dawning horror. Her breath—just beginning to come back—caught in her throat. "So it *is* possible. Somebody fired at us."

"I'm sure of it." His growl came from deep within. "I'm a dead man if I try to get on the embassy grounds." He cast her a sidelong glance. A muscle jerked at the corner of his mouth. "And you won't live long, either. If we're together."

Tightening his grip on her hand, he headed back toward the subway station they'd just left.

Pamela studied his profile as she strove to keep up. His jaw was thrust forward, his eyes narrow. She could almost hear his silent curses as he pushed her aboard a train.

Catching her breath, she slid thankfully onto a seat. "We'll call the embassy and get somebody to pick us up," she suggested, remembering Fred Altman, the trained driver who had saved their lives in Washington. "The Pentagon gave me a name to call when we were ready to leave Moscow. He'll know how to get us out of the city."

"Why didn't you ask for help when you rescued me?"

"Because I wasn't sure you were in that apartment," she said. "Our embassy people couldn't lodge an official complaint with the Russians based on a few thumping noises."

"If you'd called your contact, he could at least have supplied a car and driver." His tone was coolly disapproving.

She shook her head. "The Pentagon warned me not to do anything illegal or I was on my own." She held up her hand, ticking off her violations on her outstretched fingers. "I used a false name, I claimed to be from a Russian government agency, and I hired a prostitute to occupy your guard so I could get in that back room." She managed a wry laugh. "Then, I walked out of a Russian general's apartment with his prisoner. So I've already done exactly what the intelligence people warned me not to. I'll be jailed as a spy if the Russians find out.''

A look of wonder spread across his face. ''You risked your life against Pentagon orders, without any chance of help?''

She felt her face flushing, more pleased than embarrassed by his admiration. ''The intelligence people thought you came here voluntarily, that all I'd have to do is knock on the door, you'd answer, and we'd talk. They had no idea you'd been kidnapped.''

The cynical twist to his mouth told her he disagreed. ''If they found out where I was, then why didn't they know I'd been kidnapped?''

The train jerked to a stop. ''I'll explain everything when we get to the hotel,'' she said.

THE GRACEFUL CURVING lines of the French-built Kosmos Hotel loomed ahead of them. A wide walkway from the street led to a broad terrace. Pamela stopped before they reached the terrace, a sense of helpless frustration sweeping over her. ''We'll never get you in my room without somebody seeing us.''

''Can't we slip in a back entrance and avoid the lobby?''

Pamela took a deep breath, fighting her weariness. The drizzle had turned into a cold misty rain. If they didn't find shelter, they'd soon be soaked.

''The lobby isn't the problem,'' she said. ''It's watched, but we look like American tourists. I doubt anyone will stop us. The problem is getting in my room without being seen by the *babushka* ... er ... woman who hands out room keys on the floor.''

Mingled with her fatigue was a desperate sense of urgency. ''We've got to think this through before we do something foolish.'' Turning, she started toward a park in the next block.

Matt fell into step beside her. "Maybe we should check into another hotel under different names. Since you speak the language, we could pretend to be locals."

Pamela sighed with frustration. "We can't pass as locals. In Russia, everybody carries an identification document. You can't check into a hotel without showing it."

His tight expression relaxed into a smile. "Then I guess we're stuck with your hotel." Tiny droplets of water ran down his face from the misty rain. The shoulders of his suit were soaked.

Through her lined raincoat, Pamela could feel the chill. Stopping, she faced him and took his hands. They were like ice. She rubbed them, keenly aware of the shiver rippling through his big body. "You must be freezing. We've got to get you inside."

"I'm okay," he said. "After five days stretched out on that stinking bed, this rain is just what I need. We'll talk under that monument where it's dry."

Ahead rose a massive structure with gold-embossed figures of a man and woman on top. Matt and Pamela huddled near an outside column, partly protected from the misty rain. Kiosks selling everything from chewing gum to cheap jewelry lined both sides of the pavement beyond the monument. Every time Pamela returned to Moscow, there were more of the small stands, a sign of the country's increasing democratization.

She lowered her voice. "We can't go back to the hotel. As soon as the *babushka* reports there's an unregistered man with me, General Vactin will know where you are." She paused, feeling helpless. "I still think the embassy's the answer."

"I've got bad vibes about contacting the embassy." His worried eyes studied hers intently. "Before I get lured into Leavenworth or some other military prison, I want to know what's going on."

Pamela told him about the leave orders she carried, about the notarized letter from Colonel Reed assuring Matt would not be prosecuted, about the passport Norm Duncan had given her to be certain he would face no diplomatic hurdles.

Matt grunted. "They're typical intelligence types. They thought of everything." Matt's handsome face twisted into a frown. "They're also masters of lies and deceit. The orders are probably fake. Just like the passport and the letter."

Screams of frustration tore at the back of her throat. "The Pentagon wouldn't set us up like that."

"Don't bet on it," he returned.

"For crying out loud, Matt," she pleaded. "You've got to level with me. What did you do to get yourself into this mess?"

"The same thing you did," he said, his voice low and raspy. "I listened to Eric Goodman's story about a monster spider."

"Then that's why you were being kept prisoner here in Moscow? So the Russians could question you about it?" Pamela could hear the doubt in her voice. From Matt's hurt expression, she could tell he heard it, too.

"You don't believe me." It was a statement, not a question.

"There are some things I've been wondering about," she began cautiously.

"Like what?" He bent his head slightly forward, listening.

"What did you tell this General Vactin?" she asked.

"Nothing," he said flatly. "I considered myself a prisoner of war and gave only my name, rank and serial number."

An old man in an overly large jacket shuffled past them. Pamela waited until he was gone to ask another question. "They didn't torture you?"

Matt shook his head. "No physical torture, but every time I refused to answer his questions, Vactin threatened to kill both of us."

"Both of us?" Pamela's voice came out sounding like a squeak. Her chest felt as if it would burst from the tension.

"Yes. You and me." His brow furrowed, he examined her face. "That's the club he held over me. It worked getting me over here. You certainly didn't think I left you after—"

She raised a hand to interrupt him. "That's why you went with them voluntarily—because they threatened to kill me, too?" Relief surged through her. Why had she ever thought he'd walk out on her?

He pressed his lips together in a firm, hard line. "Last Saturday morning, after I left you, they were waiting for me in my room. They forced me to shower and change clothes so it'd look like I left voluntarily. If I hadn't done what they said, I'm sure they would have killed us both."

Pamela swallowed with difficulty, her anxiety increasing as she pictured the scene. "How did they get in your room?"

"The Washington's an old hotel," he said. "It doesn't have a secure card system like the newer places. They must have bribed someone to get the key. They also had the key to your room. And since I'd left while you were asleep, the bolt wasn't locked from the inside. They could have walked right in."

Pamela clenched her hands so tightly they hurt. Deliberately, she relaxed them. "How did they know we were in that hotel, Matt? We didn't find out ourselves until just before we left Tacoma."

He gave her a guarded smile. "Good question. Exactly how did your friends at the Pentagon find out where I was here in Moscow? Maybe General Vactin's spies located us in the Hotel Washington the same way."

The blood rushed from her face as she realized his implication. "You've got to be wrong, Matt," she said, her words choking in her throat. "It's bad enough that we might have been set up. There can't be a connection between General Vactin and the Pentagon."

"Maybe not, but we can't overlook the possibility." He grabbed her shoulders and squeezed them. "Thank God you're okay. You can't imagine how many hours I spent worrying they'd done something to you, too."

A band tightened around Pamela's chest. "Somebody did try to kill me—when I left the hotel Saturday morning," she said, her breath coming in quick gasps.

His features contorted with shock and anger. "Tell me what happened."

In a few concise sentences, she described the sniper attack outside the Hotel Washington. The incident, she told Matt, had led to her three-day stay in the secluded town house in Alexandria, Virginia.

He expelled his breath. "Thank God the brass had enough sense to put you somewhere safe."

"In that town house, nobody knew where I was," she said.

"Are you registered under your own name at the hotel?" he asked, finally seeming to appreciate the challenge of remaining anonymous in Russia.

She nodded. "But there's no reason for anybody to be looking for me in Moscow. I doubt your General Vactin would suspect the Pentagon of sending me to bring you home. But he'll probably check with the Intourist Bureau for your name." Pamela's voice thinned. Suddenly, this whole situation overpowered her, and without warning, she began trembling.

Matt took her arm. "How long's it been since you had a good night's sleep? Or something to eat?"

She forced out a stammering reply.

"I thought so when I saw those dark circles under your eyes." He turned her in the direction they'd come. "Let's go back to your hotel." He squeezed her arm. "Don't worry. We'll figure something out."

MATT CURSED HIMSELF when he realized how beat Pam was. He'd been so elated at seeing her that he hadn't noticed the hollows under her eyes or the slight quaver in her voice. When he finally got her back to the hotel lobby, she was leaning heavily on his arm.

"Is the *babushka* the main person we have to worry about?" he asked, as they crossed the crowded lobby to the elevators. Men in business suits sat on every piece of vinyl-upholstered furniture. More were standing. The high-ceilinged room was blue with tobacco smoke.

"If we could get by her, we wouldn't have a problem." Pam sneezed loudly into a tissue she grabbed from her pocket. "Unless my room is bugged, of course. Maybe the hotel bugs rooms where U.S. military officers stay. I'm registered as a U.S. Air Force captain."

"We'll have to assume it is," he said. "As for this key woman, what about tipping her to keep her quiet?"

"It's risky, but it might work," Pam said thoughtfully. "These people all need money."

They got out of the elevator on the twentieth floor. Instantly, Matt saw what Pam meant. A glass barrier with a door separated the elevators from the hallway. A gray-haired woman sitting at a desk inside pressed a button to admit them.

Pam handed the woman a card with her room number written on it. Eyeing Matt, the woman exchanged the card for the room key. Matt did not return the woman's gaze. He'd read somewhere that people who didn't want to be recognized should avoid eye contact.

But he knew exactly what she looked like. Sixtyish. Barrel-chested with toothpick legs. Wearing a white blouse and long dark skirt.

Pam reached inside her bag and pulled out a handful of bills. The woman's eyes widened.

"My friend wants to stay with me for a few days," Pam said. "He's from another hotel, and we don't want his wife to find out."

The woman riffled through the bills. "Not enough," she said in broken English. "I lose my job if they find out."

Pam smiled. "The same amount tomorrow morning. And the morning after that."

The woman grunted. After a few minutes of haggling, she agreed to Pam's terms.

INSIDE THE ROOM, with the door safely locked behind them, Pamela put her fingers to her lips. They didn't dare talk. If the room was bugged, a couple of words spoken by a male voice could lead General Vactin to them.

When she'd hung her raincoat in the closet, she handed Matt the room-service menu and a pencil. He made a small checkmark beside the boiled chicken. They'd have to share, she realized.

She went to the phone. Her voice sounded stilted and unnatural to her, and she struggled to brighten it. "I haven't eaten anything for at least twenty-four hours," she said into the receiver. "Please send extralarge helpings." In addition to Matt's chicken, she ordered soup and the only two vegetables on the menu—potatoes and brussels sprouts. But only one glass of milk, plus a large bottle of water.

"Knock loudly," she added. "I might be in the shower."

When she'd hung up, Matt pointed to the bathroom. "You first," he mouthed silently. She nodded gratefully, so exhausted her nerves throbbed.

Her suitcase lay open on one of the room's two double beds. She took out a pink satin robe and a cotton nightgown, then put the bag on the floor. She'd hang things up later, when she wasn't so tired.

She quickly ran hot water into the tub. Then, as she scrubbed her aching body, she pictured him in the next room.

Even with a week's growth of beard and wearing a wrinkled suit, Matt roused her blood. Pamela knew she erected barriers to keep herself from falling for the wrong man. So how had this by-the-book officer, who was so unlike the swaggering fighter pilots she usually dated, managed to get past those barriers?

In her mind's eye, Pamela saw his deep-set hazel eyes, flashing with the authority of command. Was he telling the truth about his abduction? Or was he following the orders of some Pentagon general plotting an operation she couldn't begin to imagine? Was that how Colonel Reed and Norm Duncan knew exactly where to find him? Were the two of them and Matt and the mysterious General Vactin all working together?

Too weary to agonize over it, she dried herself off and put on her nightgown and robe. With the water running in the tub to confuse a possible eavesdropper, she returned to the room.

Matt had stripped to his shorts and T-shirt. *The same shorts and T-shirt I saw him in on that bed,* she thought, with a painful twinge in her chest. His suit was hanging neatly at the opposite end of the closet from her uniform. She resisted the ridiculous urge to move it close, so their clothes would be together.

He'd barely closed the bathroom door, when the bellboy—a man about Matt's age—arrived with the food. "Yes, bring it in here," she said loudly, so Matt would hear.

The bellboy busied himself taking the tray from his cart and setting it on a small table near the window. "You would like some company this evening, *da?*" He didn't look up when he spoke.

Pamela felt the blood drain from her face. Had the *babushka* said something to him about Matt? "Company? What kind of company?" She had to force the words out.

The man gave her a sideways glance. "Whatever kind you want."

Suddenly, Pamela understood. Her face burned. "No," she answered shortly. "I'm not interested."

"No problem." He rolled the cart toward the door.

When he'd left, Matt came out of the bathroom. He wore a towel around his waist and a mischievous expression on his face.

He grabbed the note pad. *GLAD YOU WEREN'T IN-TERESTED!!!* he printed in large capital letters.

She took it from him and wrote: *NOT WITH YOU HERE.* She broke into a wide smile to show him she was kidding.

He turned back toward the bathroom. She touched his bare shoulder, very aware of the strength and warmth of his flesh. She pointed to the food. "Let's eat before you shower," she said silently.

He shook his head. "No way. I stink," he mouthed.

He looked so serious, Pamela could hardly keep from laughing out loud. What did she care how he smelled now that they were together again? She tried to tear her gaze away from his bare chest, but her eyes kept dropping from his face to his shoulders to the dark V of hair leading below his towel. She caught him staring at her, beaming his delight at her glances.

Taking his arm, she went with him to the bathroom. "I like you no matter how you smell," she whispered in his ear, highly conscious of his musky odor. When he stepped inside the bathroom, she turned the television set on loud. Between it and the running water in the bathroom, the soft sounds they made in the room would be obscured.

When Matt finished his shower, he brought another glass from the bathroom and offered to share his milk. But Pam insisted she wanted only water. Since they had only one set of silverware for both of them, they traded the fork and spoon back and forth, so relaxed about using the same implements, that by the end of the meal they were feeding each other like newlyweds.

"Do you have a razor?" he whispered, his mouth close to her ear. With the TV blaring a U.S. soap opera in Russian, he was certain no listening device could pick up his whisper.

She went to her suitcase and pulled out a plastic disposable one—just like the ones he'd put in his own bag. Peering over her shoulder, he saw she packed the same way he did—socks and underwear neatly rolled, pants and shirts laid out flat so they wouldn't wrinkle. He and Pam were so much alike, it was uncanny.

He'd taken one step toward the bathroom, when there was an authoritative knock at the door. Glancing at Pam, he saw her face blanch. Had the old *babushka* given them away?

Chapter Ten

Matt wanted to punch whoever was outside the door, whoever was turning Pam's beautiful face to the color of porcelain. He felt her hand on his arm, shoving him toward the bathroom.

"Just a minute," she called. Her voice, though edged with tension, sounded tired.

Damn! What kind of man hid in the bathroom while his woman took all the risks? *His woman.* He'd never thought of anybody before in exactly those words. Inside the bathroom, he left the door ajar and the light off so he could see and hear.

"Who is it?" she called.

"Bellboy to pick up dishes," came the answer.

Matt let his breath out in an irritated gasp. He recognized the voice. This was the same man who'd asked if she wanted company for the night. Matt felt himself stiffen. If the bellboy made even one suggestive comment, he'd flatten him.

Settle down, he told himself grimly. *Pam can handle this loser.*

She stayed by the outside door. "The dishes are over there."

The bellboy passed by the bathroom, inches from Matt's eyes. A big man, he strained the buttons of his blue uniform. Over the blaring TV, Matt heard faint clinking sounds.

"You have good appetite tonight." Matt bristled at the man's comment. The burly Russian was attracted to her. Matt could hear it in his voice. When he'd asked if she wanted company, he was probably referring to himself.

Matt pictured her by the half-open hall door. She'd be clutching her satin robe at the throat. He could hear rustling sounds as she shuffled her bare feet on the carpet, could feel her impatience at the bellboy's slowness.

The sound of clinking dishes grew louder, and the bellboy's broad chest came into view. "If you need anything, ask for Anton." The man was so close, Matt could smell his sweat. He held his breath, certain the Russian could hear him breathe.

"Thanks, Anton," Pam said.

The dishes rattled again, and the door closed with a hollow thud. Matt heard her lock it with the chain. He waited half a second before leaving the bathroom.

When he came out, Pam was still standing near the hall door. Her skin color had returned to normal, but her eyes, locked on his, were wide with repressed alarm.

He held out his arms, and she came into them with a whimper, like a child's cry. He cradled her against him, rocking her gently in his arms.

"We're safe for tonight," he whispered.

He led her to the bed where her suitcase had been. She slipped her robe off. Matt groaned inwardly when he saw her maidenly white cotton nightgown. Though it covered her completely, his experienced eye detected the suggestive curve of breast and hip. He didn't let himself respond. Tonight she needed rest, not the passionate attention of a man who wanted her so badly he hurt.

Matt pulled back the blankets and tucked her in. With great effort, he managed not to show his desire.

After he shaved, he took a cold shower. This was going to be a very long night.

PAMELA AWOKE WITH her back curled against Matt's chest. What a wonderful way to wake up, with his arms around her. Still half-asleep, she lay motionless, savoring the wonder of being safe and warm, and the knowledge that he was here to face today's perilous adventures with her. She'd slept more soundly than at any time since Eric's death.

Was he awake? Probably not. She felt the rhythmic rise and fall of his chest and heard his even breathing over the subdued chatter on the television. He must have turned the volume down, but not off, last night. Did he think they'd make noise during the night, noise that the TV would mask? She smiled, imagining his thoughts.

Something about Matt felt right to her, as though they were operating on the same frequency. She closed her eyes and pictured his face—his smouldering hazel eyes, the tiny cleft in his chin, his long face, his broad high forehead.

Moving out of his embrace, she turned on her other side, facing him. His eyes were wide open, locked on hers. They contained a sensuous flame that sent a delicious pulse throbbing through her loins.

"You're awake," she whispered.

His eyes widened. "I've been awake for hours, waiting for you."

The drumbeat in her loins strengthened. She yearned for his touch, but was afraid of it, too. Could she risk another intimacy when she suspected he might be lying about his abduction?

He slid toward her on the double bed. When he pulled her to him and held her, Pamela didn't resist. She locked herself in his embrace, drowning in the velvety moistness of his mouth.

He deepened the kiss, and the delicious feel of his hungry lips on her face, on her throat, wiped any regrets from her mind.

Her nightgown inched up her thigh as she moved against him. He was naked, she realized suddenly, quivering with awareness.

He caressed her thighs, her belly. His gentle massage sent currents of desire racing through her. The very air around them danced with electricity.

Suddenly, her cotton nightgown seemed dreadfully in the way. She needed his warm flesh against hers. Regretfully, she moved a few inches away.

His questioning eyes focused on hers. "What's wrong?" he whispered.

"My nightgown." She pulled at it. He helped her slip it over her head.

His eyes explored her body, then stared into hers again. "My God, you're more beautiful than I remembered." His voice was a whispery murmur. "Thinking about you nearly drove me crazy during that hellish week."

Bending down, he took the tip of her breast in his mouth. As his tongue tantalized the nipple, a hot surge of desire turned her loins to liquid. She moaned out loud, unable to stop herself.

He held her close for an instant. Then he inclined his head toward the TV set, which sat on a dresser across the room. "I'll turn up the volume so we won't be heard."

She watched him walk to the TV. What a magnificent creature he was, with his runner's well-muscled legs and smoothly rounded behind. His back tapered from broad shoulders to a slim waistline. When he turned and came toward her, the sight of his full arousal so drew her gaze that she had to force herself to look away.

Matt didn't stop to analyze what had happened to them. All he knew was that in the short time he'd known her, Pam had struck a chord somewhere deep inside him. He didn't question how or why he felt the way he did. Not now. Not with her waiting for him on the bed, her soft warm eyes beckoning.

Leaning over her, he studied the expression in those eyes. Innocent and filled with love, they made him feel possessed with extraordinary powers. As he lay down next to her and began stroking her silken flesh, he delighted in the way she

warmed to his touch, her own hands eager to caress him.
Her fingers trailed down his neck, his belly, his groin. He
guided her hand to him, inviting her to touch his swollen
manhood. Slowly, she caressed his hardened flesh, feath-
ering her fingers over the moist tip.

Matt couldn't suppress an involuntary moan. Her eyes
flew open and stared deeply into his. The expression of
pleasure on her face was enough to send him perilously close
to the edge.

Balancing on a thin wire, he took her mouth again.

She stopped her intimate stroking and moved her hips so
she was directly under him. When he entered her, she rose
to meet him. Matt put his hands beneath her, drawing her
tight against him and reveling in her warmth all around him.

She was his, and he was hers. They belonged together.
Without moving, he stared down at her, wanting her to
know how wonderful she made him feel.

Her eyes blinked open. Wild and dazed with passion, she
stared at him.

"Thank you, Pam," he whispered, his whole being com-
mitted to her happiness.

Pamela dug her fingers into his shoulders. Her hands caressed the firm flesh, his muscles taut yet supple. She
breathed his musky smell, letting it become part of her.

Closing her eyes, she wrapped her legs around him and
pulled him closer. Her body's fullness made her gasp. But
when he tried to inch backward, afraid of hurting her, she
arched higher, forcing him in deeper. She burned for him,
ached for him, needed him with every breath she took. She
couldn't let him stop. As he thrust into her, the pleasure was
so intense she had to bite her lip to keep from crying out.

His thrusts, slow at first, deepened and became more
rapid.

For Pamela, nothing existed except Matt. She was
wrapped with him in a fiery cocoon of sensations that wiped
out any other thought.

Her tremors began slowly and built to a wrenching peak. She hovered for an intense moment before tumbling over the edge. His movements continued, deeper and more rapidly than before.

She reached another peak, and then another and another. Finally, when all feeling was drained out of her, she felt him stiffen. He clutched her tightly, and a groan escaped his fevered lips. Then, incredibly, her spasms began again, and she soared once more—a golden bird against a white-hot summer sky.

For an instant, she was conscious of nothing but intense pleasure. Then, as the tremors lessened, he collapsed half on top of her, his skin moist and smooth against hers.

Pamela didn't move. She didn't want to release him, didn't want to lose this wonderful feeling of being joined to him.

A few seconds later, he lifted his chest over her, his weight on his elbows. When she opened her eyes, he was staring down at her with such an expression of awe and tenderness that her heart melted.

"The more I know you, the more I realize how alike we are." His whisper was soft in her ear.

"I know." She wriggled to one side.

He inched away, facing her. "But?"

So, he'd guessed she had some doubts.

"You were too easy to rescue." She felt her face flushing at admitting her doubt. "That makes me wonder if you've told me everything about your capture."

He didn't look away. "I thought the rescue was a little too easy myself. Let's go somewhere and talk about it."

Matt turned away to retrieve her robe. Pamela put it on, but paused halfway to the bathroom, frozen in midstep.

The announcer on the early-morning news was broadcasting a story about a woman who'd drowned in the Moskva River.

"Galina Nazarov's body was found..."

Horrified, Pamela stood rooted to the floor. Her mind refused to accept what she'd just heard. The announcer couldn't be referring to the Galina who had gone with her to General Vactin's apartment. Not *that* Galina. Not the pretty young woman with the face of a girl. She felt the blood draining from her face. If Galina had been killed, there could be only one reason. Pamela took deep breaths, struggling to regain her composure.

She felt Matt's hand under her elbow, guiding her to the nearest bed.

His brows drew together in a worried frown. "What's wrong?"

Trembling, she sat down. "Galina Nazarov was the prostitute who helped me rescue you."

He didn't seem to understand. She tried to organize her jumbled thoughts. "A woman named Galina Nazarov was just found drowned."

He still seemed confused. Grabbing the white note pad, he wrote: *HOW DO YOU KNOW?*

Pamela took a deep breath. No wonder he was confused. Since he didn't understand Russian, he had no idea what the announcer had said. The walls closed in on her, trapping her. They had to get out of here, go someplace where they could talk above a whisper without the TV blaring a few feet away.

She hoped this awful news didn't mean the prostitute had been tortured to make her talk. Before she died, had she told General Vactin about the blond woman who hired her, the woman who spoke Russian with a foreign accent?

Hurriedly Pamela scribbled on the tablet. *I HEARD IT ON THE TV.* Understanding flooded his face.

She leaned close to his ear. "We've got to go outside where we can talk."

He nodded his agreement.

She wrote again on the tablet. *WE'LL MEET BY THE SPACE MEMORIAL. YOU CAN SEE IT FROM THE HOTEL LOBBY.* She printed the words carefully, to be certain there'd be no mix-up. The last time they'd made love, he'd disappeared right afterward. That mustn't happen again.

OPENING THE DOOR, Pamela peered down the hall. The *babushka* she'd tipped yesterday was on duty again. There was no one with her, but the door to a nearby room stood half-open. Pamela knew the *babushkas* used this room as a rest area to gossip and smoke. Would she—and Matt, when he left—be secretly observed from there as they left the floor?

Her nerves raw, Pamela headed toward the desk, another day's bribe in hand. The woman gave her a welcoming smile. Pamela placed the money on the table. Instantly, it disappeared into the woman's shapeless dress.

"My friend will be leaving soon," Pamela said, searching the woman's face. Were hidden eyes watching from the darkened lounge? Pamela concentrated on keeping her voice level. "My friend has the key to the room. You can give him the card."

"No problem," the woman replied in her broken English. Several of her teeth were missing, giving her a haglike look.

Pamela took a long look at the crack in the lounge door, but could see nothing. A foreboding chill crept over her. Was she doing the right thing by meeting Matt outside the hotel so they wouldn't be seen together? The last time they'd separated, she'd had to travel halfway round the earth to find him.

She paused, on the verge of going back after him.

The woman gave her a questioning glance.

Yanking her bag off her shoulder, Pamela opened it and rummaged around inside to give herself a moment to think. She and Matt were harder to identify separately than together. Meeting outside was less risky than walking with him through the lobby.

Smiling brightly, she held up a lipstick. "Oh, here it is. I thought I'd forgotten it."

The old *babushka* grinned back, her faded blue eyes
sparkling. She waved a thin hand in mock contempt. "You
are young, beautiful girl. Why you need such things?"

Pamela examined her lined face. By keeping quiet about
Matt, was this old woman doomed to meet the same fate as
the pretty little prostitute?

HAD SHE BEEN FOLLOWED? Apprehensively, Pamela
glanced around her.

Above, the space memorial's sculpted rocket swooped
toward the heavens with a trail of blue metal smoke behind
it. A single car was parked near the hotel's broad terrace. No
one was inside. A man and woman hurrying up the terrace
stairs toward the lobby didn't glance in her direction. She
caught herself glancing uneasily over her shoulder, alert for
any movement that might be threatening.

Pamela waited for Matt near one of the spruce trees by the
space monument. They'd be safe meeting here unless she'd
been followed. She didn't think she had been. Hadn't she
spent the past half hour observing everyone who came near
her? But she was no professional. She doubted she could
spot a trained operative.

Still, nobody was shooting at her, which was a victory of
sorts. Pamela permitted herself a wry smile. A woman was
in deep trouble when she measured her success by the number of shots fired at her. The thought shattered her equilibrium.

Nervously, she paced along the row of trees, waiting.
Where was Matt? They'd agreed to meet here in exactly half
an hour. The time was up. Could it happen again? Could he
simply disappear into thin air, the way he had before?

At least it wasn't raining this morning. Thin sunlight filtered through a high overcast. Pamela hugged her lined
raincoat more closely about her, glad she'd worn her black
slacks. April in Moscow was about forty degrees cooler than
in San Antonio. Lord, but she wished she was at her apart-

ment right now, with Matt sitting beside her at her swimming pool.

She glanced at her watch. Ten minutes late. Her stomach clenched tight. She knew she should have stayed with him. She paced to a spot where she could keep an eye on the lobby.

"Hi." Matt's voice sounded abruptly from behind her.

Spinning around, she stared wordlessly at him, relieved at his sudden appearance.

"Sorry I startled you," he said, grinning. "I came around the long way, in case anyone was watching from the lobby."

She couldn't help grinning back at him. "I'm just glad you're here." She wanted to hug him, but couldn't risk drawing attention. "Did the *babushka* give you a hard time?"

"No." His face went grim. "I'm late because I saw one of the general's men in the lobby. I'm sure he was looking for me."

Pamela's heart lurched. "Did he see you?"

Matt shook his head. "I don't think so. He was near the front desk. I stayed out of sight until he left. The general doesn't know I'm staying with you, or else his men would have come to the room last night."

Nervously, she took his arm and started toward the Prospekt Mira *Mitro* station. She'd noticed many of the ubiquitous vendor stalls on a walkway near the station. They could mingle with the crowd there without being noticed.

"It won't be long till they figure out who rescued you." She shuddered inwardly at the thought. "He's bound to have my description by now. If the prostitute didn't give it to him, your guard at the apartment did. All the general has to do is show the guard my picture in that newspaper article, and he'll know who I am."

They crossed the street and headed down the tree-lined sidewalk. The subway station was in the next block.

"The connection isn't as obvious as you make it sound," Matt said. "Nobody would guess from Sharplett's newspaper article that you spoke fluent Russian or that the U.S. intelligence people would pick you for a job like this.'' He lengthened his stride, but Pamela had no trouble keeping up with him. She stared at his sober profile.

"If Vactin's the least bit suspicious, all he has to do is check with the Intourist Bureau for my name." She didn't like to sound pessimistic, but Matt had to know what they were up against. "Sooner or later he's going to, if he hasn't already. Maybe that's what his man was doing at the Kosmos." She bit her lip, hearing the quaver in her voice.

They reached the row of vendors' stalls. As she'd hoped, a crowd of fifty to a hundred people milled about in the area, some lined up for soft drinks and candy in lieu of breakfast, some hurrying toward the underground train station.

Pamela stopped walking. "We've got to get help from the embassy, Matt. That's the only way we'll get out of here in one piece."

His brows drew together in a dubious frown. "I thought we already agreed that wouldn't work."

"We'll have to make it work," she insisted, determined to convince him. "It's the only chance we've got."

"I'm not so sure," he said.

Pamela stared directly into his eyes. "Be serious, Matt. What other way is there?"

"By using our passports to get on a plane and fly out of here," he answered. "I'm sure you have yours and—" he patted his jacket pocket "—thanks to Vactin's oversight, I also have mine."

"You've got two," she said. "The one in your pocket and the one I brought for you, just in case."

"How convenient." His mouth twisted into a cynical smile. "The Pentagon thinks of everything."

Pamela heard the sarcasm in his voice. Did he suspect the Pentagon Intelligence Agency of setting him up? The notion raised the hair on the back of her neck. Hadn't she herself suspected Norm Duncan and Colonel Reed of some sort of collusion with General Vactin? She couldn't believe Vactin had simply *overlooked* the passport in Matt's jacket pocket. He must have left it there on purpose. But why?

"When they gave me that passport for you, the intelligence people didn't know the Russians had abducted you," she explained, not voicing her doubts. "They thought you could come home whenever you wanted to, as long as you had a passport and visa. They gave me an extra, just in case you didn't have yours on you when you decided to come home."

They stepped into line at one of the kiosks, being careful to keep plenty of space between them and the people around them so they wouldn't be overheard.

"In a sense the Pentagon was right." His face was grim. "I'm about ninety percent sure my abduction wasn't sanctioned by the Russian government. That tinhorn general was operating on his own."

"Why, for heaven's sake?" Her voice rose in surprise. "That 'tinhorn general' is the senior military officer in this country's space program. He'd be risking everything to abduct an American air force officer without his government's approval."

"I don't care who he is. He must have a personal reason for what he did." Matt scowled. "You know more about this country than I do. Do you think it's standard operating procedure for the government to arrest and hold people the way they did me? Especially now that the cold war's over?"

"No," she answered. "That's one reason I thought you might be involved in this somehow."

"You're kidding!" His shocked expression mirrored his startled words.

She shrugged. "I thought our government might be working with the Russians on this UFO thing. And that you might be a part in it."

He stared at her, dumbfounded. "What's the other reason?"

She forced Eric's accusation—that Matt was involved in his accident—out of her mind. That was something she never intended to tell him about. He'd be devastated to know one of his pilots had voiced such a charge.

"The same reason I told you about—that your rescue seemed too easy," she said. Her brow furrowed as she remembered the news story about Galina. "But maybe it wasn't as easy as we thought, Matt. If that poor girl was killed to get her to talk—"

"Or to shut her up," he added. "And remember, somebody shot at us when we got near the embassy."

At the head of the line, Pamela pointed to two bottled orange drinks on the kiosk's shelves and waited for the proprietor to hand them to her. She paid for them and gave one to Matt.

Sipping their drinks, they started down the crowded walkway with kiosks on each side. The sun penetrated the clouds more strongly now, brightening the littered walkway.

Pamela studied Matt's profile. "After killing Galina and shooting at us, do you really think General Vactin's going to let us simply get on a plane and fly out of here?"

"I don't think Vactin can stop us *except* by shooting us," Matt said. "Once we're on a plane, we're safe."

"But until then, we might be shot at any minute?" She grabbed Matt's arm with her free hand. Somebody was waiting for them out there, no matter where they went. Somebody with a face they wouldn't recognize, lurking in the shadows. Somebody who wanted them dead.

"We've got to at least make a try for the embassy," she argued, stepping up her pace. "The people at the Pentagon told me to take you there. That the embassy would arrange for us to get back home."

Matt gave her an annoyed glare. "Do you always follow orders, right to the letter?"

She returned his glare. "I try to. Especially when my life's at stake." For a long moment, neither of them spoke. Then her expression became determined. "I'm going to the embassy, Matt. Don't try to talk me out of it."

"That's one of the places Vactin's people will be watching." There was a warning edge to his voice.

"For you. Not for me." She stopped at the end of the row of kiosks.

"They probably have your description," he reminded her. "You said so yourself."

"I'll have to chance it." She paused. "I'll meet you under the arch where we were yesterday in exactly two hours."

His brows drew down, and his angry glare softened. "Please don't go there, Pam. It's too dangerous. Somebody's sure to spot you."

Girding herself with resolve, she shook her head. "Nobody will see me going onto the embassy grounds. I'll call the name I told you about and let him pick me up in a car."

He took a deep breath. "I wish you wouldn't go, Pam." His voice was thick and unsteady. "I'm afraid something will happen to you. I don't want to lose you."

She forced a confident smile so he wouldn't see how scared she was. "Haven't I already proved you couldn't lose me if you wanted to?"

PAMELA TOOK A *MITRO* TRAIN to Red Square. In the lobby of the huge Rossia Hotel, she found an outside phone and dialed the number of the U.S. Embassy.

Hesitantly, she asked for Brian Chapman, the name she'd been given at the Pentagon. The mere mention brought instant results. Without asking who she was, the operator connected her.

"Do not identify yourself," a man's voice said, before Pamela even opened her mouth. "I know who you are. Please answer my questions but say nothing else."

Pamela gripped the receiver with trembling hands. The name Brian Chapman must be a code name, telling the embassy who she was.

The beating of her heart quickened, and the rustling sounds in the busy hotel lobby faded. The only noise she heard was the raspy voice on the telephone. It spoke rapidly, as though time was terribly important.

"Are you alone?"

"Yes."

"Did you find the *package* you came for?"

"Yes."

"Can you bring it to the GUM in half an hour?"

"No. The package isn't with me."

"Then come by yourself. Someone will meet you by the front entrance."

The line went dead.

Chapter Eleven

It was a little after ten o'clock in the morning when Pamela arrived at GUM, the huge state-run department store on Red Square. She was twenty minutes early. The walk from the Rossia Hotel had taken less than ten minutes.

Hurriedly, she joined the throng of shoppers crowding through the central entrance of the elegant nineteenth-century building. She'd be less conspicuous inside than loitering in front, waiting for someone she wouldn't recognize.

Inside, the emporium looked like an elegant stateside shopping mall, with its marble floor, white storefronts and elevated walkways. The shops lined up on both sides of the wide center corridor featured names like Christian Dior, Samsonite and Karstadt.

Pamela paused near a group of Western Europeans gathered around a fountain and pretended to listen to the tour director, who spoke in a language she didn't understand. While she lingered, Pamela studied the people passing by and searched for any strange movement, any gesture that seemed hostile, any quick glance of recognition.

Thank God the embassy realized somebody was after her and Matt. That must be why Brian Chapman, or whomever the code name represented, was taking these elaborate security precautions.

She waited until exactly ten twenty-five before leaving the protective shelter of the building. Who would meet her? How would she recognize a legitimate American official?

A group of teenage boys stood near the main entrance selling postcards out of their jacket pockets. One detached himself from the group and came to Pamela. Tall and thin, with a square face and straight dark hair, he looked about seventeen.

"Very nice postcards," he said, holding a packet out for her to see.

"No. I don't buy such things," she said in Russian, hoping to sound like a native so he'd go away.

He pressed closer to her. "Please look." Quickly, he flipped the cards over, shielding the packet with his body so only she could see it. Her eyes widened. The word *CHAPMAN* was printed on a slip of paper inside the transparent plastic cover.

"Very nice postcards," he repeated, this time in Russian.

Pamela fumbled in her purse. "How much?"

The boy named a price, and she passed the money to him. As soon as he'd handed her the cards, he turned away.

Trembling, Pamela examined them. Written on one was an address only three or four blocks away. She thrust the cards into her shoulder bag to show to Matt. Then, curbing her impatience, she headed for the address at a leisurely pace.

It belonged to a commission shop, selling goods brought in by private individuals. In the dingy window was a display of tarnished brass samovars. She tried to see into the shop, but her view was blocked by some sort of screen.

For a long moment, she hesitated on the sidewalk outside, her heart pounding. Finally, she pushed the door open and went in.

No one was there. A musty smell, like old clothes in a long-locked trunk, enveloped her.

On surrounding shelves were household appliances, spare pieces of china and other used items. In front of her on the counter stood a lamp, its base shaped like a woman's body. Pieces of the torn shade drooped down about the figure like a shroud.

Nervously, Pamela gazed around the shop. *"Zdrastvuytye,"* she called out. "Hello? Is anybody here?"

She took a quick, sharp breath when a gnomelike man bobbed out from behind one of the display shelves. His eyes met hers. Without saying anything, he inclined his head toward the door at the rear of the shop. Was someone waiting for her there?

Nodding her understanding, Pamela threaded her way through the dusty display shelves and piles of used items. Her hand trembling, she opened the door.

There was an empty alley beyond. Where was Brian Chapman? She stepped out of the shop, wincing as the door slammed behind her.

Then she heard the low rumble of a car's engine. Coming fast, a black sedan rounded a curve in the alley and screeched to a stop beside her. The door burst open.

"Get in," ordered a man in the back seat. "I'm Brian Chapman." With his neatly combed black hair and grey business suit, he appeared presentable.

Pamela scrambled inside and yanked the door shut.

"Get us out of here," he said to the driver. The car shot forward.

Then he extended his hand to Pamela. "I'm Douglas Fosdick, Captain Wright, the political officer at the embassy." Gravely, he shook the hand she gave him. "Brian Chapman is a code name. Sorry about the theatrics, but we don't want the Russians to know how much we want Major Powers back. So we're keeping a tight lid on everything connected with this operation."

He appraised her with obvious admiration. "Congratulations on the success of your mission. How'd you talk Powers into coming back home with you to face the music?"

To face the music? What was he saying? Dumbfounded, Pamela stared at the man beside her. Slick-looking, he had a high widow's peak that gave him a hooded, reptilian appearance.

"Then you don't know he's been kept prisoner?" she asked. "That he was abducted against his will?"

A curtain descended over Fosdick's face, masking his expression. "Is that what he told you?"

"That's what I know." She thrust her chin out. "He was tied to a bed when I found him."

"So you waltzed in, untied him, and the two of you walked away together into the sunset. Mission accomplished." Fosdick's sarcasm made Pamela see red.

"It wasn't quite that simple," she began, making an effort to keep her voice calm. In a few words, she described her first visit to General Vactin's apartment, then explained how she'd hired the prostitute to keep the guard busy while she freed Matt.

"It was a setup," Fosdick said. "Powers has collected his money from the Russians, and now he wants to go home. So, he claims he was abducted and held prisoner. Of course, the Russians are more than willing to play his game—that was probably part of the deal. What better way to make a hero out of a traitor?"

"The prostitute's dead," Pamela announced defiantly. "Killed because she helped us."

Fosdick shrugged. "In this part of the world, prostitutes are expendable. Her death helped convince you his story was true. Right?"

"Yes." Pamela was becoming more infuriated by the minute. "But there's one thing you won't be able to explain. Why were we shot at when we tried to go to the embassy for help? Obviously, the people who kidnapped Major Powers didn't want him to talk to anybody there."

Fosdick's expression didn't change. "Did you see someone with a weapon?"

Reluctantly, Pamela had to say no.

"Did you hear the shot?"

"I heard a loud, cracking noise. Matt—Major Powers—said it was from a rifle."

Fosdick leaned back. "You're too trusting, Captain Wright." His cold brown eyes took her in. "You heard what could have been a car backfiring. You didn't see anybody with a rifle. You just took Powers's word for it."

Pamela recoiled from his glance. "If his imprisonment was a setup, how did they manage to have him tied up like that when I got there? Did they keep him tied up all week, just in case somebody came to rescue him?" Let this smug embassy officer answer that, if he could.

But Fosdick didn't bat an eyelash. "Easy," he said. "They knew exactly when you'd be there."

Her mouth dropped open. "That's impossible. I didn't even know myself."

"Yes, you did," he corrected. "You knew when your plane would arrive in Moscow. So did General Vactin. He figured you'd show up at his apartment within twenty-four hours."

Pamela couldn't believe what she was hearing. "How could he possibly know anything about me or my flight schedule?"

The embassy officer gave her a sly smile. "I suspect he found out about your schedule the same way we now know that the Russians paid a lot of money for the information Powers passed to them."

His smug confidence shattered her defiance. A horrible suspicion broke through the barrier in Pamela's mind, and her doubts came flooding back. Could Matt have been lying all this time, just as she'd feared? Her mouth opened in dismay.

"How . . . how can you be so positive?" She hoped he'd give her the same old runaround about classified sources, so she wouldn't have to believe him. After the closeness she'd felt with Matt, she refused to presume he was lying.

"This is highly classified, but I figure you've got a legitimate need to know." Fosdick lifted a thin eyebrow. "We're
reading General Vactin's mail. That's why we're so positive."

Pamela's heart sank to her shoes. *Intercepted communications.* If the Pentagon was intercepting General Vactin's
messages, no wonder the intelligence people knew what he
was up to.

"That's how we discovered where Powers was hiding,"
Fosdick went on. "That's how we know exactly how much
he was paid for his information. Vactin spelled it out in one
of his messages."

A sick, empty feeling washed over Pamela. Had her trust
in Matt been horribly misplaced?

The car had left the busy downtown streets and now
glided through a parklike area with little traffic. "Where to
now, Doug?" the driver asked. His familiar tone led Pamela to think they were associates, not the civilian equivalent of officer and enlisted driver.

They're CIA, she realized, her nerves tensing. *And they
want to get their hands on Matt to question him about espionage.*

Fosdick leaned toward her. "Where's Powers now?"

"Waiting for me near the hotel." Pamela kept her answer purposefully vague.

"Can you bring him in?" The CIA man's face was eager, like a trained bloodhound who's found the scent.
"We're not being followed. We can pick him up right now
in the car."

"No," she said abruptly, not sure exactly what she meant.

He gave her a quizzical look. "You *do* intend to bring him
in, don't you, Captain Wright?"

Though she was trembling inside, she assumed her stern-
est, most poised expression. "That's what I came all this
way for, Mr. Fosdick."

"Then what's the problem?" His alert brown eyes
scanned her face.

The problem is that I love Matt Powers. I won't throw him to the wolves, no matter what he's done.

She met Fosdick's gaze without flinching. "I'm going to do what's right, Mr. Fosdick."

"You don't have much choice, Captain. Be careful what you decide. If you go along with Powers in his deal with the Russians, you're as guilty as he is."

"I'll remember that," she promised, her head high.

"I'd advise you to call Brian Chapman within the next twenty-four hours." His voice was taut with warning. "And when I pick you up next time, you'd better have Major Powers with you." He paused. "Or be ready to return home without your *package* and admit you failed."

Pamela met his ultimatum with a stony silence.

A few minutes later, the black sedan dropped her off near the Kosmos Hotel, but she didn't go inside. As soon as the embassy car was out of sight, she headed for the park where Matt waited.

SHOCK AND ANGER LIT Matt's hazel eyes, as Pamela repeated what the CIA officer had told her.

"Somebody's framing me," he declared, his voice inflamed.

"What about the messages from General Vactin that the Pentagon intercepted?" Pamela kept her voice down. Nobody appeared to be watching them, but over the noon hour a crowd had gathered in the park. Someone in their vicinity might be listening.

"It's got to be some kind of trick, Pam." She could tell he was controlling himself with an effort. "Nobody paid me to come here, and I certainly didn't tie myself to that bed."

"For a man who'd been tied up a week, you were in pretty good shape," she said softly.

He stared at her, his eyes ablaze. "What are you saying? That you think I'm guilty, too?"

A suffocating sensation tightened her throat. "I don't know what to think, Matt. Everything that CIA man said made sense."

For a long minute, he didn't answer. Then, finally, he nodded. "You're right. I *was* in good shape. Because they let me exercise every day, and they fed me well. Vactin didn't want me to look abused when I was rescued—or when my body was found." He emphasized the last words.

Pamela glanced uneasily over her shoulder. She saw nothing suspicious, only crowds of unsmiling people, many with their faces turned upward to catch the weak rays of the sun.

"Then you think General Vactin sent phony messages to fool the Pentagon?"

"It wouldn't be the first time Russians have tried to put one over on Americans. The process is called *disinformation*."

Pamela struggled with her uncertainty, wanting with all her heart to believe him. "But we're not in the cold war, Matt. Why would General Vactin try to make the Pentagon think you were selling secrets?"

Matt shrugged. "Like I said, I think the general has a private ax to grind. He knew our country would lodge an official complaint with his government if word got out that an air force officer had been abducted. Then his own government would be after him, and his game—whatever it is— would be up. So he made my abduction look voluntary."

The nagging in the back of Pamela's mind refused to be stilled. "Good heavens, Matt, the man's in charge of this country's space program. What could he be up to that the government doesn't know about?"

Taking her arm, Matt led her across the brownish grass to a secluded area away from the monument and kiosks. Her running shoes sucked muddy water when she lifted her feet.

"Something profitable for him," Matt answered grimly. "And something that's got to do with that UFO Eric

Goodman saw. He questioned me about it for hours every night.''

"A powerful general spent hours questioning you personally?" She listened with bewilderment.

Matt nodded. "I wondered why he didn't use a trained interrogator."

"Maybe he didn't trust anybody else." Pamela told herself to be careful. In spite of the mass of evidence against Matt, she was starting to believe in him again. "But you never told him anything?"

"No." His brows lowered in a frown. "But I thought about that monster spider of Goodman's all the time I was tied to that bed." His gaze softened. "And about you, of course."

"Interesting combination," she murmured. "Me and the monster."

"And about what you told me about the inside of the capsule and your father's drawings," he returned quietly. "I think I figured out what your isosceles triangle is."

Pamela's heart caught in her throat. "What?"

"A navigational device—at least, that's what Goodman saw inside the capsule."

"But the air force doesn't use anything like Eric described to navigate." She paused, examining his face. "Or does it? You're the expert."

He shook his head. "Not to my knowledge. But maybe somebody else does. Maybe that capsule used a lighted panel with the exact outline of the place it wanted to find."

Pamela heard her blood pounding in her ears. Matt might be right. "But what does that have to do with my dad's sketch?"

His hazel eyes narrowed. "Pilots take reconnaissance photographs of terrain they fly over. Your father's photos were top secret, so he couldn't keep them. Maybe he drew pictures of places he thought were interesting—a sort of memento of the secret work he did."

In her excitement, Pamela paced back and forth. "He'd do something like that. Yes, he would." She held out her hands to Matt. He squeezed them.

"It was a lake," she said. "Those sketches on the wall were of lakes he flew over on his reconnaissance missions."

He grinned at her excitement. "That's what I thought, too." But his smile faded quickly. "There must be a million lakes with the shape of a triangle. How do we find the one Goodman's capsule was hunting for?"

"Simple," she said. "I go to the library and look in an atlas."

He took her arm and started walking down a tree-shaded path. "You're the supreme optimist," he said fondly. "Of all those millions of lakes, how do you expect to pick out the right one?"

"Simple," she said again. "It's a noticeable body of water, and it's located somewhere along one of my father's flight paths. It should be a snap to find."

"You know your father's flight paths?" There was disbelief in his voice.

"On his reconnaissance flights over the USSR?" she said. "You bet. Down to the mile. It took years and years, but the Pentagon finally released the information to me."

Stepping up her pace, she led him back to the crowd near the monument. "Do you mind waiting for me again, while I make a short trip to the library?"

He shook his head. "This time I'm coming along."

"Not a good idea," she said firmly. "I'll be a lot safer by myself than with an escaped prisoner a Russian general is gunning for."

He let out his breath in an exasperated snort. "You're right, of course. I'll wait for you here, near the monument."

SINCE THE HOTEL WAS on the way to the subway station, Pamela stopped there to use the bathroom. The *babushka* on duty at the desk gave her a quizzical glance when she exchanged her card for the room key.

"Your friend is coming later?" she asked, her voice low. She clasped and unclasped her thin hands on the tabletop. Her eyes darted back and forth between Pamela's face and the long hallway before her.

Why was she so nervous? Turning, Pamela glanced down the hall. No one was in sight. But the door to the lounge was ajar again. A shadow, blacker than the darkness within, moved across the opening. As she watched, the door inched open wider.

A wave of stark terror washed over her. Someone waited inside that room, watching her every move. This time she was positive. Who could it be? What did they want?

Don't make them suspicious, Pamela.

To protect the old woman, she leaned down close to her ear to answer her question. "My friend's gone to his hotel, but I'll come back with him later."

Without moving her head, the *babushka* glanced sideways at the partly opened door. Pamela couldn't tell if the movement was a reflexive gesture or a conscious attempt to warn her, but it made her even more certain someone watched from inside.

Pamela drew her breath in slowly so she wouldn't look panicky. Had someone sent the hidden watcher to arrest her and Matt? Or was the watcher a friend of the *babushka*, trying to get a good look at the rich American willing to pay a small fortune for a night with her lover?

Forcing herself to smile brightly, Pamela shook her leather shoulder bag. "Tomorrow morning you'll have your reward, as usual."

Squaring her shoulders, Pamela went down the hall to her room. The bed had been made and fresh towels hung in the bathroom. As far as she could determine, her things hadn't been touched, except to dust under them. But she couldn't escape the suffocating premonition that something was dreadfully wrong.

Hastily, she ran a comb through her hair and used the bathroom. Then she stood in the middle of the room, focusing on the beds, the dresser, the TV. What was out of place? Her gaze centered on the trash baskets. Of course they were empty, now that the maids had been here.

The empty trash baskets. Her stomach clenched with sickening intensity. Where were the notes she and Matt had written last night?

In the trash baskets.

Why in the world hadn't they flushed them down the toilet? By now someone must have read them and realized there were two people in the room. Was that why a hidden watcher waited behind a half-closed door?

Matt couldn't come back here. It wasn't safe. She wasn't even sure she'd be safe coming back herself. Or that she'd be permitted to leave the hotel.

On her way down to the lobby, Pamela half expected to hear a shouted command to stop and to feel a big hand on her shoulder. But nobody intercepted her. Finally, weak with tension, she found herself outside.

Trying not to hurry, she made her way to the Prospekt Mira subway station. Once aboard a train, she transferred twice, finally getting off near Red Square. After mingling with the crowd at GUM for half an hour, she left through a side door.

On the street again, she caught a taxi. Could anyone still be following after the convoluted course she'd taken? Tense with apprehension, she gazed out the back window. No cars behind her turned when her cab turned, nothing indicated she was being followed.

But how could she be sure? She was an amateur. The notes she and Matt had left in the hotel room were abundant proof.

The Russian State Library loomed ahead, its portico supported by square black pillars. Bronze busts of Russian literati stared sightlessly at her from niches along the facade. She paid the driver and got out.

Dashing up the wide staircase, she felt as vulnerable as a housefly buzzing against a kitchen window. At any minute, she expected to hear the crack of a rifle, to feel the stunning impact of a bullet between her shoulders.

When she reached the relative safety of the portico, she stopped, gasping for breath. At a more leisurely pace, she strode inside and entered a room off the high-ceilinged foyer.

Instantly, the familiar smell of parchment and binding glue enveloped her, restoring her equilibrium. *Books*. She expelled her breath in a long sigh. In a library, there was nothing to be afraid of. No one would attack her here.

Women worked behind a counter, answering requests from a long line of patrons. Finally it was Pamela's turn.

"Kak vam pamoch?" a woman asked. "How may I help you?"

Pamela explained that she wanted to see a world atlas. The woman showed her how to fill out a request slip. Half an hour later, with the book in her hands, she sat down at a reading desk.

First, the former Soviet Union. Carefully, Pamela traced her father's route across each of the republics. From its eighty-thousand-foot altitude, his Blackbird—still the world's most advanced reconnaissance aircraft—could survey more than one hundred thousand square miles of the Earth's surface in one hour. Keenly aware of the plane's capabilities, she examined every square mile of ground her father would have photographed.

Two lakes fit her general parameters: one near Yakutsk in eastern Russia and the other in central Kazakhstan. But neither looked exactly like the detailed sketch her father had drawn. She copied the names and coordinates on a tablet in her bag.

Next, she followed his route across Afghanistan and Pakistan. Nothing. Sighing, she turned to the map of the subcontinent. Had she been wrong about the meaning of her father's sketch? Matt would be even more disappointed than she was if she didn't find the lake. She'd been so sure it would be in the former Soviet Union. That's the area her father had been photographing, the one he was interested in. He'd flown over the other countries, but she didn't think he'd taken pictures.

With her finger, she followed the Blackbird's route south down the Indian corridor. Nothing. She traced the route again.

Then she saw it. A tiny isosceles triangle etched in blue on the map's green surface. It was upside down from her father's sketch, with the tip facing southeast. That's why she hadn't seen it right away. Her pulse pounding, she turned to another page with a large-scale depiction of that area.

And there it was. The lake was the exact outline of the sketch she remembered in her father's den. Carefully, she wrote the name on her tablet. *Lake Mewar.* It was located near a town called Jahangir in west-central India. Her father had flown almost directly over the lake and town on his way to the Indian Ocean.

Pamela felt like she'd just won a twenty-million-dollar lottery. She couldn't wait to tell Matt.

Heady with success, she tried to ignore the questions that nagged at the back of her mind. What if Norm Duncan could find no connection between the lake and the capsule? Where did that leave Matt?

And what if Matt wasn't telling the truth about his abduction? What if the Pentagon was right in its interpretation of General Vactin's messages? Where did that leave her?

Look on the bright side, she told herself sternly as she returned the atlas and went outside. They'd won, she and Matt. Surely the authorities would believe him after he gave them this information. With it, Norm Duncan at the Pentagon could track the elusive capsule. Pamela herself was one step closer to learning the truth about her father's disappearance. And about Eric's death. Bright sunlight heightened her euphoria.

Filled with happiness, she flew down the library's long staircase and hurried toward the nearest *Mitro*. She and Matt were about to be released from their terrible burden of fear and suspicion. They'd be normal Americans again—back in the United States, where they could get on with their lives. She had to get to him, to tell him, so they could take refuge at the embassy and begin the process that would take them home.

She swung around a corner to a narrow street lined with small shops. The subway station was in the next block. Breathing heavily, she slowed her pace.

Suddenly, she became aware of a sound behind her. The purr of a car's engine. Why didn't it pass? She glanced over her shoulder. A black, Russian-made Volga sedan pulled up at the curb. A man got out. She breathed more easily. If someone were following her, he would have stayed in the car. Or he would have shot her by now. This man must be a shopper.

Pamela sensed, rather than heard, the footsteps behind her. A big hand closed on her arm. She tried to twist away and felt wrenching pain in her shoulder.

He was wearing a dark suit, not a uniform, but that didn't stop her from recognizing him. The face of Matt's guard smiled down at her. His mouth was set in a vicious grin. He no longer looked like the big strapping kid who'd opened the apartment door yesterday.

"Hello, pretty census lady," he murmured, his eyes glinting. "Please come with me."

Nausea rose in her throat, choking off her screams.

Chapter Twelve

Paralyzed with fear, Pamela couldn't move, couldn't speak. She froze as the guard leaned toward her, his big body blotting out the sun.

Then, over the thudding of her heart, she heard a sharp cracking sound. The guard's iron grip on her arm loosened. His big body toppled forward. Pamela caught a last glimpse of his twisted frame sprawled on the narrow sidewalk, his face in the mud, as she dashed headlong toward the nearest shop.

Behind her, a woman screamed. Pamela heard another cracking sound, and the wood splintered in the doorframe beside her.

It didn't make sense. Whoever had shot the guard wanted her dead, too. But he'd missed. Somehow she was alive, unharmed, free to run. She had to get to Matt so they could flee to the embassy for refuge. She burst through the shop's door, slamming it behind her.

Suddenly, she smelled fresh warm bread and realized she was in a bakery. A stoic throng of customers—apparently unaware of the action on the street—clustered in front of glass cases stacked with long loaves. Gasping for breath, Pamela glanced around her. Where was the rear door? She had to get out of here before someone connected her with the fallen guard.

She elbowed her way toward a door behind the counter.

A stocky man in an apron blocked her. "You can't go through there," he said in Russian.

Pamela didn't bother answering. With one quick jab, she punched him in the chest. He jerked backward, a surprised look on his face. She ran past him without looking back.

In the kitchen, two women filled trays with fresh dough ready for the oven. Pamela headed for the only other door. It had to lead outside. She yanked it open. Her heart dropped. A storeroom. Inside was a toilet and a pile of filled flour sacks. Momentary panic threatened to overwhelm her. Frantically, she searched for an outside door.

The shop owner burst into the kitchen. "Stop her," he yelled. In the distance, Pamela heard the up-and-down blare of a police siren.

Her heart in her throat, Pamela slammed the storage room door and glanced around her. Then she saw the outside door. It was behind an oven, almost hidden. She fled toward it, her feet barely touching the floor. The shop owner bolted after her.

She couldn't let herself get caught. After the laws she'd broken, an encounter with Russian justice would be almost as hazardous as exposure to the guard's killer on the street outside. With a last burst of energy, she reached the door and yanked it open.

The air in the alley stank of exhaust fumes. But to Pamela, the polluted atmosphere was the sweetest smell in the world—the smell of freedom. Breathing deeply, she took off running.

RIKER SAT ON A CIRCULAR concrete bench, his gaze fixed on the entrance to the Kosmos Hotel. The woman would not escape him again. Sooner or later she would return. Now that he knew where she was staying, his task was as good as completed.

Smiling, he ran his fingers over the refitted violin case beside him, its knobby surface reassuring him of success. The case held his sniper rifle, an Austrian Steyr SSG 69.

With its telescopic sight, the weapon could accurately bridge the distance between him and the hotel entrance. To fire, he'd take cover in a row of evergreens behind the bench where he sat.

Riker had already decided to do the job here at the hotel. Why waste time following her? Now that he'd killed Major Powers, he might as well take care of Captain Wright while he had the chance.

Riker had spotted Powers following her, too, of course. At first he hadn't been certain the big brown-haired man *was* Powers, not until Powers had gotten out of the car and joined her in front of that bakery shop. Though Riker had seen Powers only from a distance, he'd known who Powers was from his broad back, his straight brown hair, the dark suit he was wearing. It was the same suit Powers had worn coming out of the hotel in Washington, D.C. Besides, the Wright woman knew no one else in Moscow.

Why had Powers been following her? They must have been playing some kind of game designed to throw pursuers off the track. Well, they were amateurs, and they'd failed.

His gaze trained on the lobby entrance, Riker was acutely aware of everyone leaving and entering the busy hotel. No one would see him fire the shots at Captain Wright. Just as no one had seen him kill Powers an hour ago. Riker's aura of invisibility would protect him—as it always had. He'd practiced the art of blending in—of using the very commonness of his appearance to disappear—for so long that it had become part of him. He doubted that even Otto, the most perceptive of creatures, could identify the gray-brown color of his eyes.

Riker stiffened, thinking of his employer's massive white body. Otto would not be pleased that the Wright woman had gotten away again. When Powers fell, his body had blocked Riker's aim. Then, instead of bending to help Powers as Riker expected, she'd disappeared inside the nearest door. So his shot at her had missed.

Captain Wright wouldn't get away again, he assured himself. When she returned to the hotel, she'd die. Moscow had become a lawless city, as crime-ridden as New York or Los Angeles. No extensive manhunt would be launched to find her killer.

PAMELA SPENT THREE HOURS riding subways, dodging in and out of public buildings and riding taxis to obscure places around Moscow. Everywhere she went, she imagined hidden eyes watching her. Would she hear the shot that struck her? she wondered, hating the paralyzing fear. When a car backfired on Arbat Street, her whole body jerked with shock.

Matt's guard must have followed her from the Kosmos Hotel. She had no idea who the sniper was or why he'd killed the guard and then shot at her. All she knew was that she'd been followed by one man, maybe two. She mustn't let it happen again. Her life and Matt's depended on her vigilance.

When she finally reached the park where she'd left Matt, he was nowhere near the monument. A stab of fear flashed through her. What if they'd been tailed when they left the hotel early this morning? What if General Vactin had spirited Matt off again?

The scenario didn't make sense, especially since she'd seen General Vactin's lackey shot to death. But nothing made sense anymore. Everything was shrouded with a weird craziness where two and two didn't add up to four, and her best friend died because he saw an unbelievable monster.

Wearily, she leaned against one of the monument's concrete pillars and covered her face with trembling hands. She couldn't lose Matt. Not now. Not after they'd come this far. Nothing could come between them.

The air stirred with the soft rustling of someone behind her. Even before she whirled to face him, she knew it was Matt.

A thousand pounds lifted off her chest. "Thank God! Are you okay? Where were you?"

"I'm fine. Just staying out of sight, waiting." His long, rugged face tightened with concern at her anguished appearance. "The question is, how are you?"

Standing next to him beside the monument's concrete pillar, she let him take her hands. She marveled at the warm, safe feeling flowing through her now that they were together again.

He pulled her hands close against him, warming them with his body. "What's happened?" he said, searching her eyes. "Tell me about it."

Pamela sagged against him. "I was so scared when you weren't here. I was afraid you'd been shot, too." Her voice came out sounding weak and whispery.

"Shot?" He eyed her with concern. "Who's been shot?"

For an instant, Pamela couldn't speak. The scene came back to her vividly, flooding her mind with images and sensations. The guard, his dark suit stained with blood, lying facedown in the mud. The warm smell of the freshly baked bread. The muted blare of the police siren, coming closer, ever closer.

"Your guard." She had to force the words out, unconsciously glancing over her shoulder. "The one at General Vactin's apartment. Somebody shot him. And almost got me, too."

His eyes widened. He clutched her hands to him as if he feared she would vanish. "Where?"

"A couple of blocks from the library." Once she'd found her voice, the words flowed nonstop. She told him everything that had happened—her certainty that someone was watching her in the hotel, her discovery of Lake Mewar in the atlas, the guard's shooting and, finally, her frantic escape from the bakery.

When she finished her story, he put his arm around her. Drawing her close to his side, he led her across the soggy grass toward a different path from the one they'd taken earlier. "Thank God you're okay." There was a huskiness to his voice she'd never heard before.

She smiled at him, letting his warmth seep into her. His hazel eyes brimmed with tender concern. Just being with him gave her courage, gave her the strength to go on.

For a moment they walked silently, watching a flock of tiny black birds peck at the brown grass a few yards from their feet. Suddenly he laughed, but his face was grim.

"My troops would never believe this scene," he said. "Hard-nosed, by-the-book Maj. Matt Powers running from the law like a common criminal."

"Up till now, you've had no choice," she said.

His lips curved in a cynical smile. "Sure I did. I could have turned myself in to your embassy friends and gone to jail. That's what I advise my men to do when they get in trouble. Airmen, I say, you tell the truth and pay the consequences. In the United States Air Force, there's no other way."

Pamela leaned toward him and put her hands on his face, twisting his head toward her so she could see his eyes. "You're right. You're a hard-nosed officer, but that's what makes you strong."

"I'm strong, all right." She could almost taste the gall rising in his throat. "Some filthy terrorist tries to kill me and my woman, and I sit here helpless."

"Do you think it was the same man that fired at us yesterday near the embassy?"

He shook his head. "No. That had to be Vactin's man. This sniper is somebody else."

"I still don't understand," she said, feeling stupid.

The birds at their feet suddenly stopped their pecking and soared off, chirping noisily. A young couple came down the path toward Pamela and Matt. Their arms entwined, they seemed engrossed in each other, but Matt waited until they'd passed to answer.

"This sniper must be the same man who tried to force us off the road in Washington," Matt said. "The same man who took a shot at you outside the Hotel Washington. It's pretty obvious that someone besides General Vactin wants us dead."

Pamela stared at him in disbelief. "Why did he kill the guard?"

"I think he screwed up," Matt answered thoughtfully. "Was the guard in uniform?"

The horrible image appeared again in her mind. The body, facedown in the mud, blood oozing through the hole in his back. "No. He was wearing a dark suit."

"Like the one I've been wearing ever since I left Washington?"

She nodded.

"And he was about my height and had brown hair about the color of mine?"

She nodded again, with sudden understanding. "From the back, he could have been mistaken for you."

"That's what I think happened. Our sniper killed the wrong man." His lips twisted into a cynical smile. "General Vactin's not going to appreciate losing one of his people."

"Do you think he knows who did it?"

He took her arm and started down the path out of the park. "Your guess is as good as mine. But one thing's for sure—both the sniper and the general want us dead."

Lake Mewar, Jahangir, India

OTTO RECOGNIZED THE VOICE as soon as he picked up the telephone receiver. As usual, the connection from Moscow was abominable—thanks partly to Otto's patched communication system to hide his location. But General Vactin's deep tone crackled over the thousands of miles, his gritty voice unmistakable.

"Call off your assassin, Otto. He just killed one of my best men."

A warning flare went up in Otto's mind. How did the general know Riker was in Moscow?

"Impossible, Dimitri." Otto was careful to keep his voice even. "Riker doesn't make mistakes."

"He did this time." There was a long pause. "Either that, or he was following your instructions. Did you order my man's elimination?"

"Don't be a fool," Otto returned, not wanting to upset the delicate arrangement between himself and Vactin until he knew exactly what had happened. "Why are you so certain it was Riker?"

"The man who was killed had just gotten out of a car. The driver spotted Riker." Vactin laughed, a bitter, rumbling sound. "Perhaps your invisible killer isn't quite as unnoticeable as you think."

Otto sank deeper into the chair cushions. Though the den was cool and dark, he could feel heat rising to his face. Riker's targets were Matthew Powers and Pamela Wright. He must have killed the wrong man. How could he have been so careless?

"Explain something to me, Dimitri," Otto said, probing for the reason behind Riker's mistake. "Why did you abduct the American air force major—I believe his name is Powers—and hold him prisoner?"

Vactin's strangled gasp told Otto he'd hit pay dirt. This was something Vactin hadn't wanted him to know. But Otto *did* know. As soon as Riker reported that Powers had left the Hotel Washington with two Russians, Otto had suspected Vactin was behind the abduction.

Otto smiled to himself. The heat in his face began receding. "I sincerely hope you didn't snatch Powers thinking he could tell you more about my operation."

"I...ah, of course not, Otto." The general was stammering like a schoolboy.

"Then why *did* you take him prisoner?"

After a long silence, Vactin spoke. "As military commander of my country's space program, I wanted to learn more about the UFO described in the American newspapers. How could I know the capsule was yours?"

Vactin paused. Otto could almost feel the other man's sweat.

"Didn't it occur to you that the capsule portrayed in the article matched mine in size and in its ability to take off and land independently?"

"I had no idea," Vactin returned, speaking more rapidly now. "Believe me, Otto, I respect the terms of our agreement."

"Which are?" Otto prompted.

"I provide the launch vehicle for your satellite, no questions asked."

"Correct." Otto showed his mastery in his voice. "And you're very well paid for that, aren't you, Dimitri? And for telling your government lies about what I'm doing."

"You don't have to rub it in," Vactin said in his broken English. "We both know the terms."

"Good." Otto let the stimulating feel of victory flood through him. "So tell me, Dimitri, what was your man doing when Riker shot him? I trust there was no connection between him and Maj. Matthew Powers."

For a long minute, Vactin didn't answer. Otto figured the general was beginning to suspect the man's murder was deliberate—a warning to Vactin for snooping into Otto's business.

When Vactin finally spoke, his tone was subdued. "My driver must have made a mistake, Otto. I'm sure it wasn't Riker who shot my man."

"Good," Otto said again.

After he hung up, he sat silently in his darkened den, luxuriating in the afterglow of victory. Riker had made a careless mistake, but Otto—with his genius for manipulation—had managed to turn it into a triumph.

THE EVERGREENS MADE grotesque late-afternoon shadows on the muddy path leading to the sidewalk out of the park.

Pamela eyed the sidewalk, suddenly fearful. Could some-one be lurking near the hotel, waiting for her and Matt?

She clutched his arm. "We can't go back to the hotel."

"No. We're going to a phone," Matt said. "Then you're going to call your contact at the embassy and let him send you home."

"Send *us* home," she declared firmly. "When we tell the Pentagon about that lake in India, they'll find out what Eric saw. You'll never be court-martialed, even if they don't be-lieve your story about being abducted."

Matt stopped and gave her a hard look. "You're right about one thing," he said, "I don't intend to be court-martialed for something I didn't do."

His defiant tone made Pamela's breath catch in her throat. He wasn't going with her to the embassy. She knew without his telling her.

"You've got to turn yourself in, Matt," she insisted. "If you don't, the Pentagon will believe you're a traitor."

"Oh, I'll turn myself in," he said, "but first I've got to check out that lake for myself. It's probably a wild-goose chase, but I might find something to help my case."

Pamela felt her pulse leap in her throat. *India.* "You're going to Lake Mewar to find Eric's spider monster?" She caught her breath. "Thank God. I was afraid you were go-ing after that sniper."

"Much as I'd like to string the guy up by his thumbs, I'm not a fool." There was no humor in his smile.

They reached the *Mitro* station. As they waited for a train headed toward the city's center, Pamela eyed the ornate carving on the massive marble columns, the domed ceiling, and the chandeliers that belonged in an opera house in-stead of lighting up a hole in the ground.

"Do you think we'll see subway stations like this in In-dia?" she asked innocently, as they boarded a train and sat down. With a jerk, it began moving.

"*You're* not coming with me." His voice was stern. "It's too dangerous."

Pamela didn't let his tone bother her. "Since nobody knows we're going, we'll be safer in India than we are here. There'll be no sniper waiting for us, no General Vactin to kidnap or shoot us."

She let a pleading note creep into her voice. "Besides, this lake is connected to my father somehow. For the past twenty years, a good part of my life has been dedicated to finding out what happened to him. Don't you think I've got a right to ask a few questions?"

"Sure you've got the right." His doubtful expression didn't match his agreement. "But you'll pay too high a price for going, Pam. I can't let you do it."

Now he had her dander up. "You don't have anything to say about it. If you don't want me to go with you, I'll go alone. But I *will* go."

He sighed, deep in his chest. "Pamela, Pamela. You're the same kind of person I am—law and order, by the book. Are you certain you want to throw your air force career away on a wild-goose chase like this?"

"I'm positive." But her words concealed the first rumblings of inner doubt. Was Matt right? Would she be throwing her career away by going with him to India?

"You'll be disobeying a direct order to report to the embassy here in Moscow," he reminded her. "So you'll be considered a deserter." He paused, his eyes filled with concern. "You'll also be accused of stealing government money to take a nice little vacation."

Pamela felt her face flushing. She glanced down at her waist where she carried the concealed money belt containing the thousands of dollars Colonel Reed had given her.

Matt followed her eyes. "That *is* how you planned to pay for your trip, isn't it? With the Pentagon's money?"

"We won't be taking a vacation," she argued weakly. Even to herself, the excuse sounded flimsy. "Nobody can call me a thief. I've never stolen anything in my whole life. I don't even keep library books over their due date."

"Tell that to the judge when they summon you to your court-martial." Matt's voice was bitter.

They got off at a *Mitro* station just as elaborate as the Prospekt Mira near the Kosmos Hotel. This one featured mammoth stained-glass windows with lights behind them. Not a single candy wrapper or other scrap of paper littered the huge area, a sign of the respect the local people felt for their subway system.

"Now let's go someplace and make that call to the embassy." Matt put his arm around her and squeezed her affectionately.

RIGHT UP TO THE TIME Pam dialed the number from the lobby of the Hotel Rossia, Matt wasn't sure what she'd decided. By going to India with him, she'd be risking her commission, her career and her life. He could see her inner turmoil reflected in the sober frown on her pale face. What would she do?

Part of him desperately wanted her to come with him. He didn't want to separate from her, not even for a few weeks. He'd miss her too much.

Another part of him wanted her safely home, where she could take up her life in the precise, orderly fashion she was accustomed to. Eric's monster spider had turned Matt's life topsy-turvy. He'd found inconsistencies in himself he hadn't been aware of—inconsistencies that meant he would never be the same person again. The changes felt uncomfortable, humbling somehow. He didn't want Pam to have to experience that. He didn't want her exposed to any more danger and disruption.

She said something into the telephone. Though she spoke in English, she had her back to him and he caught only a few words—enough to know she was talking to the embassy. When she hung up and turned to him, she was smiling.

"The visa office at the Indian Embassy is closed since it's Saturday." She patted her money belt. "But for a little something extra, the man on duty will be glad to give us visas."

So she hadn't been talking to the U.S. Embassy, after all. She'd be with him, thank God.

"What's our story when we get there?" He tried to frown—to show her he didn't approve of her decision—and failed miserably.

She grinned back at him. Her expressive face shone with determination. "We're U.S. military officers on a short Moscow leave, and we've decided to return home via India. We'd like to stop there for a few days and spend the rest of our money."

"No wonder they're helping," Matt commented dryly. He opened the lobby door for her, and they started across the wide street toward Red Square and the nearby subway station.

Pam didn't smile. Matt could see her determination in the firm set of her jaw.

"The Indian Embassy shouldn't be a problem," she said. "Nobody will watch for us there." She paused. "But the airport's different. We'll have to be terribly careful at Sher-emetyevo."

He nodded soberly. "Call and find out when the next flight leaves for Delhi. We'll arrange to get our tickets at the last possible minute."

The traffic light changed before they reached the far side of the wide street. She quickly headed toward a marked pedestrian area near the center.

"It might be best to buy our tickets and board the aircraft separately."

"Good suggestion." Matt glanced nervously at the cars and buses lumbering by. Exposed like this in the center of the street, they'd be easy targets for anyone in the vehicles surging past them. But no one came close. When the light changed, they hurried on to Red Square and from there to the *Mitro* train that would take them to the Indian Embassy.

SUNDAY MORNING DAWNED gray and chilly, with the smell of rain in the air. Pamela hugged her raincoat about her, glad to be outside the dusty terminal where they'd spent the night. Matt stood far ahead of her in the line of people waiting to board the big Aeroflot passenger jet. For the past five hours, ever since arriving at the international departure building of Sheremetyevo Airport, they'd exchanged barely a glance. They'd also sat apart on the bus taking them from the terminal to the aircraft. Now, watching him approach the boarding stairs, she expelled her breath in a grateful sigh.

Maybe they were going to make it to India, after all. During the long night in the stuffy terminal, she'd had her doubts. Twice security guards had asked to see her passport. She'd had to purchase her ticket, the first guard said, or she couldn't wait in the terminal. From that point on, her name—and Matt's—were on the Intourist Bureau's list of Americans leaving the country.

At least they'd been able to wait in the more comfortable first-class waiting room the rest of the night. She'd huddled in her seat, avoiding Matt's eyes, certain they'd be stopped by the Russian authorities.

Ahead of Matt, a group of Indian women mounted the stairs to the plane, their brightly colored saris blowing in the chill wind. Pamela leaned forward, willing each leaden minute to pass. Why was the line moving so slowly? Finally, Matt reached the top of the stairs and entered the cabin.

She glanced toward the terminal building off to her side. While she watched, a man burst through the door and sprinted toward the line of people waiting to board the plane. The building was a long way off, and she couldn't make out his face.

A cold knot formed in her stomach as he drew nearer. Wearing a dark, official-looking suit, he held something in his hand. As he approached, Pamela recognized him. It was the CIA officer, Douglas Furrydick.

And he was running straight toward her.

Chapter Thirteen

When the CIA officer bounded up to Pamela, at least ten passengers remained ahead of her in the line waiting to board the Aeroflot jet.

"I don't know what you think you're doing, Captain," Fosdick said, panting from his long run. "But whatever it is, you'd better think again." He grabbed a sheet of paper from his briefcase and waved it in Pamela's face.

She kept her trembling hands at her side. "Unless that's an official order putting me under arrest, don't try to stop me, Mr. Fosdick." She heard her voice, stilted and unnatural.

Fosdick thrust the paper at her. "Read this." His widow's peak seemed more pronounced, hooding his face like a cobra's.

Grudgingly Pamela took the sheet of paper. It was an unclassified message from the Pentagon Intelligence Agency to the U.S. Defense Attaché, Moscow—the proper chain of command for an order to her. The words jumped out at her.

INSTRUCT AIR FORCE CAPTAIN PAMELA WRIGHT TO RETURN TO WASHINGTON ASAP. HER MISSION IS TERMINATED. RYAN.

Her heart sank. General Ryan, the commander of the Pentagon Intelligence Agency, had ordered her to come

home immediately. She couldn't disobey without risk
court-martial.

"What did you tell them to get such quick action?
asked, mockingly, to hide her anxiety. "That I'm a
coat spy, ready to sell out my country for a few measly
lars?" She inched forward as the line moved.

Fosdick glanced sideways at the Indian man in fro
her. "Please lower your voice," he murmured, his n
close to her ear. "You're being recalled because you
sion has failed. It's pretty obvious your *package* is in
sian hands."

She started to deny his charge, but swallowed her w
If Fosdick thought she'd failed, he must believe Ma
cided to stay in Moscow. So he hadn't spotted Matt b
ing the plane.

"Why didn't the defense attaché deliver this messa
she asked. "It was addressed to him."

A shuttered expression closed over Fosdick's face.
attaché was worried when he couldn't reach you at th
tel last night. He asked for my help."

"And so, naturally, you came right to the airport
hunch I'd be here." She stared directly at him.

His neutral expression revealed nothing. If he resente
cynical jibe, he didn't show it.

He met her gaze. "That's right," he said smoo
"Moscow closes up tight after eleven-thirty. Since
weren't in your hotel room, this was a logical place to
for you."

The Indian man was approaching the boarding s
Only a few more feet to go, and she'd be out of Fos
reach.

He grabbed her arm. She jerked it away and fro
hoping Fosdick wouldn't want to draw attention by
moning the Russian police.

"If I know what you're up to, maybe I can help," l
fered, his mouth twisted in a half smile.

"What I'm up to? I'm surprised you haven't figured it out for yourself, Mr. Fosdick." Searching frantically for a reasonable explanation, she took the first step up the boarding stairway. When the answer came to her, it was so obvious, she wanted to laugh out loud.

"I'm on my way home, of course, simply following orders." Her boldness amazed her. "Since my *package* wouldn't come with me, I'd already decided to go back to Washington—even before I saw General Ryan's order. I decided to go by way of India so I could see the Taj. Sort of a consolation prize, you might say."

He stared at her, his disbelief momentarily breaking through his closed expression. "If you're on your way home, why didn't you check out of your hotel?"

She gave him her sweetest smile. "I wanted to confuse anyone who might be watching me." Reaching in her shoulder bag, she pulled out her room card and handed it to him over the heads of the people behind her. "Would you mind checking me out?"

He took the card, his masked expression unchanging. Did he believe her? Probably not. But at least he wasn't stopping her.

"Thanks," she called, from midway up the stairs, watching him turn toward the terminal. A moment later, she reached the top and entered the cabin.

PAMELA AND MATT MET at the back of the plane, huddling there as it flew south over the Ural mountains. Since they weren't sitting together, this was their first chance to talk since they'd boarded.

Quickly, Pamela described her encounter with Fosdick. She kept her voice low, out of earshot of the people waiting to use the toilets.

"Matt, we've got to get off at the first stop. The CIA knows this flight terminates at Delhi. They'll have people watching for us there."

He shrugged. "So what."

So what? she wanted to scream. *What if they pick us up?*

"It's not likely they'll stop us," he went on, inadvertently answering her unspoken questions. "With our Indian visas and those phony leave orders you brought for us, they'd have a heck of a time convincing Indian authorities to detain us." For a long moment he was quiet, thinking. "Besides, they don't want us cooped up in some filthy Indian jail. They want us back at the Pentagon. The worst they'll do is keep an eye on us."

She clutched his hand as a new thought struck her. "If Fosdick spotted me getting on this plane, maybe the sniper did, too. What if he's got somebody waiting for us in Delhi?"

Ignoring the passengers standing near them, Matt put his arms around her and held her close. "We'll take evasive action when we get there. If anybody's after us, we'll lose them."

Pamela clung to him, not feeling safe, even in his arms. The sniper had followed her from Washington. She'd been in Russia less than twenty-four hours when he'd picked up her trail again in Moscow. He'd kill them both if he caught up with them.

Shuddering, she stared past Matt's shoulder at the backs of the seated passengers in the rear of the plane. Even now, he could be aboard this Aeroflot jet, ready to attack when they reached India.

RIKER BOARDED the Air India flight, his ears still smarting from Otto's scathing rebuke.

"You killed the wrong man," Otto had growled into the telephone. "What's the matter with you, you fool? Are you getting careless in your old age?"

Riker's gut clenched with cold hatred. But the hatred wasn't for Otto—he had every right to be mad. No, Riker's hatred was for Pamela Wright and Matthew Powers. They'd gotten away, again. And this time, they'd managed to get him in trouble with his employer. Not that Riker was afraid of Otto. The bald man needed him too much to risk action beyond a vicious tongue-lashing. But he didn't like appearing foolish, either. And these two people had made him appear very foolish.

"Who did I kill?" he'd asked Otto, when his employer had finished his sarcastic tirade.

"A Russian friend of the woman," Otto said.

The bald man's evasive reply told Riker that Otto knew exactly who the dead man was—and that he'd had a connection to Pamela Wright.

How did I know she had friends in Moscow? Riker asked himself, settling into the seat for the tedious flight to India. And why had Otto issued this urgent summons to join him at the palace on Lake Mewar? Riker was reasonably confident it had something to do with Wright and Powers.

Riker's anger evaporated. Instinctively, he knew Otto was giving him one last chance to settle the score.

DELHI'S INDIRA GHANDI Airport smelled of curry, cardboard and stale cigarettes. Social smells, Pamela thought, made by people who laughed and cried and made noise. Lots of noise. It bombarded her from all sides. Voices over the loudspeaker. Conversations of people around her. The hum of the luggage conveyer belt. The rattle of carts with metal wheels that needed oiling. The clarion cries of tour guides calling for their clients in a multitude of languages.

After the silence and plodding lethargy of Moscow, the clamor and vitality of Delhi were overpowering. So was the heat. She'd already shed her raincoat and sweater. They rested hotly on her arm. Even in her pink cotton shirt, she could feel dampness under her arms and on her back.

Would the killer come after her and Matt in the crowded terminal? Probably not. His chances to escape would be better outside. But that didn't lessen her fear. Anxiously, Pamela scanned the crowd, searching for any threat. A hopeless wave swept over her. She wouldn't recognize a threat unless it jumped right in front of her, waving a weapon.

Deplaning passengers, as well as those boarding, had to go through a metal detector. She didn't glance back at Matt as she stepped through the device and showed her visa. But she was keenly conscious of his comforting presence about twenty passengers behind her in the line. They'd decided to meet in two hours at a five-star hotel recommended by a stewardess on the flight. Two hours would give them enough time to elude any would-be pursuers and to buy light clothing more suitable for the hot weather.

Please, God, don't let anything go wrong, Pamela prayed as she started across the crowded terminal. Though she sensed no trouble, she cast suspicious glances at the people near her, watching for an ordinary-looking Caucasian man who might be a killer. She looked for the CIA, too. When a woman in a green silk sari gave her a quick once-over, Pamela wondered if she could be an intelligence operative. Or maybe the agent of the killer. Could the woman have a weapon hidden in the shimmering folds of silk? Pamela forced herself to look away.

Her eyes hurting from the brilliant sunlight, she surveyed the scene outside through the smudged glass terminal doors. When Matt strode by her, he didn't glance in her direction, but she could almost hear his frantic order as he passed. *Get out of here now, Pam!* She watched him cross the driveway and climb into an orange-and-black taxicab.

A moment later, an unmarked black sedan glided after it. Could the sedan be following Matt? She tensed, straining to see inside, but the car's windows were dark. The vehicle had an official look, like a government car. Was it a diplomatic vehicle from the U.S. Embassy? *Or the Russian Embassy?* A tremor ripped through her at the thought. Her gaze dropped to the license plates, but the distance was too great for her to make out the numbers.

The familiar helpless feeling flooded over her, leaving her hollow and empty, like she was inside a fragile, broken shell.

If Matt was in danger, there wasn't a thing she could do about it until they met at the hotel. She didn't dare follow and try to warn him. That would only attract their attention to her.

She waited inside the terminal for another ten minutes. Then, after quick glances to the right and left, she dashed to the taxi stand. She heard no running feet behind her, no loud cracking noises that meant someone was shooting at her. Out of breath, she slid into the back seat of one of the boxlike vehicles.

"Delhi," she gasped. "Take me downtown."

As she yanked the door closed, the car shot forward.

A small statue of the six-armed god Siva stood on the taxi's dashboard draped in marigolds. The driver wore a black turban and a grey-white shirt. Though one of his front teeth was missing, he smiled broadly at Pamela's reflection in the rearview mirror. No one in Moscow had smiled at her with that kind of friendly enthusiasm.

Outside the airport perimeter they joined the tide of trucks, buses and bicycles surging toward town. The lush green of the grass, the purples and wines of the bougainvillea, the blues and reds and yellows on the brightly painted trucks—what a change from the eternal brown of Moscow in April.

And in Delhi, she discovered, everybody honked. Signs on the backs of trucks read HONK PLEASE, an order all drivers took seriously. In Moscow, frivolous honking was frowned on. In Delhi, the noise assailed her ears as the exhaust fumes in the air assailed her nostrils. But when she closed the windows, the heat turned the car into a furnace.

Leaving the taxi at Connaught Circle, a dilapidated downtown shopping area, she found a store open on Sunday and bought some cotton skirts and blouses, a pair of sandals, some underwear and a nightgown. She left the place wearing one of her new outfits—a green print skirt and a pale pink blouse. The lighter clothes provided welcome relief from the heat.

Had anybody followed her? She didn't think so, but to play it safe, she changed cabs twice on her way to meet Matt at the hotel. When she arrived at three o'clock, he was already there, leaning against one of the columns in the white marble lobby.

Pamela caught her breath at his changed appearance. His wrinkled blue suit was gone. In its place, he wore tan slacks, an aqua polo shirt and brown leather sandals, projecting an image that radiated masculine vitality. Like the other men in the magnificent lobby, he looked as different from the wretched poor outside the hotel gates as this hotel looked different from the hovels she'd seen near old Delhi.

For a brief instant, his eyes met hers, but he didn't speak. She sensed his relief on seeing her and felt him watching her as she went to the counter. As agreed, they registered separately and let bellboys show them to their rooms. If anyone was watching, they'd be less recognizable apart than together.

What a relief, Pamela thought, as the door to her room clicked shut, leaving her alone. No glass barrier shut off the rooms from the elevator in this hotel. No old *babushka* waited in the hallway, watching her every move. No listening devices were hidden in this room. In a moment, Matt would join her and they could do whatever they darn well pleased, without fear of being overheard.

A pleasant glow flowed over her as she anticipated their night. Free and unrestrained, they could relax and enjoy being together. She hungered to be in his arms again.

He'll love my new nightgown. She smiled to herself at the wanton thought. How smooth the satin material had felt against her skin. How he would delight in helping her take it off.

For a long minute, she sat silently on her king-size bed and savored the luxurious room, glad the Aeroflot stewardess had recommended one of Delhi's best hotels. Mahogany furniture, a marble bathroom, thick carpeting, silk wallpaper—they owed themselves some comfort after what they'd been through.

Pamela tried not to think about the car that had seemed to follow Matt's trail. He'd arrived here safely, hadn't he? Maybe she'd been wrong. Or maybe he'd been able to elude it.

But what if Fosdick was right and Matt was still working for the Russians? Could whoever was inside that car have been following Matt's taxi to meet with him? Not to spy on him or do him harm, as she'd assumed?

What a preposterous notion. She shrugged it aside. If Matt was working with the Russians, he wouldn't be here in India.

The phone jingled. She picked it up.

"How's your room?"

Her heart leapt at the sound of Matt's voice. "Simply beautiful."

"Mine, too," he said. "I'll be down in about half an hour, after I shower and shave."

"I'll be waiting," she murmured.

Five minutes later, she luxuriated in her own tub, letting the warm water soothe her weary bones. Should she get dressed again? she wondered, a little surprised at herself for asking such a question. Or should she meet him at the door in her new nightgown?

Two weeks ago, the thought would have been outrageous. The old Pamela Wright didn't do bold things like that. But the old Pamela had disappeared outside that Moscow bakery, when the guard had released his grip on her arm and toppled to the sidewalk, a rifle bullet between his shoulders. Life was too precious to waste hiding behind some imagined impropriety.

This Sunday afternoon, meeting Matt at the door in her new gown seemed exactly the right thing to do. She laughed out loud, thinking of his delighted reaction to seeing her and the intimacy that would follow.

The telephone rang again. Grabbing a towel, she stood and reached for the bathroom extension.

"Give me another fifteen minutes. You caught me in the tub." Her voice was a paean of joy.

"Sorry to interrupt." Pamela turned to stone. The voice wasn't Matt's.

She clenched the phone with paralyzed fingers. "Who... who is this?"

"Brian Chapman," came the code-word answer. "Your life's in danger. You must leave Delhi immediately."

Now she recognized the voice. Douglas Fosdick. "How did you find me?" she gasped.

"Simple," he said. "I picked the best hotel in town and asked for you."

Her stomach clenched. "Then someone... someone else might also find me."

"You mean the sniper?" Fosdick said. "The sniper who killed the soldier you were with near the library yesterday?"

Pamela gripped the phone so tightly her hand hurt. She'd been careful not to mention the attempt on her life to the CIA officer, knowing that would give him grounds to detain her.

"How did you find out?" Her voice quavered noticeably, in spite of her effort to steady it.

"The Russian authorities came to us for help." He paused. "That's how I know your life is in danger. I also know your *package* is with you. He was being paid for information, just as I said. If you stay with him, you'll be accused of the same crime when you get home."

It couldn't be true. Matt couldn't be lying to her. Pamela's heart took up an odd, off-beat rhythm. Through a dizzying haze, she heard it beating like a drum in the elegant bathroom.

"You've got to be wrong." She heard doubt in her voice and hated herself for it.

"You've been warned," Fosdick said. "Get out of that hotel and back to the States before it's too late. The embassy there in Delhi can help."

Click. The line went dead.

MATT TOOK ONE LOOK at Pam's blanched face when she opened her door and knew something was terribly wrong. She was dressed in the same skirt and blouse he'd admired downstairs in the lobby, but her serene smile was gone. Her mouth and throat appeared constricted, as though she was about to scream.

He followed her into her room and swept her into his arms, smoothing her hair with his hand. At first, she clung to him with the intensity of a small child. Then, suddenly, she backed away.

"Matt, we've got to get out of here." Her whisper was edged with panic.

"Sit down and tell me what's happened," he urged, leading her to the sofa near the window.

She began talking before she reached it. "I just got a call from Fosdick in Moscow."

Matt felt heat rising to his face. "What did he want?"

She clasped and unclasped her fingers in her lap. "He says the Russian government has confirmed you were being paid for information."

Matt shook his head back and forth. "This gets better and better. Now the Russian equivalent of the CIA is collaborating with our intelligence people to bring me to justice." The idea was so ridiculous, he couldn't keep the sarcasm out of his voice. "I suppose they're claiming I had something to do with the death of that soldier."

He could see the quick flicker of doubt in her eyes. It made him want to smash his hand through the wall. She still didn't trust him, in spite of all they'd been through.

"No, but Fosdick says the sniper probably knows where I am." Her voice trembled when she spoke, and her face was so white he thought she might faint.

"He's just saying that to scare you, Pam. Fosdick was able to find you quickly because he knew you were bound for Delhi. The sniper has no way of knowing that."

"He had no way of knowing I was in Moscow, either." Fear, stark and vivid, glittered in her eyes.

Matt tried to think of something reassuring to say. He couldn't. She was right. They had to leave.

"Give me five minutes to get my things," he said quickly. "Lock your door behind me and don't open it till I get back. We'll get to Jahangir tonight, even if we have to charter a plane."

Nodding, she ran to the closet and began throwing things in paper bags. "Hurry," she said.

But he didn't start down the hall away from her room until he heard the hissing thunk of the night latch sliding into place on her door.

AFTER THE AIR FORCE JETS Pamela was used to seeing, the tiny plane looked as flimsy as a paper kite. But it could fly, its middle-aged pilot assured her and Matt at Delhi's Safdarjang Airport.

With one short runway, Safdarjang looked like a small county airport back in the States—except that it wasn't off in the wilderness somewhere, but near the government buildings of downtown Delhi. Railroad tracks ran along one side.

Like many of the structures she'd seen from her taxi window, the airport's few square brick buildings were crumbling from lack of care. Dust and exhaust fumes permeated the air. When she sneezed, her tissue caught black-colored grime.

"Many retired Indian air force officers keep their planes at Safdarjang Airport," the clerk at the hotel had told Matt when they checked out. "You shouldn't have difficulty locating one to take you wherever you want to go—if you are willing to pay his price." They hadn't liked asking the hotel clerk—knowing it would make them easy to follow—but could think of no other way to find out, since it was Sunday and most businesses were closed.

Now, strapped into the back seat, Pamela glanced at the crumbling buildings hurtling past them as their tiny craft sped down the runway. She shut her eyes, ordering herself not to get sick.

Once they were airborne, wind blew through the cockpit, taking away the oppressive heat and most of her nausea. Matt turned and smiled at her.

"This should be fun." His eyes glowed with a special brilliance.

The look of eagles, she thought fondly. *He gets it when he flies.* Lord, she wished she enjoyed flying. She wasn't looking forward to the next four hours in this flimsy little plane.

Still, the trip had a bright side. She and Matt were together—and nobody was shooting at them. Since no one but the pilot knew exactly where they were going, they should be safe in Jahangir—for tonight and maybe tomorrow. But would that be enough time to ferret out Lake Mewar's secrets?

Jahangir. What would they find there?

IN THE CRIMSON TWILIGHT, the Mogul Babur Hotel rose from the dark banks of Lake Mewar like an evil palace rising from the River Styx. Pamela stared at it from the taxi's window, a cold knot in her stomach. With the sunset turning its domed terra-cotta towers to scarlet, the place seemed drenched in blood. She blinked, half expecting the hotel to wash into the lake.

"This is the first place Fosdick—or anybody else—will look for us," she said uneasily to Matt, who sat beside her in the cab. "Maybe we shouldn't stay here. I've got bad vibes about this place."

"It's the only decent hotel in town." He squeezed her hand. "Besides, we shouldn't be here long. Only a few hours, later tonight. If we don't get some answers right away, we're both going to end up talking to a judge as soon as we get home."

Or we'll both be dead. With frightening clarity, Pamela recalled the image of the soldier's body, facedown in the mud.

Matt caught her eyes, trying to read her thoughts. She forced herself to smile reassuringly.

"Fosdick was right about one thing, Pam," he said. "By coming with me, you exposed yourself to charges of espionage."

"The answers are here," she said, with a confidence she didn't feel. "All we have to do is find them." Why couldn't she be one-hundred-percent positive Fosdick was wrong about Matt? Why did these nagging doubts still plague her, even after Matt had denied Fosdick's accusations?

The taxi drove through a wrought-iron gate to a circular driveway in front of the hotel lobby. Up close, the former palace looked even more eerie than it had from a distance. Stone by polished red stone, the building was now crumbling slowly into the murky waters of the lake. Signs of decay were everywhere—from the cracks in the red rock, to the missing corner sections.

But the decay didn't diminish the grandeur. Inside, the red stone floor of the wood-paneled lobby was covered with an immense Oriental carpet in an intricate red, black and gold design. Awed, Pamela stared at silk wall hangings of royal elephants and maharajas wearing turbans and shoes with curled toes. She half expected to find an Indian version of Count Dracula on duty behind the counter, but the clerk who greeted them looked young and very ordinary.

"They are copies of the wall paintings in Jahangir Palace," he told her, noticing her interest in the wall hangings. "The palace is not far. We have tours from the hotel."

Pamela leaned toward the clerk. "I'd like to see it," she said, ignoring Matt. They'd decided to register separately again.

"How about the lake?" she asked. Might as well start asking questions now, she thought. "Do you have tours?"

"Yes, but only during the daytime and not to the island. The hotel boats go only a few miles out. If you want to go farther, you could hire somebody else. But be careful. Some boats are not safe."

Pamela's ears pricked up. "Island? What island?" She heard Matt move closer, felt his big body next to her.

"In the center of the lake. Mr. Otto Von Meinhoff lives on the island."

"Who's he?" She tried not to let her excitement show. "Have you ever met him?"

"No." The clerk shook his head. "Mr. Von Meinhoff is what you call a recluse. He owns a big business here. He employs many people but never comes to Jahangir."

"Excuse me?" Matt interrupted, smiling congenially at Pamela. "I overheard what you were telling this woman," he said to the clerk, "and I'd like to take the tour first thing in the morning. Where do I sign up?"

The clerk inclined his head toward a door opposite the lobby entrance. "On the dock. But you'll need to go right away. The sunrise tour is very popular. Most of the seats are already gone."

Matt grinned at Pamela, his hazel eyes twinkling. "Are you interested in the dawn tour?"

She shook her head. "That's too early for me." While Matt was gone tomorrow morning, she'd try to find out more about the recluse—Otto Von Meinhoff—in Jahangir.

Matt moved closer. "Then could I register first, so I can go sign up?"

She stepped to one side. "Be my guest."

He quickly handed over his passport, signed the necessary forms and followed a bellboy out of the lobby. She guessed he'd go to his room first, then to the dock to examine the boats and sign up for the dawn tour.

Pamela studied the young clerk. "What's Mr. Von Meinhoff's business?" she asked, hoping she sounded disinterested.

He didn't look up from the form he was completing. "Manufacturing television sets, radios—that sort of thing."

Communications equipment. She tensed, then forced herself to relax so the clerk wouldn't see how interested she was. She ventured another question. "What's the name of his company?"

"Mogul Babur Manufacturing Company."

Surprised, she leaned toward him. "The same name as the hotel."

The clerk grinned. "He owns the hotel."

An idea leapt into Pamela's mind. Since this was Sunday, when many businesses closed in India, what better time to take a look at Mr. Von Meinhoff's operation? But she had to go before it got too dark to see. And she couldn't let Matt worry about her if he got back before she did.

As she left the hotel, she stuck a note under his door telling him where she'd gone and promising not to get out of the taxi until she'd returned. Ten minutes later, she was on her way to Ram Singh Road, the location of the Mogul Babur Manufacturing Company.

MATT DIDN'T BOTHER signing up for the dawn boat tour. As soon as the clerk mentioned the island, he'd decided to reconnoiter it tonight. He spent the next hour on the dock, lining up a boat willing to take him there. Unlike most of the others moored at the decrepit wooden pier, this one appeared reasonably clean and safe. Outfitted with panel seats under a sloping roof, the boat had once been used to ferry passengers back and forth to the island, the owner told Matt proudly.

It would be dark when they arrived, he said, his stained yellow teeth against his brown skin. But his boat had lights, so they would be safe. The round trip would take about three hours.

Matt started back to the hotel to touch base with Pam before he left. He reached the lobby door and pulled it open.

Three men waited inside—a civilian, a Russian colonel and an Indian colonel. From the way they tensed, he knew they were waiting for him.

He twisted around in a desperate attempt to charge back through the door. There was an ominous click behind his head—the sound of a pistol being cocked.

"Don't move, Major." The voice came from his left side.

Matt felt the unmistakable pressure of cold steel against his neck.

Chapter Fourteen

Another weapon jabbed Matt's back. Behind him someone said something in Russian. For a tense moment, he barely breathed.

"Raise your hands and turn around, Major." The accent was American. So, there were two men next to him, an American and a Russian. Counting the civilian and the uniformed Russian and Indian colonels facing him, that made a total of five. Too many to fight.

Carefully, Matt turned and raised his hands. The civilian edged toward him, his gun drawn. Small and wiry, he had a high widow's peak flecked with gray at the center.

"I'm Douglas Fosdick from the U.S. Embassy in Moscow," he said.

Fosdick! What was he doing here? Matt eyed the CIA agent warily. "You can put the gun away. We're both on the same side."

"I'm not so sure, Powers." But he stuck the weapon back in a holster under his jacket. "Either you answer my questions, or I'll turn you over to the Russians." He inclined his head toward the stocky Russian colonel standing next to him.

The CIA in bed with a Russian colonel? What kind of a setup was this?

Fosdick's mouth turned down in a thin-lipped frown. "The Russians claim you've been selling subversive information to a general named Dimitri Vactin."

"That's a dirty lie." Matt glared at Fosdick. "All that Vactin got from me was my name, rank and serial number."

"And I suppose you didn't go with Vactin's people willingly when you left Washington?" Fosdick's voice dripped with sarcasm.

"Would it do me any good to say I didn't?" Thank God Pam wasn't across the lobby waiting for him. Could he warn her, so she wouldn't be scared half to death when these armed thugs walked up to her?

"The clerks at the hotel in Washington didn't see any guns pointed at you or any knives at your throat," Fosdick observed, his wiry body coiled, like a rattler ready to strike.

"Vactin's men threatened to kill both me and Captain Wright," Matt declared. "They had a key to her room. If I hadn't followed their orders, they would've walked right in and shot her."

The Indian colonel, about Fosdick's height but not as muscular, gestured toward some sofas at the far end of the lobby. "Why don't we sit down, gentlemen?" He nodded toward three enlisted men in Indian Army uniforms standing at ease near the registration desk. "I guarantee we won't be disturbed."

Glancing around, Matt noticed that guests entering the lobby were being escorted to the garden terrace by hotel personnel.

He felt a jab in his back. "Take it easy," he growled over his shoulder. "I'm not armed."

The jab came again. Harder.

"You're wasting your breath," Fosdick said. "Boris doesn't speak English."

"Tell him to knock it off. He's making me nervous."

The officer beside Fosdick said something in Russian and the jabbing stopped.

Fosdick turned to the Indian colonel. "Tell your men to watch for Captain Wright. The desk has her passport with her picture on it."

Matt stiffened. Had Pam left the hotel without telling him? What could she be up to and where had she gone?

Fosdick caught Matt's startled reaction. "You mean you didn't know she'd left?" Fosdick's grin was sardonic. "According to the hotel clerk, she hired a taxi. She told him she wanted to go on a tour of Jahangir before it got too dark."

Hiding his anxiety, Matt walked to the nearest couch and sat down, his back to the glass lobby door. He eyeballed the Indian colonel who dropped to the sofa opposite him that faced the door. "She's not armed, Colonel. She might run when she sees your men, but she's no threat to them or to anybody."

"They won't shoot her, Major, if that is your concern." The colonel was a small-boned man with delicate features and a well-modulated tenor voice. Matt wondered how much control he had over the three enlisted men.

If only Pam would give herself up without a fight, she'd be in much less danger. *But she'll resist*, he thought, clenching and unclenching his fists. That's the kind of spunky woman she was. Why had he let her talk him into coming along? He'd known how risky this trip would be.

Fosdick sat beside Matt on the sofa. The others stood behind the Indian colonel. The enlisted men took up positions about fifteen feet away, facing the lobby entrance, their rifles in their hands.

Matt eyed the three men standing behind the colonel. Two were Russian officers in uniform. He pegged the third as an American, probably a Company man like Fosdick.

One of the Russians was short and stocky, one tall—a Mutt and Jeff combination. The American, much younger, looked like a college fullback.

"What's going on here, Fosdick?" Matt asked. "Is the CIA working with Russian military intelligence these days?"

Incredibly, Fosdick nodded. "Welcome to the brave new world of Russian and American collaboration, Powers."

Dumbfounded, Matt leaned back against the sofa cushions. When he'd mentioned the notion to Pam, he'd been joking. Obviously, Fosdick wasn't.

After a moment's thought, Matt smiled. "I'm flattered. The intelligence services of three major world powers are all after me." He glanced toward the Indian colonel. "I'm assuming you're from Indian intelligence, Colonel?"

The colonel's pencil-thin mustache didn't so much as twitch. "That is correct, Major." His glaring eyes were as dark as mahogany.

Matt turned back to Fosdick. "So what did I do to deserve all this attention? There has to be more to it than the mere abduction of a U.S. Air Force officer by a Russian general."

Fosdick hesitated. "I can't release—"

The stocky Russian standing behind the couch broke in. "He needs to know."

Fosdick shrugged. "It's your story. If you want to tell him—"

The Russian circled the couch and sat down beside the Indian colonel, facing Matt and Fosdick. "Gen. Dimitri Vactin was arrested this morning."

Momentarily struck speechless, Matt eyed the two men opposite—the Russian square-faced and determined, the Indian detached and darkly handsome. So, Matt thought, he'd been right about Vactin's involvement in something illegal.

"I'm glad you cornered the scoundrel," he said to the Russian. "I didn't think he had government approval when he kidnapped me."

The Russian examined Matt through narrowed eyes. "He claims you went with his people voluntarily. But if he is lying, we will find out."

"Other than kidnapping me, what was his crime?" Matt asked. "Skimming cream off the top?" When he saw the

Russian's puzzled expression, he rephrased the question. "Was he taking money for himself that belonged to the government?"

"Exactly." A bulldog of a man, the Russian stood and began pacing between the two sofas, keeping his eyes on Matt. "The government authorized him to sell our SS9 rockets so other countries could use them to launch their satellites into space. Vactin was keeping nearly ten-percent profit for himself. He says he used this *cream*—as you say— to pay people like you for information to protect his operation."

"Surely you don't believe him." Matt didn't restrain his incredulity. Nobody could be that stupid.

The Russian grunted a noncommittal answer that could have been yes or no. "He broke the law. That is what matters. The murders of the prostitute and the soldier who killed her—"

Matt tensed, shaken by this new information. So his guard had been the prostitute's killer. He must have murdered her less than twenty-four hours after she seduced him.

"—led us to the apartment where you stayed," the Russian went on, not noticing Matt's stunned reaction.

"Where I was kept a prisoner," Matt corrected, leaning forward. "What was the connection between the prostitute and the soldier and the apartment?"

The Russian cast Matt a venomous frown. "Since you were staying there, I'm sure you already know, Major."

"Enlighten me, please," Matt growled, hoping to find out how much the Russian Intelligence Service knew.

The officer stared at him skeptically and went on. "A friend of the dead woman told us the prostitute had a meeting with a soldier at that apartment a few hours before she was found in the river. The police were looking for him when he, too, was murdered."

"The Ministry of Security came to us when they learned the murdered soldier had left his car to talk to an American woman the moment before he was shot," Fosdick broke in.

"How did they figure that out?" Matt asked.

"Witnesses," Fosdick returned with a smug expression. "The driver of the car the soldier was riding in and the owner of the bakery shop." He grimaced. "You people didn't cover your tracks very well. The *babushka* you bribed at the Kosmos Hotel became very cooperative when she was assured she wouldn't have to return your money. And the colonel here got the people at Safdarjang Airport in Delhi to tell us where you were headed. We flew here in an Indian Air Force plane."

Fosdick tensed and leaned forward.

Here it comes, Matt thought. *The real reason the CIA and Russian intelligence came chasing after us.*

"IS THIS THE WAY to Ram Singh Road?" More dismayed by the minute, Pamela stared through the taxi window at the line of wood and tin cubicles lining the rutted dirt street. In front of each crude shelter, iron pots swung over low fires. Did families actually live here? Was this how they cooked?

People were everywhere. She gasped as a little girl in a ragged dress dodged the taxi's front fender.

"This is quickest way," the driver replied in broken English. "Sorry. Not best part of Jahangir."

A cow ambled across the road. The driver hadn't stopped for the child, but he did for the cow. The animal, though just as scrawny as the child, obviously had priority. Pamela knew the cows were sacred, but couldn't understand the driver's apparent disregard for human life. A suffocating sensation tightened her throat when she viewed the awful poverty.

As the taxi waited for the cow to pass, its engine idling, the pungent smell of burning dung, dust and curry drifted inside. So did five or six big black flies. Pamela rolled up her window, but that seemed to attract them to her head. Hastily, she rolled it down.

"They leave when we move," the driver predicted, unperturbed by the pesky nuisance to his passenger.

A girl about ten appeared at Pamela's open window, her hand outstretched, her black eyes pleading. Pamela dug around in her purse and came up with a rupee. Instantly, many more children materialized, all with hands outstretched.

The driver honked, waved his hand and yelled something in Hindi, but they didn't leave. Pamela found some coins and flung them outside. Laughing and jumping, the youngsters caught them before they hit the dusty ground.

After the cow had ambled past, the taxi started ahead with a jerk. Two teenage boys ran after it, pounding on the fenders. When Pamela spread her palms in a *that's all* gesture, they made fists and shook them at her, their skinny brown arms flailing.

A tense knot tightened inside her. Suddenly, this deprived neighborhood seemed unsafe. What would she do if a mob forced the driver to stop? The Pentagon's money seared her hip, reminding her she was a fugitive in a strange land, a fugitive carrying thousands of dollars in cash. This driver, though recommended by the hotel, might even be working with a gang. Was that why he'd picked a route through such a destitute area?

She quickly rolled up the two back windows. The flies were better company than threatening hands.

The taxi bumped along the rutted dirt road for another mile or so.

"Ahead is Ram Singh Road," the driver said, over his shoulder. "Number 813 is to the left."

A few minutes later, he nodded toward a squat brick building painted white. Pamela took in the emerald-green lawn dotted with bright red bougainvillea bushes, the low brick wall painted white to match the building.

After the appalling poverty only blocks away, the headquarters of the Mogul Babur Manufacturing Company had all the earmarks of a deliberate attempt to draw attention away from the destitution. Could it also be designed to distract interest from whatever Mr. Von Meinhoff was doing on his island?

To Pamela's surprise, a European-looking group was being escorted toward the building from a green-and-yellow tour bus.

The taxi driver stepped on the gas. "You will have to run to catch up, but I'm sure they will let you go with them."

"You mean they take people through the building, even on Sunday nights?"

"Seven days a week," the driver said, with obvious pride. Apparently, the Mogul Babur Manufacturing Company was a source of considerable local satisfaction. He pulled in behind the tour bus. "I will wait here for you."

Pamela checked her watch. She'd already been gone half an hour. Would Matt worry if she were a few minutes longer?

Since he stopped at his room first, he's probably not back from the dock yet, she reasoned. And even if he was, their time was running out. This might be the only chance she'd have to get a firsthand look at Mogul Babur's operation. Her skirt fluttering, she sprinted after the last of the group, now disappearing through the front door.

"WHAT WE NEED TO KNOW from you and Captain Wright," Fosdick gritted at Matt, "is what you're doing here in Jahangir."

Through the latticework bordering the lobby's ten-foot-high walls, Matt could see the fading evening dusk giving way to night's darkness. Where was Pam? Why hadn't she come back yet?

He gave the CIA officer an extremely dirty look. "We're on our way home by an indirect route."

Patiently, Fosdick rephrased his question. "In case you didn't know, Powers, General Vactin commanded a vast nuclear arsenal as part of his job with the space agency." He lifted an eyebrow in an expression of pained tolerance. "It's in the interest of every living thing on this planet that we find out exactly what he was up to.''

Matt concealed his mixed emotions. Was Fosdick on the level or was he playing another of his shadow-world games?

"We think General Vactin was involved in more than stealing our government's money,'' the Russian intelligence officer interjected. ''We will find out the whole story eventually. But you can perhaps help us hurry.''

"He means you can speed up the process,'' Fosdick said.

"I know what he means.'' Matt stalled to give himself time to think. Were these intelligence people lying to somehow trap him and Pam? Unlikely. Given the potential threat the Russian general posed, could Matt afford not to trust them?

He leaned forward. ''You don't give me much choice, Mr. Fosdick.'' His gaze took in the other men and returned to Fosdick. ''Are you certain the Russians should hear my story? You told Captain Wright you didn't want them to know how important the United States considered me.''

Fosdick smiled congenially at the two Russian officers. ''That was before we knew General Vactin was operating outside army authority.'' His voice was as smooth as glass. ''Since this matter deals directly with their government, of course I want them to hear what you have to say.''

"All right, then.'' Succinctly, Matt told them about the capsule Eric Goodman had seen and the navigational device he'd described to Pam. ''The outline Captain Goodman saw aboard the capsule was the same shape as Lake Mewar.''

An astounded silence followed his brief story.

Fosdick's face mirrored his disbelief. ''Are you saying your pilot actually saw inside that flying saucer after the monster crawled out of it?''

Matt nodded. ''I didn't believe it, either, at first.''

"But you said the pilot spoke only in general terms about the triangular-shaped outline.'' Fosdick's brow creased with doubt. "Why are you and Captain Wright so sure it's the exact outline of this lake?"

"Because Captain Wright's father flew over Lake Mewar twenty years ago in an SR-71. She clearly remembers a scale drawing he made of it, probably from a classified reconnaissance photo."

Across from Matt, the Indian colonel's eyes widened. "Then the United States has been interested in this lake for more than twenty years?"

"I have no way of knowing that, sir," Matt said. "All I know is that the capsule my pilot saw used a navigational device with a shape similar to this lake. We—Captain Wright and I—thought there might be a connection. That's why we're here."

Fosdick let his breath out in a long sigh. "Why didn't she tell me this?"

"You didn't believe anything we said," Matt returned shortly. "All you seemed interested in was getting me home to face a hanging judge. Unfortunately, I'm still—" He stopped speaking when one of the Indian enlisted men approached the colonel and said something in a language Matt didn't recognize.

The colonel turned to the Russian officer next to him on the sofa. "There is a telephone call at the desk for you."

A moment later, the stocky Russian returned. "General Vactin is dead," he announced. For a moment there was only stunned silence.

Finally, Douglas Fosdick spoke. "How?"

"Suicide in his cell. He hung himself."

Sure he did, Matt thought, meeting Fosdick's skeptical gaze. The Company man didn't believe it, either.

The hairs stood up on the back of Matt's neck. Somebody didn't want Vactin to reveal the truth to the Russian Intelligence Service. Was his killer even now stalking Pam?

THE MOGUL BABUR Manufacturing Company was a model operation with every television tube inventoried, every speck of dust filtered by the powerful air-conditioning system. The company claimed to manufacture television sets and radios, and that's exactly what it was doing—in the best-kept building Pamela had seen in India.

Halfway through the tour, she returned to her waiting taxi, convinced nothing illegal was going on. *It's a front, pure and simple,* she thought, admiring the building and its grounds as the taxi pulled away.

On the way back to the hotel, Pamela kept her windows closed and the doors locked. The darkness hid much of the appalling poverty, but one area stank so badly of garbage that she had to breathe through a tissue to keep from gagging. She sighed with relief when they drove through the hotel's wrought-iron gates. Ahead lay a driveway swept clean of debris. In the covering darkness, the red-rock structure no longer reminded her of an evil palace. After her glimpse of life outside, it seemed a sanctuary from the grinding poverty.

The taxi moved slowly toward the canopied lobby entrance. Was Matt worried about her? She'd been gone longer than she anticipated—nearly two hours. Peering over the driver's shoulder, she half expected to see his big frame stationed outside the entrance waiting for her. Instead, she saw a jeeplike vehicle parked at the curb.

"Is that a police car?" she asked the driver uneasily.

He shook his head. "Is army car, madam. Another one in lot."

A nervous shiver shot down her spine. "What lot?"

"Car lot over there." He inclined his head to the left. "I see through bushes when we drive in." Apparently there was a parking lot, camouflaged by heavy growth, beside one wing of the hotel.

The taxi stopped in front of the entrance. Pamela hesitated. Could the Indian Army be here to arrest her and Matt?

Not likely. They'd broken laws in the U.S. and Russia, but none in India.

She paid the driver and got out of the taxi. All senses on full alert, she paused outside the glass doors, staying off to one side where she couldn't be clearly seen from the lobby. When the uniformed concierge started to open the door for her, she shook her head. Quickly she peered inside.

How odd. Three Indian Army enlisted men, their rifles in their arms, stood facing the door. She shrank farther to the side and stepped backward, not wanting to draw their attention. Judging from their positions with their backs to the room, she figured they were protecting someone. She gazed beyond the soldiers to see who it was.

Matt! And he was with two uniformed Russian officers! Ice spread through her stomach. Though Matt's back was to her, she knew it was him. He was still wearing his aqua polo shirt, and she recognized the authoritative way he held his head. A shorter man in a dark suit sat beside him. She couldn't see his face.

An Indian officer faced Matt on the opposite sofa. One of the Russians sat next to the Indian. The other stood behind him, alongside a civilian. While she watched, the Russian on the sofa turned and said something to the two men behind him.

Translating Matt's words, she thought, swallowing the sob in her throat. Judging from the presence of the Indian officer, the Russians must have enlisted the help of the Indian Army in their search for the flying saucer.

Pamela's throat ached with defeat. Fosdick was right, after all. Matt had been working with the Russians from the very first. Why else would he be talking to them? Her heart felt bruised.

What a gullible fool she'd been! How could she believe his story about a mysterious, early-morning abduction and five days' imprisonment in that Moscow apartment? It had all been part of a devious plan designed to ferret out Eric's secrets about the capsule and her father's about his reconnaissance missions.

At last she knew the truth. Much as Pamela wanted to deny it, the evidence was staring her right in the face. Her legs turned to water as the knowledge twisted and turned inside her. What other explanation could there be for a meeting between Matt and these Russians? No wonder they'd gotten here so quickly. He must have told them exactly where he'd be.

She told herself to be strong and willed her legs not to collapse under her. But nothing could erase her deep sense of hurt and betrayal.

Well, the Russians couldn't have found a more naive target, she thought, swallowing hard. She'd been only too willing to tell Matt everything she knew. So what did he plan to do with her now? She didn't doubt his strong feelings for her. Would he expect her to go back to Moscow with him?

He knows me better than that. She went rigid. *But what about his Russian colleagues? Will they let me go home, knowing I'll tell the Pentagon everything that's happened?*

Her gaze focused on the three Indian soldiers inside. Every time the concierge opened the door for a hotel guest, they looked up, as though they were watching for someone.

Watching for someone. She felt the blood rush from her face. *My God, that's what they're doing. Watching for me!*

At that instant the concierge swung the door open for a couple leaving the hotel. A soldier stared straight at her. Recognition widened his eyes. He lunged toward her, yelling.

Matt twisted around on the sofa. For an instant, his eyes met her horrified gaze. Then she whirled and darted toward the circular driveway.

Please, God, don't let them catch me. She had to phone Doug Fosdick in Moscow. Otherwise, the Pentagon would never know she'd been taken prisoner. Or killed.

Behind her, two soldiers burst through the lobby door.

"Stop, madam!" the concierge shouted after her, his voice a piercing shriek.

Pamela reached the driveway. There were no taxis waiting in front. But near the far end of the drive, a boxy black-and-orange vehicle she recognized as a taxi pulled out of the car lot on the other side of the hotel.

She flew toward it. Heavy feet thudded after her. She wasn't going to make it.

Then the taxi roared down the driveway and screeched to a stop beside her.

"Get in," the driver yelled.

Pamela fumbled with the back-door handle. Her nervous fingers couldn't get it to work. Behind her, she heard the soldiers gasping for breath.

She twisted the handle, jerked the door open and threw herself inside. She'd barely yanked the door closed when the car, its tires screeching, did a U-turn in the driveway and took off in the opposite direction.

She'd made it. She'd gotten away.

For a moment she could do nothing but pant.

Then, over her thumping pulse, she sensed a movement next to her. She wasn't alone on the back seat of the darkened taxi. Icy fear twisted around her heart. She turned her head.

A man sat beside her. Though there was nothing distinctive about his square, plain face, she cringed in terror.

Instinctively, she realized this man was the demon who haunted her nightmares, the sniper who always knew exactly where she was. Now he was sitting only a few feet away, close enough to reach out and clutch her throat.

She grabbed for the door handle. Jumping from the moving car would be infinitely better than what he might do to her.

"Don't even think about it, Captain." His voice was neutral, expressionless, his eyes as cold as bits of dry ice. Her stomach clenched in terror.

Without seeming to move, he held something near her head.

Trembling, she stared up the steel barrel of a snub-nosed revolver.

"DON'T SHOOT HER," Matt yelled after the pursuing Indian soldiers. Fosdick and the Indian colonel were right behind them. Ahead, Pam's taxi sped toward the street beyond the hotel gates.

The colonel shouted an order. His men stopped and shouldered their rifles.

Thank God, Matt thought, relieved. *They didn't shoot.* Pam might be scared half to death, but at least she was unharmed.

"We should have no trouble finding her," the colonel assured him, his mustache twisting upward in a benign smile. "With only a million population, Jahangir is not a big city, and she is a stranger."

"Let's do it," Matt said, sprinting back to the lobby. To him, anyplace with a million people seemed a big city to search for one small woman.

The next hour was the longest he'd ever spent. With Fosdick beside him, he listened while the colonel spoke on the telephone to the police, the airport, the other hotels. Each time the colonel hung up, he shook his head. No one had information about a blond American woman wearing a bright pink blouse and a green patterned skirt.

"She has no passport," he pointed out. "She can't check into a hotel or leave the city without one."

"She can hire the taxi to drive her," Matt said, his voice hoarse with frustration.

The colonel shook his head. "The police are watching the roads. If she tries to leave the city that way, they will detain her."

"How about by boat?" Matt asked. "There must be a thousand boat owners willing to take her to another city on Lake Mewar."

The colonel dialed another number. He said a few words in Hindi. When he hung up, his face was grim. "She's been seen at the Mogul Babur dock getting on a company boat with a man.''

Matt fought his sudden spurt of anger. ''You mean she was right here at the hotel dock, and we let her get away?''

''No. The company dock is about two miles north of here.'' The colonel looked puzzled. ''That dock is guarded. I'm surprised they let her through.''

For a moment, Matt was speechless, unable to understand what had happened. Why would Pam risk a trip to the island with a stranger? Then, suddenly, the pieces clicked neatly into place.

''They didn't *let* her through.'' His voice shook with a horrible new insight. ''They put a gun to her head and forced her aboard the boat.''

His gut twisted into a million knots. Wherever Pam was, she must be terrified, like a helpless animal caught in a trap. Whoever had taken her would pay dearly for this crime.

Chapter Fifteen

Riker called Otto from the deep-hulled boat used to ferry guests and workers back and forth between the island and the lake's shore. Before speaking, he activated the scrambler mechanism that would prevent eavesdropping.

"I've got the woman." He didn't bother to keep his voice down. The Wright woman was bound and gagged at the other end of the boat and probably couldn't hear over the roar of the engine. But it didn't matter if she knew they were speaking German or even what they said. For her, there would be no return trip to Jahangir.

"How about the major?" Otto asked.

"I arrived after they checked in and was unable to get them both. After I deliver her, I'll pick him up."

"Good." Otto's satisfaction was evident. "If he gives you any trouble, shoot him. I will find out why they are here from Captain Wright."

"Do you want me to ask her now, *Mein Herr?*" Riker licked his lips. "My interrogation methods are very persuasive."

He heard the high-pitched squeaks that meant his employer was chuckling. "You are a barbarian, my friend. The woman would die of fright before she told you anything." The squeaking stopped, and he paused. "No. I will find out from her myself. There is another matter I wish to discuss with her, as well."

Riker knew better than to ask what that other matter might be. He was well aware of what happened to men—even high-ranking men like that general in Moscow—who snooped into Otto's business.

"There's something you should know," he said carefully. "She was being pursued by the Indian authorities when I...uh...intercepted her outside the hotel."

There was a long silence. Riker could sense his employer's concern.

"When you return to Jahangir for the major, find out why," Otto said finally. "It's always better to know what's behind such actions by our esteemed countrymen."

"Very good, *Mein Herr,*" Riker said. "Where should I bring the woman? I'll be at the island dock in about half an hour."

"Bring her to the freight elevator. Someone will meet you and take her off your hands."

The line was dead before Riker could say goodbye.

PAMELA CROUCHED ON the hard stone floor in almost total darkness, her ear flat against the cold metal door. Was anyone outside?

She heard nothing but the persistent hum of the ventilating system and the ominous drip, drip, drip of water. Where was the sound coming from? Panic rose in her throat when she thought of this room flooding. Judging from the long ride down the elevator, she was far beneath the lake's surface. Could there be a leak somewhere, a leak that might inundate this chamber?

She tried to force her terror away. But when she concentrated, all she could visualize was Matt's face. How astonished he'd looked when he saw her through the lobby door.

A terrible ache seared her heart. Her throat tightened until she could hardly breathe. How could he have lied to her so consistently, for so long, if he loved her? And she couldn't believe his love had been nothing but a pretense—he'd been too ardent, too devoted.

Swallowing hard, Pamela forced her pain away, willing herself to be strong. She was alive and unhurt, and the awful man who captured her had gone. She'd heard his boat roar into the night as she stepped aboard the cavernous elevator, a grim-faced guard beside her. When they'd reached this cell carved from solid rock, the guard had cut her bonds and shoved her into the darkness, slamming the door behind her.

Why had he cut her loose? she wondered uneasily. Because there was no hope of escape? Or did her captors want her to stay in reasonably good shape until...until what? Her insides clenched tight, as she wondered what they were going to do to her.

Carefully, she stood and backed away from the door. A tiny shaft of light from the hallway outside pierced the uneven crack underneath. Above the door, the red eye of an armed alarm system glowed menacingly in the darkness. Now that her vision had adjusted to the gloom, she identified two white plastic chairs along one wall. The room contained no other furniture.

Where was the light switch? She studied the wall beside the door. In the darkness, she couldn't spot it. Methodically, she ran her fingers over the area. The surface was rock, like the floor. That made her task easier. The switch should stick out from the wall. Half a second later, she found it.

Before she flicked it on, she paused, listening. Anyone outside would notice the light under the door. As she listened, she heard the faint creaking of the elevator.

Someone's coming.

She froze, her heart in her throat. Metal clanged against metal as the elevator doors opened. Two voices spoke in German. One, high-pitched and resonant, might have been a woman's. The other sounded like the grim, Teutonic-looking guard who had brought her down.

The red alarm light flicked off, plunging the room into almost total darkness. Pamela backed away as far from the door as she could get. The voices drew nearer, coming down the long hallway.

The door burst open. Light flooded in from the hallway, blinding her. Squinting, Pamela strained to see who stood in the doorway.

Two black figures were etched against the brilliance of the hall. One reached for the light switch. An overhead fluorescent tube blazed into life. Pamela blinked, then shrank back against the rock wall.

The massively obese man peering at her from across the room didn't look human. He had absolutely no hair on his chalk-white albino body—not on his head, not on his face, not anywhere she could see. In spite of his tremendous bulk, the skin on his face and neck hung in ugly, drooping folds. He wore slanting dark glasses that gave him an odd, Oriental cast.

He shuffled into the room. As he moved, Pamela eyed his corpulent body. Bulging white arms emerged from the sleeves of a tentlike yellow sport shirt. His legs were partially covered by dark green hiking shorts that couldn't hide the sagging layers of fat on his thighs.

He searched her face. Pamela stared back at him. Was this pathetic creature responsible for the days and nights of terror she and Matt had endured? What in the name of heaven did he plan to do to her in this barren rock cell?

"IF YOU WON'T GO to that island after her, then, by God, I'll hire a boat and go alone." Matt started down the dock.

"Get real, Powers," Fosdick snapped. "Von Meinhoff is an Indian citizen. Let them take care of him."

Matt couldn't suppress his cold rage. "You mean the way they took care of him during the twenty-plus years he's been living on that island? He's probably paid them enough bribe money to support the entire Jahangir police force."

"Just how is it you think you're going to help her get away?" Fosdick's voice rose in exasperation. "The place is guarded. You go out there, you'll get yourself shot. What good will you be to her then?''

Matt stopped walking, his anger turning to remorse. ''She was right there, practically inside the lobby. Why couldn't I get to her in time?'' His voice broke. He cleared his throat to hide his anguish.

''They'll find her and bring her back.''

''Sure they will.'' Matt inclined his head toward a cluster of Indian policemen milling around at the end of the dock. ''We'll both be on social security before they make their move.''

''They're waiting for the company boat,'' Fosdick said. ''When it returns, they'll question whoever's aboard. Then they'll make their move.''

''She could be dead by then.''

''If Von Meinhoff wanted her dead, he wouldn't have taken her to the island.''

At the end of the dock, the policemen stirred. In the distance, Matt heard the faint roar of an outboard engine. Would the crew admit they'd taken Pam aboard?

''COME OUT HERE, under the light, where I can get a good look at you, Captain Wright.'' The albino's voice, though high, was as resonant as an androgynous rock star's. ''We need to talk.'' He shuffled slowly toward Pamela.

Her pulse began to pound erratically. Trying to move backward, she dug the heel of her sandal into the bare rock behind her. But it was hopeless—there was no escape. She caught a strong scent of baby talcum as the albino drew near. He grabbed her arm with a small, well-manicured hand. She jerked away.

The guard, standing near the hall door, took a step toward her. The albino shook his head, and the guard stopped.

''Come here, Pamela Wright.'' The albino took her arm again. This time she didn't jerk away. There was no sense resisting. He led her a few steps forward, till she was directly under the overhead light.

"What do you want?" she demanded. "Why am I here? I don't even know your name."

"But you do," he corrected. "You found out my name at the hotel desk. Then you went on a tour of my factory. Why, Ms. Wright?"

"I was curious." So, this was the reclusive Otto Von Meinhoff. The way he looked, no wonder he stayed hidden on his island.

His grip on her arm tightened. "Why were you so curious? Are you being paid by someone for information?"

"No...I—" She stopped, speechless, as he stared relentlessly at her face. The dark glasses hiding his eyes made him even more frightening.

He dropped her arm and motioned to the guard. "Wait outside, please."

"Yes, *Mein Herr.*" The guard turned and left. Through the half-open door, Pamela could see him waiting in the hallway, out of earshot but within easy hailing distance.

Von Meinhoff motioned toward the chairs. One was larger than the other, more like a bench than a chair. Apparently, they'd been deliberately placed in this rock chamber for her and her captor. Did he really think she'd sit here calmly, like a willing hostage, and tell him whatever he wanted to know?

"Please, let us be comfortable." Von Meinhoff shuffled to the bench and lowered his immense bulk onto it. Rolls of hairless white flesh hung over the bench's seat after he'd settled himself.

Shuddering with revulsion, Pamela pulled her chair far enough away so she couldn't smell his talcum. What she'd found a pleasant fragrance in the past was suddenly nauseating.

"Now, Pamela Wright. You were telling me why you're so curious about me. If nobody's paying you for information, you must have some *personal* reason for your curiosity." His dark glasses seemed to sink into the folds of flesh surrounding them.

"I'm just a tourist interested in this area." Even to her, the excuse sounded so flimsy she knew it wasn't believable.

"Don't try to con me, Captain." His voice sharpened. She shrank back in her chair, away from his probing stare. "Your curiosity is connected to your father and your pilot friend, is it not?"

How could he know about Eric and her father? Pamela's mind leapt ahead and found the answer. "That's what the article in the Tacoma newspaper said."

His slow smile reflected a glimmer of admiration at her insight. "I know some things about your father's accident that were not in the newspaper article."

She stiffened. "What?"

His puffy lips curved into a slow smile. "You tell me what I want to know and I'll tell you exactly how, why and by whom your father's plane was disabled. It happened right over this lake, at an altitude of 81,000 feet."

Her mouth dropped open. In the seventies, when her father's SR-71 disappeared, no winged aircraft except the U-2—another reconnaissance plane—could reach that altitude. The early satellites could, but no satellite could have shot down her father's plane.

"Are you saying my father's plane was shot down by a UFO from outer space?" Her voice trembled with eagerness.

"Not shot down," he corrected. "Disabled. The same way your friend Eric Goodman's jet fighter was disabled."

Had she been wrong about the Russians shooting down her father's plane? Or was Von Meinhoff playing her for a gullible fool, just as Matt had?

Her heart thundering in her ears, Pamela leaned toward him. "Then both Eric's plane and my father's must have been *disabled* by vehicles from outer space?"

His bland smile vanished. "I've said enough. Now it's your turn. If you want to hear more, you'll tell me exactly how you tracked me to this place."

"And then you'll kill me." The certainty brought bile to her throat. The room swam dizzily around her. She looked at Otto Von Meinhoff's inhuman face and saw her own destruction. Her death meant as little to him as a baby bird's to a prowling cat.

His mouth, surrounded by ugly rolls of sagging flesh, spread into a cynical smile. "Of course I'll kill you. What reason do I have not to?"

Pamela stared down at her fingers, which were twisted nervously together in her lap, the knuckles white. He couldn't let her live. She already knew too much. As soon as she told him what he wanted to know, she'd be dead.

His penetrating, high-pitched voice went on. "But there are very painful ways to die. If I turn you over to Riker, your death will be long and difficult. You remember Riker, don't you, Captain? He's the man who brought you to me."

Von Meinhoff stopped speaking. Pamela followed his gaze. A man strode rapidly down the corridor toward the guard. Icy fear spiked through her when she saw who it was. *The man Von Meinhoff called Riker.* The demon had returned.

Both he and the guard trotted into the room. Nodding toward a communicator on his belt, Riker said something in rapid-fire German. Then he helped Von Meinhoff to his feet. The three men left as quickly as Von Meinhoff's slow shuffle would permit.

The metal door closed behind them. A second later, the alarm light flashed red. Once again, Pamela was alone in the solid-rock cell. If she didn't get out before they returned, she was as good as dead.

FROM ACROSS THE LAKE, the roar of the boat engine increased. Matt could see lights as the craft approached the landing pier. He turned, poised to sprint toward the Indian authorities gathered near the boat's docking space at the end of the pier.

Doug Fosdick caught his arm, stopping him. Matt whirled toward the shore. Fosdick's CIA colleague jogged down the wharf toward them. Two armed soldiers at the shore side of the dock prevented a crowd of curious onlookers from following.

"I've got news," the CIA officer said, when he'd reached them.

"What's up?" Fosdick barked.

"The colonel's just talked to Von Meinhoff on the phone. He claims no knowledge of Captain Wright. Says if she's on the island, she came on her own. He knows nothing about her."

"He's lying," Matt muttered. He turned to Fosdick. "I've got to get out there."

"What about the man who was with her?" Fosdick snapped to his colleague.

"Von Meinhoff says a male employee was the only passenger. He brought no woman with him."

Matt stared at Fosdick. "The boat driver will verify everything his boss says. He'll lie through his teeth to keep his job."

Fosdick hesitated, then nodded. "I think you're right, Powers." He turned toward the end of the pier. "Let's go. It's time to build a fire under those Indian troopers."

PAMELA PROWLED the perimeter of her prison like a caged lioness. She might have lost the love of her life, but she didn't intend to lose her life itself in the bargain. Not without a fight.

Was there a hidden recess somewhere? Or even a loose rock she could use as a weapon? No. Not a single loose pebble was evident. The room contained only the white plastic chair and bench she and Von Meinhoff had used.

Certain now that no one was on guard outside, she jiggled the door handle. It didn't open. It must lock automatically. She'd heard no key being inserted, no bolt being shoved when Von Meinhoff entered.

She yanked on the door. Nothing happened. Made of some metal she couldn't identify, it appeared hard as steel but much lighter. Perhaps it was hollow inside and she could break through it. Picking up the plastic chair, she swung and hit the door as hard as she could. Again, nothing happened. The chair stayed intact, too. Could she use it as a weapon?

She pulled Von Meinhoff's bench to the door and stood on it. Then she picked up the plastic chair and held it high over her head. If someone came through the door, she could give him a good whack with the chair. She didn't have to knock him out or even down. Just throw him off balance long enough for her to dart through the door and yank it closed.

But how could she get someone down here to open it? Von Meinhoff had appeared disturbed at seeing Riker. Good. Something upsetting was going on upstairs. That could work in her favor. But it also might keep everybody away from her door.

She glanced up at the glowing red alarm light. If she pulled out the wires and disabled the thing, would that set off a warning at a master control panel and send somebody down here to check up on her? It was worth a try.

She flicked the light switch off and sat down on the bench near the door. Matt's face appeared in her mind. Relentlessly, she forced it aside, ordering herself to concentrate. This plan was her only chance. It had to work or she'd be dead. Squeezing her eyes shut, she forced herself to go over every move.

It was time.

Pulling the bench directly under the alarm light, she stood on it and reached for the wires leading into it. Like the light wires, they were encased in a plastic tube.

She gave the tube a jerk. Nothing happened. She jerked again, harder. The red light blinked out. She half expected to hear a horn blaring somewhere, but there was no sound.

Hurriedly, she pushed the bench back beside the door, grabbed the chair and climbed on the bench, holding the chair in both hands over her head. If her plan had worked, someone should be on the way.

From down the hall came the creak of the elevator. Seconds later, footsteps pounded toward her. They stopped outside her door. The door lever turned. The door inched open a crack, but nobody came inside.

What was wrong? Why didn't he come in?

In desperation, she yanked off her watch and threw it against a far wall. It smashed and fell to the rock floor with a jingling sound.

The door burst wide open. A man rushed inside. He paused, inches from the bench Pamela was standing on. She swung the chair at him with all her might, letting go when it slammed against his head and shoulders. He pitched forward with a startled oath.

In one quick motion, she jumped off the bench and darted through the door. Her left hand caught the handle. She yanked the door closed. Was it locked? Yes. The lever jiggled furiously, and muffled shouts erupted from the rock chamber.

Pamela didn't look back. The elevator was straight ahead. She had to escape before Von Meinhoff and Riker found she'd gone. The man in her cell might have a walkie-talkie, in which case he would now be reporting what had happened. Like a scared deer running for its life, she moved purely on instinct. Every cell in her body was focused on survival.

She reached the elevator and pressed the switch. As she touched it, she froze. A creaking sound filtered downward through the shaft. Someone was coming for her. Riker. It had to be. Oh, lord, now what should she do?

She turned and ran blindly back down the corridor. Midway, she jerked to a stop and pushed a door open.

An array of fluorescent tubes blinked on, triggered by the door. Inside were steel tables, microscopes, white refrigerators, rows of chemicals—laboratory paraphernalia. There were no inside doors. Like the cell where she'd been imprisoned, the room was a dead end.

Darting out, she dashed to the closed metal door at the end of the corridor. This entrance was big, like the elevator's, and the steady drip, drip, drip of water was louder here. Maybe the room beyond had an outside exit to the lake's surface. If this door opened onto another dead end, she was finished.

Behind her she heard the squeak of the elevator stopping. Her time was almost up. She had to get out of this corridor.

Pamela pushed the switch beside the door. It slid open. She stepped through, and it closed behind her. Overhead lights blinked on automatically.

She found herself in a room, similar to the NASA control rooms she'd seen on TV, but smaller. There were desks, computer terminals and a control panel built into a long counter. TV monitors ringed the area under the ceiling. Straight ahead was another door. Pamela let her breath out in relief. At least the room wasn't a dead end.

In front of the control panel, she saw an oversize leather executive chair. *The master's seat.* She ran to it.

Outside, feet pounded toward her. Her pursuer had checked the lab and was now coming for her.

Fighting her panic, she eyed the lighted panel in the counter. What did it control? Von Meinhoff obviously spent time here. His chair reflected the contours of his corpulent body.

Maybe she could lock the door from the outside by pressing a button. Or trigger the alarm system. Or foul up the phones. The more confusion she could cause, the better.

The footsteps stopped. In another instant, he'd be inside. She had to do something. She quickly punched each red button on the display panel. Even if she blew the place up, she'd be better off than if Riker caught her.

A lighted notice appeared on top of the panel in capital letters. WORK CYCLE BEGINS IN FIVE MINUTES

It was followed by another announcement. CLEAR DOCKING AREA. LAUNCH SEQUENCE BEGINS IN TEN MINUTES

The outside door slid open. It was Riker! He stood there, his face contorted in rage. He'd removed his dark jacket, revealing his holstered pistol snug against his white shirt.

Pamela's heart pounded. She scrambled to the inside door. It opened with a lever, just as her cell door had. She jerked it open and ran through, slamming it shut behind her. A dank, humid atmosphere swirled around her, like the warm, moist air in an indoor heated swimming pool.

She quickly scanned the door's solid metal frame for a lock to keep Riker out. None! She'd have to run. She spun around, straining to see in the dim light.

She stood on a narrow metal catwalk that ran around three sides of a huge hangarlike enclosure. Water dripped from the walls and ceiling, leaving damp rivulets on the sloping floor far below.

Her eyes widened in horror. On a platform at the far end of the vast room stood an immense space capsule, its white lights blinking.

Eric's UFO. Could it be? Was the monster inside?

Riker must have reached the door by now. She fled down the catwalk, her sandals flapping on the metal surface. Sweat beaded on her upper lip and forehead. She brushed it off with the back of her hand to keep it from running into her eyes. Her blouse and the waist of her skirt were soaked.

Glancing over her shoulder, she saw Riker burst through the door. At any moment, she expected to hear a shot and feel the slamming impact of a bullet.

Instead, she heard his running feet behind her. He was going to take her alive. She hadn't answered Von Meinhoff's questions. If she could only keep away from Riker, she might still have a chance.

He was gaining on her. The catwalk offered nowhere to hide, no place to escape to. Then she spotted an open workmen's elevator off to the side. Contained in scaffolding it would take her to the floor far below.

Dashing toward it, she clambered over the edge of the catwalk and landed on a swaying metal platform. It trembled beneath her weight. Frantically, she searched for a control device to lower it.

There it was. She kicked the knob with her toe and grabbed for one of the rope supports. Her hands, wet with sweat, slipped on the narrow line. Overcompensating, she clutched it so tightly her fingernails cut into her palms.

Slowly, the elevator moved downward. She gasped for breath, taking advantage of her brief reprieve. With this elevator gone, Riker would have to use the one on the far side. While he went around the perimeter to it, she'd have a few precious minutes to find a hiding place.

She stared up at the catwalk. Riker was still pounding toward her. Why hadn't he turned toward the other elevator?

Because there's an up-down switch on the catwalk, you fool.

Pamela looked beneath her as the elevator continued its slow descent. She was still about twenty feet from the floor.

Above, Riker reached the place where she'd been standing. Incredibly, he was smiling. The dirty rat was enjoying this cat-and-mouse game. And now he thought he had her.

Well, he's wrong.

The elevator swung to a stop as he pushed the switch on the catwalk. In a second, it would begin its upward climb.

Without looking down, Pamela knelt by the elevator's outside edge, gripped the metal floor planking in her hands and swung her body over the side. By dropping from a hanging position instead of jumping from the elevator floor, she'd have less distance to drop. Her arms tore at the shoulder sockets with her weight, but she was able to hold on long enough to slow her fall.

Letting go, she fell about ten feet to the floor and rolled as soon as she landed—the way she'd been taught in basic officer training.

Like a frightened animal, she glanced around her. She was running on pure adrenaline now, every muscle and nerve keyed for survival.

Why wasn't the elevator moving upward? Her gaze lifted to the catwalk above. Riker no longer stood there, waiting for its slow rise. She sucked in her breath. For the first time, she noticed rope ladders swinging from beneath the catwalk. When Riker saw how slowly the elevator moved, he'd run to the nearest ladder. Now he was descending like a monkey, already halfway down.

Where could she hide? From the catwalk she'd seen thin sheets of metal stacked along one side of the immense launching dock. She'd have to go around the capsule to reach the stacks, but the saucer seemed eminently less frightening than the killer stalking her.

She took off running. A raised curl of metal in the pocked floor caught her sandaled foot, and she crashed to the deck. Bright red blood dripped from a scratch on her calf, but she felt no pain.

Before she could rise, a loud humming noise filled the air. Changing to a low rumble, the sound vibrated through the dank atmosphere. Petrified, she stared toward the capsule.

A huge door slid open. A spider the size of a small house emerged—all eight legs in motion. Slowly, methodically, it crawled toward her, its red eyes blinking.

Chapter Sixteen

"Can't we go any faster?" From his place behind the police boat's coxswain, Matt scowled over his shoulder at the Indian colonel. "I can swim faster than this blasted thing."

"Patience, my friend," the colonel replied. "We should be there in less than fifteen minutes."

Cursing, Matt turned and stared into the blackness ahead. Somewhere out there, Pamela was in the hands of a madman. From the colonel's description of Von Meinhoff's freakish appearance and behavior, Matt didn't doubt he was crazy. And now he had her. Matt clenched his fists, wanting to hit something as hard as he could.

There was a religious shrine on the boat's dashboard, an idol with marigolds around it. For a tense moment, he stared at it, struggling to regain his equilibrium.

He felt Fosdick's hand on his arm. "Take it easy, Powers. Even if Von Meinhoff's as crazy as the colonel thinks, he won't kill her with two boatloads of troopers on the way."

"Don't bet on it," Matt muttered. "He's already said she's not there. You really think he's going to turn her over to us, just like that?"

Fosdick's silence made Matt even more anxious.

The excruciating ache in his chest grew stronger. Dear God, what was happening to her? He searched the darkness ahead. According to the colonel, Von Meinhoff's house was immense. He had a staff of more than eighty. Where were the lights?

Again he turned to the colonel. "We can't be on the right course. There are no lights for miles."

"Von Meinhoff blacks the place out." The colonel inclined his head to the left. "His dock is ahead. We're almost there."

Following the colonel's direction, Matt peered into the blackness. A titanic shape, darker than the starlit sky, rose before his startled eyes.

Awed, he stared at it. "The place looks like a castle."

"Exactly so," the colonel said. "Von Meinhoff brought it from Austria, stone by stone."

"You said there's a runway on the island long enough for jets to take off and land?"

The colonel nodded. "He hasn't used it for a couple of years, and it's no longer serviceable. Now the only traffic is by water or helicopter."

Matt felt a sharp jolt as the boat nudged the deserted pier. They'd arrived. Now he had to find Pam. Would he be in time?

PETRIFIED, PAMELA WATCHED the giant spider crawl toward her. From the floor where she'd fallen, she stared a long way up—past the creature's long thin legs to its bulging brown belly. The thing towered over her, its gargantuan round head swinging rhythmically from side to side like the pendulum on a grotesque clock.

Every nerve in Pamela's body screamed *Run!* but she couldn't move. In a scene out of a nightmare, she found herself frozen, glued to the steel planking beneath her.

Only a few feet away now, the creature's skinny legs carried it ever closer. Its bulging stomach hung halfway to the deck. Its red eyes blinked on and off, like the warning signal at a railroad crossing.

She heard a faint roaring sound, like water rushing into a bathtub. Where was it coming from? Before she could find out, a strangled gasp caught her ear.

Riker. She jerked her head around, shattering her paralysis. He'd stopped halfway between her and the rope ladder. Apparently as stupified as she, he was also in the monster's path. But she was much closer. It would reach her first.

No longer did Riker look like a demon. His face was frozen in an expression of pure terror that mirrored her own feelings.

She glanced back at the monster. It had taken another slow step toward her. With one more, it would be close enough to touch. Why hadn't the thing attacked her? With one sweep of its oversize round head, it could destroy her.

She rolled to one side to get out of its way. Apparently unaware of her, the creature crawled past. Now it was headed straight toward Riker.

Pamela's movement broke the assassin's trance. He leapt out of the behemoth's way. But when he moved, the monster changed its course, again heading straight toward him.

Riker yanked his pistol out of its holster and pointed it at the spider's head.

From above came a piercing shriek, a shrill keening sound that battered Pamela's eardrums. She glanced upward. Otto Von Meinhoff stood above on the catwalk, his enormous belly pressing against the guardrail.

"No!" he screamed. "Don't shoot! You'll destroy it!" His voice echoed weirdly in the cavernous launching dock.

Riker crouched motionless, the pistol in his hand.

Pamela lurched to her feet and sprinted behind the saucer's platform, out of Riker's line of fire. At any moment Von Meinhoff could order her killed. She looked around frantically, searching for somewhere safe to take cover.

A grinding vibration trembled through the air. Not daring to breathe, Pamela peered around the capsule at the monster.

A scooplike mouth on a long stem unfolded from the spider's head. Awestruck, she watched it arch toward Riker. On the underside of the mouth was a row of sharp, serrated teeth.

Riker lifted his pistol and fired. One of the creature's blinking red eyes flickered out. She expected to see blood spurt from the wound, to hear a roar of pain. Instead, there was a series of sharp clinks as pieces of something made of glass—or maybe plastic—fell to the drydock floor.

It's a machine. The spider's nothing but a machine. She sagged to her knees and sat down, weak with relief.

Above on the catwalk, Otto screamed, "No. No. Don't shoot! It is after your radio."

Riker spun around toward Otto, his walkie-talkie in his hand. "I don't understand." His words sounded hollow, tinny.

"Throw your radio!" Otto screeched.

Before Riker could move, the lower jaw of the spider's scoop shovel hit him midway across the back, impaling him on its serrated teeth. The walkie-talkie dropped from his hand. Slowly, the machine lifted him high over its head to its broad back. For an instant, he hung there, suspended over the spider's back. His eyes locked on Pamela's in a look of stunned horror.

With a shake, the scooplike jaws released him. He dropped into a hollow crater in the spider machine's midsection. Long after his scream had faded, she heard an awful grinding sound from deep within as the machine chewed up his body.

The vast dock spun around her in a dizzying circle. She swallowed hard, trying not to be sick. Putting her head between her knees, she breathed deeply, fighting her nausea.

The spider machine. Don't lose track of it. It might come for you next.

Pamela forced herself to lift her head. Attracted by Riker's dropped walkie-talkie, the thing had stopped crawling when he dropped it. Methodically, it pressed its serrated lower jaw against the steel deck, tilted its bucket upward and dropped imaginary contents into its midsection.

Whatever the machine was doing, it posed no threat to her at the moment. Perhaps because she had no radio to attract it.

Otto was above her somewhere, but she was too sick and worn-out to care. Without his gunman, what could he do to her? She didn't think he carried a weapon, and with his tremendous bulk, he couldn't climb over the catwalk to the construction elevator.

But he'd probably send somebody else after her, somebody who might, even now, be on his way. And if she managed to elude him, there'd be someone else. She was so tired of running, of being afraid. Now that she'd lost Matt, she wasn't sure the struggle was worth the pain. Huddled on the floor, she felt her resistance ebbing until nothing remained but sick resignation.

The roaring in her ears increased. She put her hands over them to shut it out. But nothing could shut out Otto's high-pitched screams. His piercing, resonant voice quavered with alarm. Straightening, she lowered her hands and glanced upward.

He was shuffling toward the far end of the catwalk, his communicator in his hand, yelling into it in German. Then he stopped walking, and his voice became more strident. He seemed to be stuck where the guardrails narrowed.

Fascinated, Pamela watched him try to free himself, rocking first forward and then backward, screaming louder with every motion. Each time he moved, he seemed to sink farther backward. Finally, he lay on the catwalk on his back, flopping around like a giant beetle unable to turn over. He kept on screaming, but the steady roaring neutralized the sound.

Now that she'd lifted her head, the roaring seemed even louder. She looked at the bright red blood trickling to the floor from the cut on her leg. Suddenly, water crept over the tiny pool of crimson, turning it pink.

Water. Where was it coming from? Even as she watched, the rising flood touched the edge of her skirt where it fanned out on the metal floor. An instant later, the liquid soaked through her sandals, cooling her toes.

Slowly, she rose and scanned the low part of the dock. She began to shake when she saw what had happened. Water gushed through two low sections of the outer wall as if a giant spigot had been turned on.

Suddenly, a third door opened in the center of the wall. Thousands of additional gallons poured in. Since the launch dock's metal floor sloped downward, the water rose gradually, with the low end filling first.

A moment earlier, Pamela had been resigned to her fate. She couldn't fight Otto and his armed assassins forever. But Otto was down, and none of his henchmen had responded to his cries. She'd survived Riker. And the monster machine, still going through digging motions in empty space, seemed unaware of her.

It's a mining device, she realized, with sudden insight. The machine looked enough like a spider that Otto had made it seem alive. Why? To disguise its real mission, perhaps, in case someone like Eric got a good look at it. Or maybe he'd had a whimsical motive—crazy men had crazy reasons.

Pamela felt the coolness of the water lapping at her calves. In the last few seconds, it had risen more than a foot. It was already halfway up the side of the platform holding the towering space capsule.

She had to get to the catwalk. But how? The construction elevators—both at the lowest end of the sloping dock floor—were already covered with water.

She stared at the flimsy rope ladders. They swung weakly back and forth, propelled by the air movements caused by the flooding water. The narrow catwalk was at least three stories above. Even rested, she doubted she could pull herself up the swaying ropes. After what she'd been through tonight, her arms and legs were so weak that she knew she'd never make the climb.

But she had to go somewhere. The water had already risen to her knees. She felt wet coolness against her thighs as the liquid soaked her skirt. She had to get to the higher part of the sloping floor.

The monster machine stood between her and higher ground. Splashing furiously, she ran toward it, trying to outrun the rising water. She reached the machine with water lapping at her heels. Hardly daring to breathe, she darted past the thing's hind legs, then its sagging midsection. She didn't let herself dwell on the memory of the assassin being ground to pieces in the creature's huge belly. If she got sick again she'd be lost.

The water was rising faster now, and the roaring deafened her. Another door must have opened, letting in even more lake water. Pamela told herself to run faster. Though she was about three-quarters of the way down the football-field-sized dock, the distance between her and the rope ladder nearest the control-room door seemed immense.

She found herself gasping for breath. Taut bands tightened around her chest. She slowed to a trot. She had to rest. If she didn't stop for a minute, her lungs would burst.

She paused. In an instant, the water rose to the hem of her skirt. Doggedly, she pushed ahead, fighting her dizziness.

She wasn't going to make it. The water reached her waist. Then she felt cool wetness under her armpits, over her shoulders. The rope ladder was still fifteen yards away, and she could no longer run.

The roaring sound increased, echoing in the vast dock like a thundering herd of buffalo. She would not leave this place—she knew it now. She'd drown here, thousands of miles from home, and no one would ever know what happened to her.

She was so tired, she could barely keep her head above water. How simple it would be to lay back and let the cool liquid cover her. In silent resignation, she glanced toward the capsule. Water flowed through its open doors. While she watched, its flashing lights blinked off.

Then, over the loud roaring, she heard someone calling her name. It sounded like Matt's voice, but that couldn't be. She must be imagining it, the same way she constantly imagined seeing his face and feeling his arms around her.

She looked up at the catwalk. *Not possible.* Yet there he was, leaning over the railing. She tried to hold her arms up to him, to show him she loved him, but the move made her head go under. When she emerged, she flailed in the water, struggling to stay afloat.

"I'm coming down, Pam," he yelled. "Get as close as you can to the ladder."

Fosdick was beside him. She blinked. The two Russian officers from the hotel peered down at her. The Indian officer was also with them. The arrival of their boat near the island must have triggered Riker's return and the resulting commotion upstairs in Otto's island palace.

Matt kicked off his shoes, climbed over the catwalk and started down the ladder, his stocking feet skipping every other rung. Midway he dropped, hitting the water feetfirst.

"Can you swim?" he yelled, when he'd surfaced.

She didn't have to answer. In three strokes, he'd reached her. "Hang on to my neck," he ordered.

Thankfully, she put her arms around his neck and shoulders. He felt so solid, so strong. *Matt.* He'd come to deliver her from the madman.

They reached the rope ladder.

"Can we just float up to the balcony?" She was surprised at how weak her voice sounded.

Tenderly, he brushed a strand of wet hair out of her eyes. "Any second that wall could open and flood this whole room."

"You mean the water goes higher than the catwalk?"

He helped her stand on a rung and showed her how to hold on. "I'm guessing it does," he said. "It might fill this whole hangar. Apparently, the capsule launches and is recovered from the lake."

Pamela followed his glance to the capsule. Only the top third showed. By now it must be filled with water, its complex instruments ruined. The spider machine was already submerged.

His hands around her waist, he urged her upward. While he stayed in the water, she took one cautious step up the ladder.

Otto's image appeared before her eyes. She looked down at Matt, who was treading water beneath her.

"Matt, Otto Von Meinhoff fell down at the far end of the catwalk. He was too obese to get up. Somebody should go get him or he'll drown."

Matt yelled up at Fosdick but the other man couldn't hear him over the roaring water.

"You'll have to tell Fosdick yourself, Pam." He reached up and gave her leg a pat to reassure her. "Get going. I'll see you up top."

She flashed him a startled look over her shoulder. "Aren't you coming behind me?"

"The ladder won't hold both of us." He gave her leg another pat. "Be careful. You won't hurt yourself if you fall—you'll just drop into the water—but you'll sure slow us down."

"I'm on my way." The thought of Matt drowning in a deluge lent new strength to her weary legs and arms. Breathing hard, she pulled herself up the swaying ladder, rung by flimsy rung.

At the catwalk, eager hands seized her arms and waist and lifted her over the barrier. She looked down. Matt was already halfway up.

"Hurry!" she called, but her voice was so weak she doubted he could hear her.

She told Fosdick and the Indian officer about Otto. The Indian yanked the control-room door open. Several uniformed men burst out. The colonel said something in Hindi and pointed toward the end of the catwalk. But before they could move, an awesome rumble echoed through the vast chamber. As the last section of the outer wall opened, a huge wave surged toward them.

Matt vaulted over the catwalk railing, his clothes plastered to his body. "Get out of here, quick!" he yelled.

Everybody on the catwalk dove through the control-room door, and all but Matt ended up on the floor in a confused tangle of arms and legs. Matt, the last one through, slammed the door shut. An instant later, Pamela felt the wall shudder as the wave smashed against it.

Matt ran to where she lay sprawled on the carpet and knelt beside her. "I was afraid I'd lost you," he whispered. He took her in his arms, cradling her against his chest. "Did they hurt you?"

She shook her head. "No, but they would have if you hadn't come to the island when you did. Von Meinhoff was on the verge of killing me when they detected your approach." She eyed the two Russian officers picking themselves up off the carpet. "What are they doing here, Matt?"

He smoothed her wet hair. "I'll explain later, darling. Right now we're alive, we're together, and I love you."

He kissed her then, hungrily, devotedly, with just enough passion to warm her blood.

"I love you, too, Matt," she whispered. "I want to be with you, no matter where you go."

Behind them, Doug Fosdick rose from the carpet. "Sorry to butt in, people. But we need to figure out how to close the doors and pump the water from that big fish tank out there." He inclined his head toward Otto Von Meinhoff's watery grave. "That saucer's going to get me a promotion and you two a couple of medals. The quicker we get it dried out, the better shape it'll be in for our technicians to examine."

The Indian colonel got up, brushed himself off and strode to the control panel. Close behind were the two Russian officers.

Matt helped Pamela stand, holding her close with an arm around her waist.

She smiled up at him. "I know someone who can tell us how to pump out the water." She started toward the corridor door. "When they left me alone to check out your arrival, I locked a guard in a room down the hall. When he finds out both Otto and Riker are dead, I bet he'll be more than happy to operate that control panel for us."

ON THE POLICE BOAT taking them back to the mainland, Pamela felt Matt's arm around her shoulders and knew she was safe at last. The terror-filled nights were behind them. No longer would she have to fear Riker, the demon who always seemed to know exactly where to find her.

"Why did you try so hard to make me think Matt was selling secrets to the Russians?" she asked Fosdick, who was sitting on her other side.

"Because that's what we believed," Fosdick returned. "General Vactin sent fake messages to his subordinates telling all about Matt's so-called plan. When we intercepted them, we thought we'd stumbled onto some devious plot."

His mouth twisted wryly. "Vactin was fooling his own government, too, of course."

It still didn't make sense to Pamela. "But why was Vactin so interested in Matt?"

"Not me personally," Matt said. "All his questions were about the capsule and where it came from."

"Exactly." The CIA officer lowered his voice. "He was so eager to discover the capsule's origin and mission, that he decided to kidnap Matt, hoping he might know something. He first heard about you people and about Captain Goodman's accident from that newspaper article."

"Tell me this," Matt said. "How did the capsule get to the launch sites without Vactin knowing where it came from?"

Fosdick smiled smugly. "Because it took off and landed under its own steam—the same way it took off and landed on the Eastern Washington desert. That landing was an accident, of course. It happened because of a navigational error. Von Meinhoff was able to correct the problem and get his capsule back.''

Pamela turned to Matt. "What do you suppose he was mining on the moon?''

On her other side, Fosdick stiffened. "Why the moon?''

She shrugged. "It's closer to earth than anywhere else in our solar system. Where else would Otto send his spaceship?''

Washington, D.C.

IN THE PENTAGON'S mezzanine basement, Norm Duncan hung up the scrambler phone and returned to his desk.

At last, he thought triumphantly, leaning back in his executive chair. As he'd suspected, the spider monster held the key to the puzzle. But he'd never dreamed the activity on the moon over the past few years could have been caused by one man, operating from a remote lake in northwestern India.

Duncan shook his head, amazed by Von Meinhoff's genius. He'd been using the spider to mine for an alloy to make a metal stronger than steel, but lighter and more durable than aluminum. His palace in India was full of the stuff.

Colonel Reed bustled into the office, fresh from the morning briefing for the Joint Chiefs of Staff. He plopped into his chair. "The chairman's hot to hear the latest on the capsule.''

"I just talked to our attaché in Delhi," Duncan began, suppressing his excitement.

Colonel Reed shot out of his chair. "What'd he say, Norm? Did he get a look at the thing?'' For an instant, he hovered near Duncan's chair, finally situating himself on the edge of his desk.

Duncan nodded. "He says the technicians have figured out why our radar and our space-tracking people at Goddard never spotted it going to the moon.''

Reed leaned forward.

Enjoying his boss's interest, Duncan took his time about answering. "When the capsule reached a certain altitude, it split into two sections. Half went into orbit as a communications satellite. The space center tracked that half." He paused.

"So why couldn't Goddard track the half that went to the moon?" Reed's eyes, owlish behind black-rimmed glasses, stared down at Duncan with fascinated interest.

"A sophisticated jamming device," Duncan replied. "Our technicians at Jahangir are studying it now. In effect, it made the capsule invisible to our tracking technology."

Colonel Reed leaned so close, Duncan could smell the coffee he'd drunk at the morning briefing.

"But the jamming device had a problem," Duncan went on. "If another aircraft got too close, it screwed up the other plane's flight-control system."

Reed let out a slow breath. "So that's what happened to Eric Goodman's F-16."

"And to David Wright's Blackbird." Duncan eyeballed his boss. "Apparently, Von Meinhoff's been using his jamming device for years. A long time ago, he figured out how to maneuver his capsules in the earth's atmosphere—even at high altitudes. He wanted to be sure nobody could track them."

"But he never figured out how to launch them into outer space," Reed finished. "That's where the Russian missiles came in."

He stood and went back to his own desk. "How much of this do we tell Captain Wright?"

"We promised her the whole story," Duncan reminded him softly.

"Of course I'll tell her about finding her father's body and the wreckage from his plane when the air force did that search twenty years ago. But this stuff about the jammer's top secret."

"So's the info about the search." Duncan studied his boss. "By the way, she wants a transfer to McChord Air Force Base."

"To be near Powers? Normally that's not done until the couple's married."

"They've only known each other a couple of weeks and don't want to rush into anything. Basically, they're both very conservative."

Reed snorted. "Conservative! After the risks they took, they could have ended up in the military prison at Fort Leavenworth."

"Or dead," Duncan said dryly. "They came awfully close."

"So they did." Swinging his feet off his desk, Reed jotted a note on his memo pad. "I'll talk to the director about recommending her for the transfer. Let me know if they want anything else. They've certainly earned it!."

THE BUDDING BRANCH of an oak tree swayed over the simple white cross in Arlington National Cemetery. Kneeling beside the cross, Pamela placed a dozen red roses on her father's grave.

"He was here all the time." She glanced up at Matt. "If only I'd known."

He pulled her up. "The Pentagon should have told you— no matter how secret his mission was and how much they wanted to keep the Russians from finding out about it."

She felt his arm around her, drawing her close. For a moment they were both silent, reliving the terror, unable to believe it was really over. They slowly began walking away, arm in arm.

Before they reached the car, he stoppped her and turned her toward him. One set of hazel eyes looked into another.

"We're so much alike," he murmured. "I didn't appreciate my own strength until I saw how strong and loyal you are."

She came into his arms. "Then the next time you go monster hunting, you'd better take me along for protection."

"Always," he promised, just before he kissed her.

#281 HUNTER'S MOON by Dawn Stewardson
Timeless Love
Dani Patton awoke to the strangest circumstances: she'd traveled through
time to 1850 Transylvania, and hooded villagers—convinced she was a
vampire—were about to drive a stake through her heart! Rescued by sexy
Count Nicholae, Dani's only hope was to convince him vampires didn't
exist…but a live killer did!

#282 DOMINOES by Laura Gordon
There was nothing P.I. Kelsey St. James enjoyed more than solving
a case. Except when her best friend was the victim. Ben Tanner, a Chicago
cop with an attitude, had his hands full with Kelsey, for if he was right,
she would be the next to topple.…

#283 SILENT SEA by Patricia Rosemoor
Dolphin trainer Marissa Gilmore was at home in the sea—until someone
tried to kill her. Was it only coincidence that Riley O'Hare was near every
attempt on her life…or did the sexy owner of Dolphin Haven have secrets
of his own?

#284 LOOKS ARE DECEIVING by Maggie Ferguson
A Woman of Mystery
Alissa Adams was afraid to sleep. In her nightmares she saw the face of
the next day's murder victim. Kyle Stone wanted to believe her—and to
love her—but a detective needed hard evidence. And then Alissa's own
face appeared in her dreams.…

AVAILABLE THIS MONTH:

#277 SHADES OF FAMILIAR
Caroline Burnes

#278 IN THEIR FOOTSTEPS
Tess Gerritsen

#279 MOON WATCH
Vickie York

#280 MIDNIGHT RIDER
Laura Pender

Where do you find hot Texas nights, smooth Texas charm and dangerously sexy cowboys?

Crystal Creek reverberates with the exciting rhythm of Texas. Each story features the rugged individuals who live and love in the Lone Star state.

"...Crystal Creek wonderfully evokes the hot days and steamy nights of a small Texas community...impossible to put down until the last page is turned."
—*Romantic Times*

"...a series that should hook any romance reader. Outstanding."
—*Rendezvous*

"Altogether, it couldn't be better." —*Rendezvous*

Don't miss the next book in this exciting series.
SHAMELESS by SANDY STEEN

Available in July wherever Harlequin books are sold.

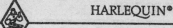

HARLEQUIN®

■ INTRIGUE®

When lovers are fated, not even time can separate them....When a mystery is pending, only time can solve it....

Timeless Love

Harlequin Intrigue is proud to bring you this exciting new program of time-travel romantic mysteries!

Be on time in July for the next book in this series:

#281 HUNTER'S MOON
by Dawn Stewardson

Better take a garlic necklace along when you travel back to drafty dark castles in remote Transylvania. You never know if you'll come face-to-face with a thirsty vampire!

Watch for
HUNTER'S MOON...
and all the upcoming books in
TIMELESS LOVE.

TLOVE3R

HARLEQUIN®

I N T R I G U E®

INNOCENT UNTIL PROVEN GUILTY...
IN A COURT OF LAW

Whether they are on the right side of the law—or the wrong side—their emotions are on trial...and so is their love.

Harlequin Intrigue is proud to continue its ongoing "Legal Thriller" program. Stories of secret scandals and crimes of passion. Of legal eagles who battle the system and undeniable desire.

Next on the docket is

> **#286 IN SELF DEFENSE**
> **Saranne Dawson**
> **August 1994**

Look for the "Legal Thriller" flash for the best in taut romantic suspense—only from Harlequin Intrigue.

HARLEQUIN INTRIGUE—NOT THE SAME OLD STORY!

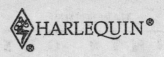

EXPECTATIONS
Shannon Waverly

Eternity, Massachusetts, is a town with something
special going for it. According to legend, those who
marry in Eternity's chapel are destined for a lifetime of
happiness. As long as the legend holds true, couples
will continue to flock here to marry and local
businesses will thrive.

Unfortunately for the town, Marion and Geoffrey Kent
are about to prove the legend wrong!

EXPECTATIONS, available in July from
Harlequin Romance®, is the second book in
Harlequin's new cross-line series, **WEDDINGS, INC.**
Be sure to look for the third book, **WEDDING
SONG,** by
Vicki Lewis Thompson (Harlequin Temptation® #502),
coming in August.

WED-2

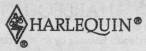

HARLEQUIN®

Don't miss these Harlequin favorites by some of our most
distinguished authors!
And now, you can receive a discount by ordering two or more titles!

HT #25551	THE OTHER WOMAN by Candace Schuler	$2.99	☐
HT #25539	FOOLS RUSH IN by Vicki Lewis Thompson	$2.99	☐
HP #11550	THE GOLDEN GREEK by Sally Wentworth	$2.89	☐
HP #11603	PAST ALL REASON by Kay Thorpe	$2.99	☐
HR #03228	MEANT FOR EACH OTHER by Rebecca Winters	$2.89	☐
HR #03268	THE BAD PENNY by Susan Fox	$2.99	☐
HS #70532	TOUCH THE DAWN by Karen Young	$3.39	☐
HS #70540	FOR THE LOVE OF IVY by Barbara Kaye	$3.39	☐
HI #22177	MINDGAME by Laura Pender	$2.79	☐
HI #22214	TO DIE FOR by M.J. Rodgers	$2.89	☐
HAR #16421	HAPPY NEW YEAR, DARLING by Margaret St. George	$3.29	☐
HAR #16507	THE UNEXPECTED GROOM by Muriel Jensen	$3.50	☐
HH #28774	SPINDRIFT by Miranda Jarrett	$3.99	☐
HH #28782	SWEET SENSATIONS by Julie Tetel	$3.99	☐

Harlequin Promotional Titles

#83259	UNTAMED MAVERICK HEARTS (Short-story collection featuring Heather Graham Pozzessere, Patricia Potter, Joan Johnston)	$4.99	☐

(limited quantities available on certain titles)

	AMOUNT	$
DEDUCT:	**10% DISCOUNT FOR 2+ BOOKS**	$
	POSTAGE & HANDLING	$
	($1.00 for one book, 50¢ for each additional)	
	APPLICABLE TAXES*	$ _____
	TOTAL PAYABLE	$ _____
	(check or money order—please do not send cash)	

To order, complete this form and send it, along with a check or money order for the
total above, payable to Harlequin Books, to: **in the U.S.:** 3010 Walden Avenue,
P.O. Box 9047, Buffalo, NY 14269-9047; **In Canada:** P.O. Box 613, Fort Erie, Ontario,
L2A 5X3.

Name: _____

Address: _____ City: _____

State/Prov.: _____ Zip/Postal Code: _____

*New York residents remit applicable sales taxes.
 Canadian residents remit applicable GST and provincial taxes.

HBACK-AJ